"*Phoebe's Light* is another work of art and heart by Suzanne Woods Fisher; a beautifully told tale that honors the early Quakers of colonial Massachusetts and their rich heritage on unique, lovely Nantucket Island. Inspired by actual historical figures, these characters and this place meld into a remarkably poignant page-turner. An inspiring start to what is sure to be a beloved series!"

—**Laura Frantz**, author of *The Lacemaker*

"Set sail on an absorbing adventure with Fisher's delightful new book, *Phoebe's Light*. Fisher brings to life Nantucket Island with her vivid descriptions and true-to-life characters. Shedding light upon Quaker customs and beliefs as well as the whaling era, Fisher plunges her readers into turbulent waters with plenty of plot twists and intrigue that lead to a satisfying conclusion."

—**Jody Hedlund**, author of *Luther & Katharina*, Christy Award winner

"You can always trust Suzanne Woods Fisher to write a compelling story that has readers turning pages as fast as they can to see what happens next. She's done it again with *Phoebe's Light*, a surefire mix of engaging characters, fascinating Nantucket Island history, and even a whaling trip on the high seas. If you like romance mixed with history and adventure, you're going to love *Phoebe's Light*."

—**Ann H. Gabhart**, bestselling author of *These Healing Hills*

PHOEBE'S LIGHT

Books by Suzanne Woods Fisher

Amish Peace: Simple Wisdom for a Complicated World
Amish Proverbs: Words of Wisdom from the Simple Life
Amish Values for Your Family: What We Can Learn from the Simple Life
A Lancaster County Christmas
Christmas at Rose Hill Farm
The Heart of the Amish

LANCASTER COUNTY SECRETS
The Choice
The Waiting
The Search

STONEY RIDGE SEASONS
The Keeper
The Haven
The Lesson

THE INN AT EAGLE HILL
The Letters
The Calling
The Revealing

THE BISHOP'S FAMILY
The Imposter
The Quieting
The Devoted

AMISH BEGINNINGS
Anna's Crossing
The Newcomer
The Return

NANTUCKET LEGACY
Phoebe's Light

PHOEBE'S LIGHT

SUZANNE WOODS FISHER

℞
Revell
a division of Baker Publishing Group
Grand Rapids, Michigan

© 2018 by Suzanne Woods Fisher

Published by Revell
a division of Baker Publishing Group
PO Box 6287, Grand Rapids, MI 49516-6287
www.revellbooks.com

Printed in the United States of America

Library of Congress Cataloging-in-Publication Data
Names: Fisher, Suzanne Woods, author.
Title: Phoebe's light / Suzanne Woods Fisher.
Description: Grand Rapids, MI : Revell, a division of Baker Publishing Group,
    [2018] | Series: Nantucket legacy ; 1
Identifiers: LCCN 2017044853 | ISBN 9780800721626 (softcover)
Subjects: LCSH: Young women—Fiction. | Quakers—Fiction. | GSAFD: Christian
    fiction. | Love stories.
Classification: LCC PS3606.I78 P48 2018 | DDC 813/.6—dc23
LC record available at https://lccn.loc.gov/2017044853

Scripture used in this book, whether quoted or paraphrased by the characters, is taken from the King James Version.

This is a work of historical reconstruction; the appearances of certain historical figures are therefore inevitable. All other characters, however, are products of the author's imagination, and any resemblance to actual persons, living or dead, is coincidental.

Published in association with Joyce Hart of the Hartline Literary Agency, LLC

18 19 20 21 22 23 24   7 6 5 4 3 2 1

To Mary Coffin Starbuck (1645–1717),
a Weighty Friend to all Nantucketers.
A woman far ahead of her times,
who did indeed build something that endured.

Author's Note

The story of Nantucket Island, nearly thirty miles out to sea off the sharp elbow of Cape Cod, begins long before *Phoebe's Light* picks up. Native Americans farmed this crescent-shaped island in relative peace and quiet, able to avoid many of the problems with English colonists that mainland Natives could not. In 1660, a group of white settlers moved to Nantucket, including fifteen-year-old Mary Coffin, hoping to build something that would endure.

Sheepherding became a natural industry for these new settlers, far from predators like wolves. In fact, sheep gave Nantucket its economic base until whaling overshadowed it. Whaling became such a great source of revenue, through the late eighteenth century and into the middle of the nineteenth century, that Nantucket Island was considered the wealthiest port in the world.

And that is when this story begins . . .

Cast of Characters

17th century

Mary Coffin: daughter of one of the first proprietors of Nantucket Island—highly revered; considered to be like Deborah the judge of the Old Testament

Tristram Coffin: proprietor of Nantucket Island, father of Mary, husband of Dionis

Nathaniel Starbuck: son of proprietor Edward Starbuck

Peter Foulger: surveyor, missionary to the Wampanoag Indians of Nantucket Island, joined the proprietors

Eleazer Foulger: son of Peter Foulger

18th century

Phoebe Starbuck: great-granddaughter of Mary Coffin

Barnabas Starbuck: father of Phoebe

Matthew Macy: cooper on Nantucket Island

Phineas Foulger: whaling captain of *Fortuna*

Silence Foulger (Silo): cabin boy
Sarah Foulger: daughter of Captain Phineas Foulger
Hiram Hoyt: first mate of *Fortuna*
Libby Macy: mother of Matthew
Jeremiah Macy: brother of Matthew
Zacchaeus Coleman: constable of Nantucket

Glossary

Language of 18th-Century Nantucket

ambergris: a waxy, grayish substance found in the stomachs of sperm whales and once used in perfume to make the scent last longer

baleen: the comblike plates of cartilage in a whale's mouth to strain plankton and other food from the water; very valuable for its strength and flexibility

boatsteerer/harpooner: crew at the bow of the whaling boat whose job is to spear the whale

broken voyage: a whaling ship that returns home with less than a full load of oil

cat-o'-nine (or *cat-o'-nine-tails*): a multi-tailed whip used to flog sailors

cooper: barrel maker

cooperage: workplace of the cooper

crosstree or *crow's nest*: the part of the ship, near the top of the mast, where the sailor on lookout duty watches for whales *cuddy*: a small room or compartment on a boat

disowned: under church discipline

elders: historically, those appointed to foster the vocal ministry of the meeting for worship and the spiritual condition of its members

Facing Benches: the benches or seats in the front of the meeting room, facing the body of the meeting, on which Friends' ministers and elders generally sat

fin up: dead

First Day: Sunday (Quakers did not use names for days of the week, nor for the months, as these had pagan origins)

First Month: January

flensing: butchering of the whale

Friends and *Society of Friends*: Quaker church members

gam: to visit or talk with the crew of another whaling ship while at sea

gangplank: a movable bridge used to board or leave a ship

greenhand or *greenie*: an inexperienced sailor making his first whaling voyage

hold in the Light: to ask for God's presence to illuminate a situation or problem or person

idler: a crewman whose tasks require daylight hours (cook, cooper, cabin boy)

lay: the percentage of a ship's profit that each crew member receives; a sailor's lay usually depends upon his experience and rank

lookout: the sailor stationed in the crosstree to watch for whales

Meeting: church

minding the Light: an expression used to remind Quakers that there is an Inward Light in each of them that can reveal God's will if its direction is listened to and followed

mortgage button: a Nantucket tradition of drilling a hole in the newel post of a household's banister, filling it with the ashes of the paid-off mortgage, and capping the hole with a button made of scrimshaw (called a Brag Button in the South)

moved to speak: an experience, in the quietness of the meeting, of feeling led by God to speak

mutiny: an uprising or rebellion of a ship's crew against the captain

Nantucket sleigh ride: a term used to describe the pulling of a whaleboat by a whale that has been harpooned and is "running"

Quaker: the unofficial name of a member of the Religious Society of Friends; originally the use was pejorative, but the word was reclaimed by Friends in recognition of the physical sensation that many feel when being moved by the Spirit

quarterboard: a wooden sign with carved name displayed on each ship

rigging: the ropes and chain used to control a ship's sails

saltbox: traditional New England–style wooden frame house with a long, pitched roof that slopes down to the back; a saltbox has just one story in the back and two stories in the front

scrimshaw: whalebone adorned with carvings

seasoning: a process to ensure that decisions are truly grounded in God's will *seize*: to tie up a sailor in the rigging as a form of punishment

slops: sailors' clothing (a ship's captain will charge his crew for any clothes he supplied)

syndicate: a group of businessmen who own a whaling ship or ships

tryworks: a brick furnace in which try-pots (a metallic pot used on a whaler or on shore to render blubber) are placed

Weighty Friend: a Friend who is informally recognized as having special experience and wisdom

worldly: having to do with secular values

1

Phoebe Starbuck flung back the worn quilt, leapt out of bed, and hurried to the window. She swung open the sash of the window and took in a deep breath of the brisk island air tinged with a musky scent of the flats at low tide. It was how she started each morning, elbows on the windowsill, scanning the water to see which, if any, whaling ships might have returned to port in the night. It was how most every Nantucket woman greeted the day.

Drat! She couldn't see the flags among the jumble of bobbing masts.

Phoebe grabbed the spyglass off the candlestand and peered through it, frantically focusing and refocusing on each mast that dotted the harbor, counting each one. And then her heart stopped when she saw its flag: the *Fortuna*, captained by Phineas Foulger, the most-admired man on all the island, in her opinion. And the ship sat low in the water—indicating a greasy voyage, not a broken one.

Today Phoebe was eighteen years old, a woman by all

rights. Would the captain notice the vast changes in her? She felt but a girl when he sailed away two years ago, though her heart had felt differently. What a day, what a day!

"Make haste, Phoebe dear," her father called up the stairs. "Something special awaits thee."

The morning sun brightened the room as Phoebe scooped up her clothes. She tugged on a brown homespun dress and combed her hair until it crackled. She wound her thick hair into a flattering topknot, pinned it against the back of her head, then covered it with a lace cap. She gave her bedroom a quick tidy-up, plumping a goosefeather pillow and smoothing the last wrinkle from the bed.

Downstairs, Phoebe smiled as she entered the warm keeping room, its fire crackling. Father, the old dear, a small and gentle man, sat at the head of the table with a wrapped bundle in his hands and a cat-that-swallowed-the-canary look on his weathered face, seamed with lines.

"There she is, my daughter, my one and only. Happy birthday, Phoebe." He rose and held the seat out for her. When he stood, she noticed the patches on his overcoat, the sheen at the elbows, the fraying threads at his sleeve cuffs. *Not today,* she thought. *Not on this day. I will not worry today.*

Barnabas Starbuck was considered the black sheep of the Starbuck line—oddly enough, because of sheep. Her father had continued to raise sheep for profit, providing a very modest income at best, despite the fact that all his kinsmen were deeply enmeshed in the whaling industry and growing wealthy for it. The gap between Barnabas Starbuck and all other Starbucks had widened enormously in the last decade.

Phoebe loved her father, but she was not blind to his shortcomings. He was a kind and generous man but lacked the business acumen common to his relations. Barnabas Starbuck always had a venture brewing. New enterprises, he called them, always, always, always with disastrous results. He would start an enterprise with a big dream, great enthusiasm, and when the idea failed or fizzled, he would move on to something else.

For a brief time Barnabas fancied himself a trader of imports. There were the iron cook pots he had ordered from a smooth-talking Boston land shark, far more pots than there were island housewives, so many that the lean-to still had pots stacked floor to ceiling. Oversupply, he had discovered, was a pitfall. Thus the pots remained unsold and unwanted, rusting away in the moist island air.

And then Barnabas had an idea to start a salt works factory in an empty warehouse on Straight Wharf but once again neglected to take into account the high humidity of the island. The drying process needed for salt production was so greatly hindered by the summer's humidity that the salt clumped and caused condensation on all the warehouse's windows.

Her father was quite tolerant of his business failures. "Just taking soundings!" he would tell Phoebe with a dismissive wave of the hand. "Part and parcel of the road to success."

What her father refused to accept was that all roads on Nantucket Island led to the harbor. Nearly every islander understood that truth and was involved, to some degree or another, in the making of tools necessary to outfit whaling and fishing vessels. Phoebe had tried to encourage her father to consider investing in sail making, blacksmithing, ironworks, rope manufacturing. Anything that would tie his enterprise to the sea. But he was convinced whaling was a short-term industry, soon to fizzle out.

Phoebe had a dread, and not an unfounded one, that her father would soon be declared Town Poor by the selectman. The Starbuck kin had made it abundantly clear that they had reached the end of their tether to bail Barnabas out of another financial failure.

And what would become of them then? The Town Poor were miserably provided for.

Not today, she reminded herself as she poured herself a cup of tea. *I am not going to worry today. Today is a special day.*

Leaning across the table, her father handed her a brown parcel, tied with twine.

"A gift? I thought we had agreed no gifts this year." And here was another sweet but conflicting characteristic to her father—he was a generous gift giver, despite a steady shortage of disposable income.

"This is an *inheritance*," he said, beaming from ear to ear. "It has been waiting for thee until the time was right."

Carefully, Phoebe untied the twine and unfolded the paper, both items to use again. Inside the package was a weathered book, bound in tan sheepskin. When she opened it, she had to squint to read the faint ink. "What could it be?" She looked up at him curiously.

"What could it be? Why, none other than the journal of Great Mary!"

Great Mary? Phoebe's great-grandmother, her father's grandmother. Great Mary's father, Tristram Coffin, was one of the first proprietors to settle the island. Mary was his youngest daughter, regarded as a wise and noble woman, a Weighty Friend to all, oft likened to Deborah in the Old Testament. "I thought the existence of Great Mary's journal was naught but rumor."

"Nay! Nay, 'tis truly hers. Passed along to me from my father and given to him by his father. 'Tis meant to be passed from generation to generation, to whomever would most benefit from the wisdom of Great Mary. For some reason, my father felt I needed it the most."

Reverently, Phoebe stroked the smooth brown sheepskin covering. "And thee has read it?"

He was silent for some time, staring into his teacup. "Truth be told, I always intended to but never found the time." His smile disappeared and he looked uncharacteristically chagrined. "The script is faint, my eyes are weak . . . Ink is so vulnerable to humid conditions." He put down his fork and wiped his mouth with his napkin. "And then . . . I have been so busy with my enterprises."

Phoebe had to bite on her lip not to point out the irony of this conversation. "I thank thee, Father. I will take good care of it, and when the time is right, I will take care to pass it on to the person who most needs Great Mary's wisdom."

It was only after breakfast, as Phoebe knotted the strings of her black bonnet under her chin, swift and taut, eager to hurry to the harbor and catch a glimpse of the *Fortuna*'s captain, that she realized the sharp point of irony was jabbed not only at her father but also at her. For she was the one in this generation, amongst dozens and dozens of Starbuck cousins, to whom the journal of wisdom had been passed.

A fine, fair morning it was, with the air washed fresh by the rain. The countryside was soft, shades of green, hints of yellows and reds with the coming autumn. Matthew Macy tipped his hat to bid goodbye to the constable and left the gaol, tucked away on Vestal Street, heading toward the wharf where his cooperage was located. A second-generation cooper, Matthew was, with the knowledge of barrel making passed down from his late father. Late . . . but not forgotten. Never that.

He filled his lungs with crystalline air, happy to be outside on this lovely morning and far away from the wretched gaol, at least for the next ten hours. After that, sadly, he was due to return.

He strode down Milk Street, turned the corner, and paused to stop and look down toward the harbor. It was a view that always affected him. How he loved this little island. Thirty miles away from the mainland—not too far but far enough. The rain last evening had chased away the usual lingering fog, and even cleansed the air of the pervasive stink of rendering whales. At the moment the sea was calm, shimmering in the morning sun, but it could change in the blink of an eye, with nary much warning, into a deadly tempest. How well he knew.

Main Street was slick from last night's rain. The markets were setting up for the day, and he had to move deftly to avoid the clusters of townspeople, horses and boxcarts, wheelbarrows and wagons. Every corner swarmed with people: seamen and merchants, black-cloaked Quaker matrons holding tightly to their children's hands, somber men in their broad-brimmed hats, rat catchers and peddlers, all going about their lives.

In front of him, he saw a bonneted Quaker maid step right into the path of a fast-moving horse. He veered around two old salts and leaped into the street to swiftly rescue the woman. As he yanked her toward him and away from imminent danger, he heard her gasp.

"Matthew Macy, take thy hands off me!"

Bother. Of all the Quaker girls on the island to rescue, *this* one had to be Phoebe Starbuck. He lifted his hands in the air to show her that he heard and obeyed. "'Tis you, Phoebe? Hard to discern who is under that enormous coal scuttle. But then, that is what the Friends prefer, is it not? To wear blinders to life going on around them."

Ignoring him, Phoebe tugged at her bonnet, straightened her skirts, and dusted herself off.

"Do I not deserve a thank-you for saving your life?"

She frowned. "Saving my life might be an overstatement." Another horse and cart thundered by, its wheels splashing her skirts, and she added, "But I am grateful for thy quick thinking."

"Had I known it was you . . ."

She glared at him. "Thee might have let the horse run me down, no doubt."

"I was going to say . . . I might have let the Quaker brethren come to your rescue. But then . . . they all seem far more interested to hurry and greet the *Fortuna* than to notice a damsel in distress."

As he looked around the street, he realized he had unwittingly spoken truth—a crowd was growing near the harbor—though he had meant only to sting Phoebe. Being around her brought out a streak of malice in Matthew that he could not restrain. He seldom left her company without cutting her, or the Friends, with some small criticisms.

As she recovered her composure, her dark brown eyes started snapping. She glanced up Main Street. "How did thee sleep last night? Was the stiff wooden plank comfortable enough for thee? And was a breakfast of gruel fully satisfying?"

"Happily, I am a man with simple needs. I can sleep anywhere and eat anything."

"How delightful. The Nantucket gaol sounds like a suitable arrangement for thee."

And then her attention was diverted by the sight of someone she spotted, and Matthew used the opportunity to excuse himself. As he rounded the corner to Water Street, he turned his head and stopped abruptly. The sun was shining down on Phoebe, lighting her like a beam. Her bonnet brim was turned up and she was smiling as Phineas Foulger, captain of the newly arrived *Fortuna* whale ship, and his abominable daughter, Sarah, approached her.

Why was Captain Foulger so soon off the ship? Most captains waited until the ship's cargo was unloaded, anxious to overlook every barrel of precious oil and ensure it was accounted for in the warehouse.

Then he saw the look on Captain Foulger's face as he caught sight of Phoebe.

A sick feeling lurched through Matthew. His mouth went dry, his palms damp.

Why should he let himself be bothered? Many a night in gaol he had reminded himself that apart from his brother and mother, he cared for no one and nothing.

———

It was hard to control the smile that strained to burst over Phoebe's face at the sight of Captain Phineas Foulger advancing in her direction among the crowds of shoppers, sailors, and vendors, his elbow guiding his daughter, Sarah. Phoebe had to suppress the impulse to call out and wave, and the even greater one to rush toward the captain. When he did draw close, he took notice of her and stopped abruptly. The corners of his hazel eyes lifted, crinkling, and she took that as solid evidence of his approval, but she could also see he clearly did not recall her. Had she changed so very much?

Suddenly seeming to remember the presence of his daughter, the captain took a step back. Sarah's cold gaze swept over Phoebe's homespun dress, and she said with a thin-lipped smile, "Hello. How pleasant to see thee."

"And thee as well." *In a pig's eye*, Phoebe thought, all the while she returned as warm a smile at Sarah as she could muster. She hoped Sarah Foulger could not tell the way her heart suddenly flew to her throat at the sight of her father, Captain Foulger, so tall and handsome. Salt-and-pepper hair, trimmed beard framing his chiseled cheekbones, sun-bronzed skin.

Behind Sarah stood a fine-boned half-Indian boy, small and thin for his years, with large sad eyes that were almost too big for his face. His knitted sailor's cap covered a head of thick brown curls. His arms were full of packages. Phoebe turned her attention toward him, mindful that she was "oversmiling" at the captain—and the sweet boy beamed in return.

Suddenly the captain's eyebrows lifted in surprise. "Well, I'll be blowed—'tis Phoebe Starbuck?"

His smile was so warm, so open, her heart leapt, capturing her devotion all over again. "Welcome home, Captain Foulger," she answered. *Oh, welcome, welcome home! You take my breath away.* "A greasy voyage, I trust?"

"Extraordinarily successful," he said. "God blessed the voyage beyond measure." His eyes appraised her. "Thee is looking . . ."

Thee's looking right womanly, Phoebe hoped were the words to come.

". . . quite contented," the captain said.

Contented? How does one look contented? 'Twas a compliment, she decided, though she would have preferred that he noticed how she had matured in his absence. "Today happens to be my birthday," she said. Why on earth was she telling him that? She supposed she wanted him to know that she was no longer a girl, no longer just Sarah's peer. Just Sarah's *seamstress*.

Phoebe rushed on. "My eighteenth birthday."

Rather than impressed, he seemed amused. "Is that right?" Sarah made a slight social cough signaling impatience and the captain glanced at her. "Sarah, did thee know it was thy friend Phoebe's birthday?"

Sarah gave her a thin smile, barely disguising her lack of interest.

The captain turned his attention back to Phoebe, hazel eyes twinkling. Oh, how they twinkled! "And what has thou received today?"

She dropped her head and lifted her drawstring purse. "My great-grandmother's journal."

The captain's face, alit with good-natured amusement only seconds ago, suddenly lost its smile and was replaced by a quizzical expression. His eyes riveted to her drawstring. "Great Mary's journal? I thought its existence was a legend."

"Nay, 'tis no legend. My father said 'tis filled with revelations of her wisdom." Of course, that was only his presumption. He hadn't read it. How could he *not* have read it? It was a baffling thought.

"As I was saying, Father"—Sarah's attention was fixed on

her father as if Phoebe were not there—"we ought to host a gathering. Friends would enjoy a gam with thee, hear of thy whale hunts, news of thy travels."

"A lovely idea," the captain said, his eyes fixed on Phoebe.

There was a pregnant pause, in which Phoebe expected Sarah to extend an invitation to her, but none was forthcoming.

"We must not delay Phoebe from her . . . shopping," Sarah put in.

Feeling the bite of Sarah's words—a dig at the fact that Phoebe did the shopping for the Starbuck household—she looked away. For all of Sarah's Quaker airs, she made full use of servants.

"Sarah, my dear," the captain said, "I see my first mate over there by the apple cart, with his eyes fixed on us."

Sarah spun toward the direction of the apple cart so quickly she nearly toppled the packages in the boy's arms. Phoebe reached out to steady the packages and the boy gave her a shy smile. Something about him touched Phoebe's heart. "Is thee part Indian?"

"His mother is a Lucayan-Arawak princess," the captain said, his gaze still on the first mate.

"And the other part?"

"Ah, who knows? A bit of this, a bit of that." The boy gave him a hard look as the captain turned to his daughter. "Sarah, dear, would thee please find out what it is Hiram Hoyt needs?" He spoke gruffly to the boy. "Silo, go along with her."

The first mate was indeed staring at the captain. Hiram Hoyt had always struck Phoebe as a mournful man, though she wasn't sure whether it was due to his scarred face, or the perpetual pipe sticking out of the left corner of his mouth that made one eye squinty, or mayhap it was his Nantucket Island heritage. His mother was a Wampanoag.

Sarah excused herself with a nod so curt to Phoebe that it was chilling, but no sooner was she out of earshot—Silo obediently trotting behind her—than the captain caught Phoebe's eyes. "I found the boy in the Bahamas and made him my cabin boy as a favor for his mother. Teaching him the ropes of life at sea, but 'tis no easy task. Silo, short for Silence. Deaf and dumb."

How sad. And yet the boy did not seem to be deaf.

The captain smiled his charming smile and Phoebe nearly melted in its warmth. "Perhaps I will see more of thee while the *Fortuna* is in harbor."

"What is the plan for the *Fortuna*?" *Please, please, please say the ship needs to be overhauled. Please stay in Nantucket for an extended period.*

But before the captain could respond, the first mate appeared at his side with Sarah and Silo and gave a nod to Phoebe. "I'm sorry to interrupt, sir, but I have a letter for thee." Hiram Hoyt slid his hand into his coat pocket. "'Twas given me by another sailor who had just returned from the Bahamas."

The captain scowled at him, and glanced at Sarah, then Phoebe. "Excuse me," he said while he slit it open and read it. His scowl deepened.

"Bad tidings?" Sarah said.

He slipped the letter into the pocket of his waistcoat. "Just a bit of ship's business to take care of."

Sarah put a hand on her father's arm. "Can it not wait? Thee has just arrived."

The captain hesitated, then warmth returned to his beautiful face. "Of course." He glanced in the direction of the harbor and Phoebe knew that something in the letter made him distracted.

Sarah tugged at his sleeve. "We must be on our way to Orange Street. I invited thy first mate to sup with us. To celebrate thy homecoming. Lunch awaits us."

Another awkward silence as Phoebe waited, hopefully, for an invitation. None was forthcoming.

"Thus we must," the captain said with a tolerant smile, "make haste." He reached out for Phoebe's hand and squeezed it, whispering, "But before the *Fortuna* sets sail, I do hope to see thee again." He reached behind her to pull a long red rose out of a vendor's bucket of flowers and handed it to her. "Happy birthday, my sweet Phoebe." In one smooth motion, he tossed a copper to the vendor. She nearly swooned.

A long motionless moment passed before Phoebe looked up to find his eyes upon her, full of her, taking their fill now. Reluctantly, it seemed, he turned away to join his daughter.

As she watched him cross the street, she felt something powerful swell her heart. *Sweet.* He had given her a rose and called her his "sweet Phoebe." She spun around, swinging Great Mary's journal in her drawstring purse, giddy as a bee in a summer garden.

Mary Coffin

15 September 1658

Tristram Jr. saw a Quaker today! I asked him how he knew, because he is the brother prone to tell outlandish tales. He said he could tell by the way the man was dressed and the peculiar way he talked.

It is against the law to have much to do with Quakers. They are supposed to be terrible! Tristram Jr. said the man didn't seem as bad as they are thought to be.

It is all most confusing. Father says that the Quakers started in England only a few years ago. They claim to be Christians, but the General Court insists they are heretics, and accuses them of uttering blasphemies. These Quakers are said to despise government and to be disrespectful to magistrates and ministers. They say they are sent direct from God, like the prophets of the Old Testament. Sent to warn others of the path they are on, but Reverend Rodgers says they try to turn people from the faith.

Father says the constable has warned everyone that they should have nothing to do with Quakers, and if a Quaker is found out, he is supposed to be whipped and locked in the house of correction until he can be sent back where he came from. Anyone found bringing Quakers here on a ship is supposed to be severely punished.

What causes these peculiar people to cross the sea and come to our Massachusetts Bay? They are not wanted here.

3 October 1658

I had a dreadful scare today. It was early in the morning and I had gone down to the pond to fill a bucket with water. We'd had a storm last night, and the pond had filled up, and even the meadow near the pond was soggy. I slipped down the bank and twisted my ankle sorely, too sore to walk on it. I tried calling out, but the pond is a long way from the house and no one could hear me. I would have to wait until someone noticed I went missing. That could take a very, very long time, especially because Tristram Jr. talks a blue streak at breakfast and wouldn't even notice I was absent. Then it started raining again, so here I was, stuck by the pond with a twisted ankle, getting soaked in the rain.

Lo and behold, who should appear at the top of the pond but Nathaniel Starbuck! He tied his horse to a tree and made his way down to the water. He checked my ankle ever so tenderly and asked me if I hurt anywhere else. Then he lifted me in his arms like I was made of cotton and carried me home, as if I was a royal princess.

It's settled. I am in love with Nathaniel Starbuck.

2

As Phoebe walked past the Pacific Bank, the manager ran down the steps to catch her and ask her in to his office. His name was Horace Russell, a gloomy man with a wattle and sagging jowls. Her heart sank as she climbed the steep steps to the bank.

Horace Russell sat behind his desk and pulled out a thick file, opening it with a heavy sigh. Her heart sunk a little further. Wattle jiggling, he informed Phoebe that her father had defaulted on yet another loan, the mortgage loan for their house on 35 Centre Street.

Relieved, she shook her head. "Thee must be mistaken. We have a mortgage button. I remember when my mother burned the mortgage papers and put them in the banister hole. I remember it vividly!" Phoebe's mother had been so proud of that accomplishment.

"There is no mistake," Horace Russell said, jabbing a bony finger at the top of the sheaf of papers. "Last year, thy father took out a mortgage on the house for a new venture."

She peered at the open file. "That is simply not possible."

"'Tis entirely possible. Barnabas Starbuck needed a loan, he said, to make an investment. The only collateral he had to offer was the house—35 Centre Street."

"And thee gave it to him? Thee did not think to let me know?"

Horace Russell stiffened. "I am letting thee know now. Consider this thy thirty-day notice." He rose to come around his desk to say he was sorry. But not so sorry that he found himself unable to tell her that the Centre Street house was going to be auctioned off in thirty days if the funds were not forthcoming.

Then he leaned close to Phoebe, too close, and softly whispered, "Mayhap thee and me, we could come up with some kind of suitable arrangement."

Phoebe gasped. He might think her poor, but she was not *that* poor. "Thee is an *elder* at Meeting, Horace Russell! Thee has a *wife*! And *eight* children."

"Nine," he said gloomily.

She frowned at him and stood up, holding her drawstring purse against her body to put space between her and Horace Russell. "I will solve this problem." Her fears of being declared as Town Poor were no longer imaginary. If the house were taken, what would they do? Where could they go? Over the last few years, the Starbuck kin avoided them as poor relations, including them in fewer and fewer gatherings. Phoebe could not blame them—her father owed money to all of them.

Ten minutes later, as soon as Phoebe stepped back inside her Centre Street home, hung her bonnet on its peg, and set down her drawstring purse on the tabletop, she mentioned her conversation with Horace Russell to her father. Barnabas's face drained of all color. Frowning, he rubbed his stomach, insisted he wasn't well, that he'd been laid low by a bad clam and ought to go lie down.

He wasn't fooling her; his chronic dyspepsia had always arrived with convenience. She built up the fire and heated water for chamomile tea to soothe his stomach, and just as she fished the tea leaves out of the pot, a knock came at the door. When she opened it, she could not have been more stunned at the sight on her stoop than if she had opened the door to a large gray squirrel.

"Captain Foulger!" she cried, both hands to her face, her eyes wide in surprise and delight.

He seemed pleased by her pleasure. "Good day, Phoebe."

"I was . . . just making a pot of tea for my father. Would thee like some?"

"That sounds delightful."

He took a very small step into the keeping room, then another. As he glanced around, Phoebe appraised the room as he might: the set of hard, straight-backed chairs, the table and mantel with no decorative flourish, the threadbare settee. Only the woven rug had anything bright to offer. Then she noticed his eyes fall on her drawstring bag set on the kitchen table. Fall there and stay. He walked toward the table and sat on a chair, his hand resting on top of the bag. "Phoebe, I'd like to know more of the journal of Great Mary."

She looked at him, startled. "But why? I'm surprised thee is even aware of its existence."

"All the Foulgers know of it. But no one knew if it was real. And if it was real, where it had gone missing to. Not until today, when thee made mention of it."

She filled two cups with tea, picked up one to give to him,

and was mortified that her hands shook so much the cup rattled noisily on its saucer. She kept her head down and quickly sat in a chair, lifted her cup, and took a sip.

The captain seemed not to notice her discomfit. "Thee has read the journal?"

"Nay, not yet."

"Phoebe, my dear, I wondered if thee might allow me to borrow it? Just for a day or so."

Dear! He called her his *dear*. "Borrow it? But why?"

He shrugged. "I have always been inordinately curious about Great Mary." He sipped on the tea. "She was said to be an oracle. A Deborah, like the judge in the Old Testament."

Yes, Phoebe knew all about Great Mary's reputation. Her shadow cast large on her descendants.

But to borrow it? She had just received the journal—thoughts and words and insights from her great-grandmother. It felt . . . private. Personal. Special.

On the other hand, if she agreed to loan the journal to the captain, it would provide an opportunity to spend time with him. She was silent for a long moment, eyes on her teacup, as if she could read guidance on its dark surface. As she wavered on a decision, her father came down the stairs and into the keeping room.

"Welcome, Phineas. Thee looks well."

The captain rose to his feet and reached a hand out to shake her father's hand. "Hello, Barnabas." He sat back down.

"Quite a greasy voyage, I heard."

"It was, it was," the captain said, looking pleased. "Substantial in every way."

Barnabas sat at the table. "Quite a large piece of ambergris, as well."

Phoebe glanced at her father. She had not realized he'd already been down to the docks to hear the scuttlebutt surrounding the *Fortuna*, but then, he did have a keen interest in all things new.

"Indeed, the ambergris was sizable." The captain dipped his head in modesty. "Word travels speedily. A French perfumery is eager to negotiate."

"How large was it?"

"The ambergris? 'Tis getting weighed and valued at the countinghouse as we speak."

"Thirty pounds, I heard. A high-quality ambergris."

Captain Foulger frowned. "'Twas truly God's great blessing."

Phoebe felt embarrassed. Why did her father need to poke his nose in the captain's financial matters?

Barnabas leaned on his elbows, and Phoebe cringed, noticing the stains on his sleeves. "Will thee stay long on-island, Phineas?"

"The *Fortuna* will be emptied of her cargo. Then she will be watered, and we will make way. If all goes well, we will be off within a month's time."

So soon? Panic tore through Phoebe. A month wasn't enough time! Usually, captains and their crew were eager for a rest on land. Most had families who needed their attention, children who needed to be reacquainted with their fathers. "What is the reason for such haste?"

"Winter migration, of course. The right whales will soon be traveling down the seaboard toward warm waters, funneled toward Nantucket by the arm of Cape Cod. Nothing satisfies Londoners but whale oil, and their consumption far exceeds our supply. The *Fortuna* must venture out and find more whales. The English appetite for candles is insatiable."

"Candles?" Barnabas's sparse eyebrows lifted. "I thought the English wanted our oil to light the streets of London."

Our oil? Since when did Phoebe's father consider himself to be part of the whaling industry?

"Candles too," the captain said. "They burn whiter, brighter, longer. 'Tis a shame we do not manufacture candles on Nantucket. Not a single chandlery on our sweet isle."

"Why? Why is that?"

"There is some secret to the process of refining. The Brown brothers of Providence buy raw material from my warehouse. Word has it that they allow no one to enter their manufactory. 'Tis all very hush-hush." He took a sip of tea. "Some enterprising fellow will figure it out soon, of that I have no doubt."

"Hmm," Barnabas said, "that is worth a ponder."

Uh-oh. Such a ponder from her father worried Phoebe. She had seen that look in his eyes before. Whatever currently held his interest would fade away and all his attention would move on to his newest fixation.

The captain finished his tea and set down his cup. "I stopped by thy home to see if Phoebe might allow me a day or so with this famous journal of Great Mary's."

Barnabas laced his hands together. "I am sorry to disappoint, but the journal must not leave my daughter's hands. It was a gift to her, and only to her."

Phoebe was startled by the strong tone of her father. He was not one to speak with authority, particularly to such a man as the captain.

Even the captain lifted his head, a puzzled look in his eyes. "I would take care to protect it, Barnabas. And return it within a day's time. Mayhap two days."

"Surely, Father, if he—"

"Nay! 'Tis my final word on the subject. The journal does not leave my household."

"The journal holds knowledge to all Nantucketers, Barnabas, not just to thy family."

"Thee be not captain here, Phineas Foulger. Not in my house."

The sharp rebuke was not lost on the captain. "Calm down, Barnabas. I have no quarrel with thee. Why, I've only just returned. I was merely looking to amuse myself whilst I have a duration on the island."

The captain rose to his feet and a wave of fear engulfed Phoebe. Her one chance to connect with the captain and it was slipping through her hands, all because of her father's unreasonableness.

But the captain surprised her again. He seemed not at all perturbed. Instead, he turned to her. "Phoebe, I wondered if thee might like to take a turn around the block on this fine day? 'Tis a rare day on Nantucket to have the autumn sunshine on us."

She stared blindly at him. "With . . . me?" Her voice squeaked and heat flooded her face. She coughed to clear her throat. "I mean, that sounds delightful." She grabbed her bonnet and cloak from the wall pegs before her father could object and hurried to join the captain at the door, fumbling with the ties on her bonnet.

As they walked along the street, passing one gray-shingled lean-to after another, she wondered if she should defend her father's bluntness or just let it pass. "I apologize for my father's injustice. He is not usually so abrupt in manner. The journal . . . it is the one inheritance his father has bestowed on him. He takes it very seriously."

"Think naught of it." The captain took her elbow, seemingly to help her over the ruts in the street, and her heart soared. He inhaled deeply. "I've missed the lady's wind of the island."

"Lady's wind?"

"There's a perfume in the air. It lacks the sting of salt."

She smiled. "That's a very lovely way to describe relentless island wind. I daresay that whatever direction I happen to walk, I will face the wind head on." As if she had beckoned it, a gust of wind ruffled her bonnet and made the ties stream out over her shoulder.

He grinned and led her to a bench under a tree on Main Street. "If thee is fond of wind, try sailing on a sloop in the middle of the Atlantic Ocean."

"Oh, how I would love it! I envy men and their sea adventures. Ships and shops, travel and trading, they fire my blood." The moment she said it, she felt the pink of her cheeks deepen to red. Too childish? Too eager? She glanced at the captain, wondering if she had spoiled his impression of her.

He was staring at her, the way a man stares at a complex puzzle he cannot cipher. "Thee has an uncommon way of looking at things, Phoebe."

"A good thing, I hope."

He laughed. "A very good thing. Thee is . . . quite refreshing, like a summer sea. In fact, I find myself caught under thy—"

Caught under what? Phoebe practically leaned forward to catch the end of the sentence, but he never finished his thought as his attention was diverted by the sight of an approaching man. Hiram Hoyt. The captain's first mate again. When he reached them, he stood in front of them, feet straddled as if he were still on a ship.

Slowly, he removed the perpetual pipe from his mouth. "I'm sorry to bother thee, Captain, but I've been hunting everywhere for thee. Thee is wanted down at the countinghouse."

"I'll be there presently, Mr. Hoyt." The captain spoke dismissively, but Hiram Hoyt did not budge.

"M' sincere apologies, sir, but they were insistent that I not return without thee."

"What's a first mate for?" Captain Foulger sighed. "Apparently Mr. Hoyt requires my full attention." He reached for Phoebe's hand.

She took his hand, or rather let him take hers, which felt small and warm when clasped in his—so smooth! It surprised her, such smooth hands; she expected them to be rough. Though of course a sea captain's duties were far removed from the harsh manual labors of his crew.

"Phoebe, child, I feel as if we've just begun our conversation."

"Yes! Yes, that is exactly my own feeling!" And then—startled by her reckless confession—she gasped and bit her lips, but the captain only offered her a beneficent smile and gave her hand a gentle squeeze before parting.

He was unlike any man she had ever met—worlds away from her father and his disastrous endeavors, or Matthew Macy's cynicism, or Horace Russell's hypocrisy, or her whale-obsessed cousins, her stern uncles, or any other man on this island. As she watched the captain stride down the street toward the wharf, heads turning as he walked, she realized that there was something in his bearing that set him apart. Her heart felt so tight it hurt.

When she returned home, she found a note left by her father that he was seeing to the sheep and would not return until supper, so she stirred the keeping room fire with the iron poker and pulled a chair over to a west-facing window. She sat down, the journal on her lap, eager to discover the profound wisdom of Great Mary. She felt goosebumps rise up along her arms as she saw the childlike penmanship of her great-grandmother. *This*, this was the mind of the woman who loomed so large over Nantucket.

Mary Coffin

3 November 1658

Sleep is impossible for me tonight. I am greatly distressed.

I saw a Quaker lady in town. I knew she was one because of the way she dressed and talked. She was speaking out on a street corner to anyone who would listen to her, and no one would, but she kept on talking.

Quakers are said to be agents of Satan himself, wandering around preaching against the church and its leaders. Patience and Margaret tell me that their father says they have horns and tails and perform evil deeds. The law prohibits anyone from having anything to do with them.

I was curious as to what this Quaker devil had to say, so I stayed hidden behind Goody Smyth's shop and listened as she spoke. She said that there is an Inward Light within each one of us, and we should all be listening to that Light. Because that Light was the Spirit of God, she said.

That did not sound like the words of a devil.

At one point, she noticed me and looked right at me, her eyes locked with mine. "Look for the presence of God, child! He is always with you!" Her face was radiant and her eyes were piercing and I couldn't tear myself away from listening to her. She spoke with such fervor, such passion. I have never seen someone express such feeling about God. Surely, anyone who acted like her in Sunday church would be strongly criticized for being overly sentimental.

As I listened, I wondered why the Quakers are thought to create such civil disorder. The Quaker threat, it is called. It is true that some of their beliefs are peculiar—despising the government or disrespecting ordained clergy. I have heard that they refer to our clergy as "hirelings." That is a strange notion, for how could anyone dare preach of God without going to seminary?

As my thoughts wandered to the Quaker threat, suddenly there was a commotion and this woman was dragged away by the constable. She did not resist him, and yet the crowd that surrounded her threw pebbles and sticks and horse droppings at her, and the constable treated her roughly.

I was upset by the sight of such needless violence on that poor woman. So much so that I started toward the crowd to put a stop to their cruelty. Someone from behind grabbed my arm. "Mary, you must not get involved. No one is supposed to have anything to do with them or they, too, will be whipped. If you speak out, you will bring harm to yourself. Or to your family."

The one who spoke so forcefully and held his grip on me so tightly was none other than quiet Nathaniel Starbuck. He led me away from the crowd, down the street, and toward home, guiding me swiftly and firmly. Nathaniel did not let go of my arm until we reached my house. Then he opened the gate for me and closed it behind me, heading off down the lane without a word.

When Father returned home that evening, he had news to tell. The Quaker woman was whipped on her naked back, her tongue was bored with a hot iron so she would never utter another word, and then she was put in the stocks for all to see her humiliation. A warning to all others, the selectmen said, to have nothing to do with these heretics.

Father said that the Quaker woman did not seem to be humiliated, but had a look of complete peace all throughout her punishment. He seemed distressed and could not sit still through dinner. He kept returning to the window, peering out with a troubled look on his face. I overheard him tell Mother that the General Court has gone too far. That it is like England all over again.

There is a dreadful storm raging tonight, pouring rain, thunder and lightning, and it is so very cold out. I cannot sleep, for I am deeply troubled about the poor Quaker woman.

I do not understand why these Quakers are so determined to share their religion. I do not even understand what the Quaker lady meant about God being the Light within us. But I must admit that I was astounded at the courage and conviction she displayed for her beliefs.

Would I ever have such conviction? I fear not. But there is a part of me that would like to have that certainty, deep down inside.

It is all most confusing.

4 November 1658

The Quaker lady was found dead in the stocks this morning. I never even knew her name.

I cannot stop crying.

3

Thoughts of Captain Phineas Foulger filled Phoebe's mind over the next few days, though she caught no sight of him, nary a glimpse. She reminded herself he was surely overwhelmed with work—seeing to the unloading of the cargo, dealing with the eager investors of the *Fortuna* and of course the lays to be disbursed for the crew. A whaling crew took no wages, but instead signed on for a lay of the future profits of the voyage. Barnabas had told her of the rumblings he'd heard that no whaleship had ever returned to Nantucket with such a full load, even excluding the chunk of ambergris found in a whale's intestines. A chocked-off ship in less than two years, he said, amazed. Unheard of! The families of the *Fortuna*'s crew wore broad smiles and paid up their debts.

Phoebe waited eagerly for First Day Meeting, hoping the captain might seek her out before Meeting started, but he treated her like all the others. Polite, respectful, but no special smile or look or word, no invitation to the gam Sarah had spoken of. Phoebe suffered in silence on the hard wooden bench—a different kind of silence than the usual quiet of a Quaker meeting. When the captain was "moved to speak," she felt a tingle start at the nape of her neck. He turned and his gaze swept over the room filled with Friends, and she imagined that it rested momentarily on her.

As she listened to his words—and not merely his words, but the strident timbre of his voice—she felt a strange constriction of her mind and heart. Oh, it was heavenly to hear God's Word spoken from the captain's perfectly shaped lips! She sat in a trance of admiration, gazing up at him. She thought she might swoon into a faint, right there, right in the utter stillness of Meeting.

Of course she did not.

The next day, Phoebe made her way toward 28 Orange Street, the residence of Captain Phineas Foulger and his thin-lipped daughter, Sarah. She would know it blindfolded—up Centre Street, a short left on Main Street, then right on Orange Street—for she had a habit of walking past it, even without any reason. Today she had a bonafide reason. Sarah Foulger had made an appointment with her, two weeks prior to the captain's return.

Phoebe had been looking forward to having occasion to visit the captain's house, a well-to-do home even amongst sea captains—a tall saltbox with blue shutters. She stood outside 28 Orange Street for a long moment, overcome by a nameless longing. As a child, she had often lingered outside this house while day turned to evening, that gloaming time, when she could remain unseen. Matthew caught her once and teased her, told her she was hungering after something that did not exist. But it did! she insisted. A perfect house, filled with a perfect family. There it *was*! And here it still was.

Two gaslight sconces flanked the door . . . burning even in daylight! The Friends frowned on opulence. If anyone else were to display such flagrant waste, the elders might have something to say about it. Anyone but Captain Phineas Foulger.

Phoebe was received by a servant into their high-ceilinged foyer and led to wait in the sitting room. She stood still for the longest while, hoping to listen for evidence that the captain might be at home. Alas, there was no indication he was present. She sighed, disappointed but not surprised. She had assumed on a weekday morning that the captain would be in his warehouse, counting his barrels of whale oil, meeting with the ship syndicate, preparing contracts for the next voyage, or whatever else it was that whaling captains did when they were not at sea.

As she waited for Sarah, her eyes soaked up every detail of the room: diamond-paned windows, scenic paper murals on the walls, fringed draperies, fashionable London-made settees, silver candlesticks from Mr. Revere's smithy in Boston. And *such* color in the rooms. Bright fabrics and rugs, bowls of flowers and greenery all about. When she was summoned to go up the balustrade staircase to Sarah's chamber (there was indeed a mortgage button on the newel post—Phoebe *looked* for it!), not a squeak could be heard on the wooden stair tread. (She *listened* for it!)

Phoebe felt a surge of pride over Captain Foulger's accomplishments. It shamed her to admit that one of Matthew Macy's criticism of her was accurate: she was overly impressed by wealth, by luxury and lavishness. Was it because her father had caused such insecurity that wealth seemed so inviting, so alluring, so comforting? An abundance of money seemed to be the answer to all of life's problems, or most of them, anyway.

A month ago, Sarah had asked Phoebe to sew a new winter wardrobe for her. Phoebe was a reluctant but skilled seamstress, grateful for the work. Very grateful.

This last spring, Barnabas's herd of sheep had been devastated by a skin condition that caused the poor woolies to lose their thick fleece. The pasture was littered with tufts of wool. The sheep of Barnabas Starbuck were no longer permitted to graze in the common area but confined to a small fenced pasture. Then the constable came across seventeen balding sheep wandering in the streets of Nantucket and impounded them.

Her father claimed he had neglected to mind the sheep because he had been distracted by the pain of a corrupt tooth . . . which had inspired him to create a dentrifice of his own invention—a mixture of cuttlebone, brown sugar, gunpowder, and saltpeter. Not a bad undertaking, even Phoebe agreed, as so many elderly Nantucketers had lost their teeth. But the problem lay in the ingredients of the dentrifice. The gunpowder and the saltpeter, combined together, became toxic to the user. Suffice to say it was a disastrous endeavor.

And Barnabas was slapped with an extra fine for the wandering sheep. (The constable's wife had tried Barnabas's dentrifice.) This was not an unusual event.

Phoebe counted on her modest income as a seamstress to cobble together a way to make ends meet, even if barely—and how she hated sewing, hated, hated, hated it!—plus she had turned away other smaller projects to take on Sarah's large wardrobe.

Today, she thought she might ask if Sarah would be willing to pay her in advance. It wouldn't cover the entire defaulted loan that her father had made, but it would be a start and might prove to Horace Russell that she would make good on the remainder. A fine plan, she thought.

So with some trepidation, Phoebe was eager to be welcomed into Sarah Foulger's grand chamber. But *welcoming* was not the word to describe Sarah on this gray morning. "Thee is late on the tide. Thy services are no longer required."

Phoebe searched Sarah's face to see if she spoke in jest, but her gaze was direct. "Sarah . . . be reasonable. I was downstairs, waiting for thee."

Sarah flicked that excuse away. "'Tisn't that. Father is sending me to Boston to have my entire wardrobe made over. He brought back bolts and bolts of fabrics of the finest quality. He traded for them in the Bahamas."

Phoebe dipped her chin. "I have made many dresses of fine cloth for Friends."

"Not these kinds of fabrics. Silks and cashmeres. And I will have mitts and fans made, even a hoop. The Boston maids are wearing corsets now."

"Corsets?"

"Corsets." Sarah spoke in a tone to suggest Phoebe might be a dimwitted child. "To help keep a woman's youthful figure. They make one's shape appear straight up and down." She made for the door. "I have much to do. Clara Swain is coming for dinner tonight. I'm on a mission to convince my father to marry again, and I believe she hopes he'll settle on her. I daresay Father has taken a fancy to her." She smiled smugly at Phoebe. "No doubt Mother would be pleased. They're first cousins, of course."

Phoebe stared at Sarah. Clara Swain! Of all people. Why, she was older than the captain and so utterly pious that even bedbugs stood at attention as she entered a room.

That night at supper, Phoebe found herself with uncommonly little to say to her father. She wondered if Clara Swain was dining at 28 Orange Street at this very moment, then abruptly dismissed the question. She had plenty of other fish to fry. Rather troublesome fish.

Matthew finished up repairing Henry Coffin's adze by midday and set it aside next to his smoothing tool. He gazed out the window—what a glorious day! The morning fog had burned off, leaving the rest of the day to a warm and slanting autumn sun. The harbor shone like glass, the masts shined on the water's surface like reflections in a mirror.

Just then a voice interrupted his musing. "Matthew?"

He spun around. In the doorway stood Barnabas Starbuck. "Is thee busy?"

"Never too busy for you," Matthew said.

As Barnabas walked into the cooperage, he picked up the adze and peered at the initials on the handle, then carefully set it down. Something was on the old man's mind.

Hands clasped behind his back, he walked slowly around the cooperage, kicking at the sawdust and wood shavings that littered the planks. "Matthew, I was wondering . . . does thee have any knowledge of candle making? Spermaceti candles, that is."

"Refining the oil for candles? Nay. I have heard 'tis a tricky process. Those who have cracked it won't share any information."

Barnabas frowned. "Exactly what I have heard."

"Someone on the island should try, though. 'Tis ridiculous to think we do not have the ability, when the whale oil is sitting right here." He pointed at the window toward Captain Foulger's warehouse.

"Indeed it is." Barnabas lifted up the adze. "'Tis Henry Coffin's?"

"Aye. I just finished its repair. You caught me thinking of closing up shop and delivering it to Henry Coffin myself. Seems a shame to waste such a beautiful day by staying indoors."

"Henry would appreciate a visit. Not sure if thee has heard, but he was recently fired by Captain Foulger."

"Fired? He'd guarded the warehouse for years. What reason was given?"

"No reason."

"Huh. That's rather hard-hearted."

"Indeed." Barnabas walked to the window and stood on his tiptoes to look at the Foulger warehouse. "Has thee seen the cargo unloaded from the *Fortuna*?"

"I can't say that I've noticed. Heard it was chocked off, though. A full hold."

"But thee hasn't seen any barrels rolled into the warehouse? Nary a single one?"

"Three ships are in port this week. 'Tis hard to discern which lighter belongs to which ship."

"Aye."

"Barnabas, what are you getting at?"

The older man's face seemed clouded as he turned to Matthew. "Nothing, m' boy. Nothing at all. Only that Henry Coffin might appreciate a visit, if thee's half a mind to it."

Matthew grinned. "I've still more than a half a mind, I hope." He followed Barnabas to the door after putting the Closed sign up. Henry Coffin, he recalled, did make a nice apple brandy from his orchard trees.

▬▬▬▬▬▬▬▬▬

Phoebe returned home from buying meat and vegetables from a farmer's cart on Main Street and found the latch-string hanging out. Her father left a note to say he was off to research candle making. She rolled her eyes. How many times had he seen Phoebe and her mother make bayberry candles in the keeping room? Dozens!

She had much to do, but she felt restless and anxious. She sliced carrots, onions, and parsnips for a beef stew, one of her father's favorites, and wondered how much longer she would be cooking in this keeping room. Thirty days! Nay, it was down to twenty-four now. How was she ever going to find the money to pay off the defaulted loan?

She picked up the poker to stir the coals of the fire, added a few handfuls of peat and a stick of driftwood to the embers, then watched the flames sputter up. After hanging the heavy iron cauldron on the crane, she stood for a long moment, absentmindedly stirring the stew. The fire was low but hot, and in the flickering of the firelight she noticed her great-grandmother's journal on the chair by the window, right where she had left it.

Fresh air. That's what she needed to clear the tangle of her jumbled thoughts.

She covered the stew with the heavy cauldron lid, grabbed Great Mary's journal, stuffed it into her drawstring purse, and headed outside.

Mary Coffin

16 November 1658

Ever since the Quaker lady perished in the night, Father has been in a stew. It is not unusual for Father to be in an outrage over the interference of government, followed close behind with a rant over the absurdity of taxation. He left England to stop the long fingers of government from dipping into his purse. And now he wants to leave Massachusetts.

Mother asked him where he thinks he will find this peace he is searching for and he had no answer for her.

It will always be in the next place, I suspect. (I did not share that sentiment aloud.)

After Father left the house, quite in a huff, Mother gazed out the small window, watching him stomp off, and said it is a man's pride that makes him so stubborn. She called it their dreadful affliction.

I am grateful to be born a maid.

5 December 1658

'Twas my dearest friend Heppy's fourteenth birthday today. I gave her a sheepskin journal, just like the one Mother gave me last February for my own birthday. I added the same warning to Heppy that Mother gave to me, to never forget the Almighty Lord is reading every word. 'Tis a bit of an intimidating mantle to wear each time I pick up my quill and dip it in the inkpot, but I suppose it does bridle my tongue from blustering on and on about my worst brother, Tristram Jr.

Heppy's birthday holds great sadness for her, and great

joy for me. Her mother died on her eighth birthday, and her father sent her to Salisbury to live with his great-aunt, a wonderfully eccentric elderly dame for whom Heppy was named—Hepzipah Childers—and who happens to be our closest neighbor.

When Goody Childers discovered that Heppy had not been taught to read, she promptly hired a tutor. And because she knew I had taught myself to read by borrowing the books of my older brothers, she asked Father to allow me to join in with the sessions. She thought I might be helpful to inspire Heppy, to provide lively discussion. (Goody Childers told Mother that I was blessed with the gift of conversation. I thought it a lovely compliment, the nicest I'd ever been given, until Tristram Jr. said it meant I never stopped talking.)

Father hesitated to agree, concerned that Mother needed my help at home. Goody Childers assured him she would provide compensation for the tutor. At that, Father smiled. Pennies and pence are dear to him.

And so began a time of great blessings. My friendship with dearest Heppy, and sitting under the tutelage of Elder Toth.

I had only seen Elder Toth at church. Our family pew sat two behind his. I was not convinced I would enjoy being tutored by such an imposing man, as wide as he is tall, but he quickly won my heart. After settling his rather portly self into his chair, he peered at us over his spectacles and uttered in his raspy voice, "Little maids, do not let anyone snuff out your fire!"

I have never forgotten those wise words from Elder Toth. They are written on my heart.

4

Phoebe walked a long way down Cliff Road, walking and walking, until she came to a stop, staring out at the meadow of the Founders' Burial Ground. Somewhere here, in an unmarked grave, her great-grandmother Mary was buried. That's how the Quakers did things: a minimum of fanfare. But there were moments when Phoebe wished the Quakers were not always so mindful of outward pride and would allow things such as headstones, so she could know with certainty where her great-grandmother's grave lay. She wished she could stand in front of it and ask questions of the woman known throughout the island for her wisdom and good judgment. The Great Lady of Nantucket she was called. How would her great-grandmother advise Phoebe about the quandaries she currently faced?

"You look like you've lost your best friend."

Phoebe stiffened when she heard the familiar voice, realizing that Matthew Macy stood just a few feet from her. She spun around to face him and thought, for just a split second, she caught an expression of longing in his eyes, here and then gone. "How long has thee been standing there?"

"Long enough to know you've got some kind of problem."

Matthew was spectacularly unconcerned about being disowned by the Society of Friends. Why, he even dropped his thee's and thou's on the morning after he had been disowned. A way of openly displaying his irreverence. Even if with but a foot, nay, but *one* toe, he must step outside the circle. Phoebe's aunt Dorcas sized Matthew up succinctly: "He not only goes out on a limb, he takes the saw along."

A queer mélange of feelings twisted within her: familiarity, caution, sorrow. Silently, she studied him. He had changed little since his return last spring. Tall as a tree, hard-muscled, thick black hair, a magnificent hawk nose, and the bluest eyes she'd ever seen. The slanting afternoon sun tinted his eyes even bluer. She was particularly vulnerable to those eyes, so she took care to keep her chin tucked whenever she encountered him. All in all, he could be quite attractive—*quite*—with a shave and a haircut, but he cared nothing for what others thought of him. "Why is thee here?"

"Had to deliver something down the road to Henry Coffin's farm." He took a few strides to draw closer to her, close enough that she caught the smell of brandy on his breath. "So what brings you here . . . to the final resting place of these old settlers?" He gestured an arm toward the large grassy field, dotted here and there with scrub bushes and trees.

She wrinkled her nose in disgust. "Thee is half seas over." *Drunk!*

He was indifferent to her appraisal. "Let me guess what troubles you. I'll bet it has something to do with you hoping to court a man as old as your father."

That was *not* true! Phineas Foulger was half her father's age.

He smirked. "But here's the real dilemma: how will you be able to tell them apart?"

Phoebe's head came up with a jerk. "I don't know what thee is talking about."

"You and the captain. He was seen paying a call to your house." He wiggled his eyebrows. "It's caused quite a stir among the Quaker matrons and maidens. Especially the ones who have hoped to set a trap for him."

"He stopped by the house, 'tis all."

"I have to hand it to the captain. 'Tis uncommon for any man over forty to be found on a whaling ship. 'Tis dangerous work. Most men his age are patching sail or shoring up slack." The sound of bleating sheep floated from off in the distance. "Or mayhap, minding fleeceless sheep?"

Was that an arrow aimed at her father? Phoebe narrowed her eyes, thinking of how she no longer liked—indeed, couldn't abide—Matthew Macy. There was a time when she found his sarcasm and mockery to be amusing. What was once witty and droll was now harsh and condemning.

She had recently pointed out that any self-respecting cooper would not accept a commission to carve figureheads for a ship. They were considered good-luck charms, to see the ships safely back to shore. Worldly, utterly profane, thoroughly secular. He had responded by saying that it was not a conflict to him because he was not a self-respecting man.

But there was the rub. For all of Matthew's annoying ways, he *was* a much-respected man. His excellent cooper skills were in high demand, he was well liked by seamen, and these two qualities made him hard to avoid. It galled her to think she once fancied him.

Matthew quirked his dark eyebrows. "'Tis a foolish notion."

"What is?"

"Captain Phineas Foulger. You've set your sights on him. As I recall, you've always had a fondness for him. I remember how, even as a schoolgirl, you would stand outside his house and stare at it."

Phoebe tipped her chin in his direction, though she didn't look at him directly. How would he possibly know of her heart's desire? She had told no one. She felt her cheeks tingle, and then her neck. She didn't want to reveal to Matthew that he had irked her, had found her out, but her next words shot out like a challenge. "What concern of that belongs to thee?"

"Well, in a way, it is. If the captain marries himself a young maid, she might convince him to stay home. And that's bad business for the cooperage."

Of course! Of course he found a way to make it all about him.

"So, Phoebe, do tell. Have you decided, then? 'Tis better to have no husband at all or to have one who is never home?"

She frowned. That was a question that circled through every Nantucket woman's mind.

"One thing I've always wondered, and you might be just the one to clear up this conundrum, being as you're such a devout Quakeress . . . Don't you think it's odd that the captain insists on being called Captain Foulger?"

Yes. Yes, Phoebe did. She found it very odd. The Friends eschewed titles of any kind to avoid pride and as a subtle reminder that all were equal in God's eyes—man, woman, white, black. Servants called their employers by their Christian name. She also had a hope that the captain would stop

56

referring to her as "my child." But she would not admit anything to Matthew Macy.

"And another question about your fine community of Friends."

She cringed, crossing her arms and holding her elbows. Once, it was his community of Friends too.

"There is a strong emphasis on love in all relationships, is there not?"

"Thee knows the theology as well as I do."

"Why is it that they seem to only love other Quakers, then? Unless, of course, a transaction benefits them financially. Then they seem to be considerably open-minded."

What could she say to that? His critique was not unfounded, but he focused on what was wrong with the Society of Friends rather than all that was right. He always had. "Not everyone is motivated solely by riches. Most Friends embrace seasoning. Most seek the Light of God in all their dealings."

"Like you?" He scoffed. "You certainly wasted no time choosing a walking oil barrel."

"Me? Me! What about thee? Thee went off to pursue oil, bone, and ambergris." She shouldn't have said that. The disaster of the *Pearl*, his father's ship, was too serious, too heartbreaking to fling in indignation. In a softer voice, she added, "I did not refuse thee for a lack of wealth, but of faith."

"You refused me because the elders told you to." His brow furrowed. "Don't deny me that, Phoebe."

"I don't deny it!" Phoebe's voice was strained, her cheeks blazing. "Yet thee is neglecting the fact that I could not disagree with them. Thee was disowned at sixteen for laughing aloud in Meeting, more than once. And thee cared not!" She crossed her arms against her chest. "Thee is faithless to the core. Nothing to stand on in a gale. Just look at what has happened to thee . . . thee finds solace in spirits and spends more time in the gaol than in thy own bed. Thee has lost all ambition."

"Have you ever wondered how it felt on my end?" He glared at her, his voice rising. "I thought I was building a future for us. I endured three long years of misery and hardship at sea. And nothing to show for it. Worse. I returned to more loss than gain. I'm still digging out of debt for the investment my father put into the *Pearl*. Three hundred pounds sterling."

When his yelling stopped, the tension between them settled as thick as the fog that covered Nantucket more often than not. The *Pearl* had been Matthew's father's grand plan to sail into a cozy retirement. He took out a loan to purchase a two-masted whaling sloop. He would not consider investors backing him in this venture, nor insurance, though Phoebe had heard that his wife, Libby, was furious with him for such stubborn thinking. Isaac Macy wanted a ship of his own, a legacy for his two sons, Matthew and young Jeremiah. When the *Pearl* floundered in a squall, she took everything with her. The investment, the cargo; worse still, the life of Isaac Macy. A tragedy that left Matthew's soul closed off to any Light of God. She worked her palms together nervously. "I am sorry, Matthew. Truly sorry."

His eyes—*such* blue, blue eyes—they went soft and she found herself melting. Then he sighed and dropped his head. "Well, things have a way of working out for the best." In a bitter tone he added, "Look at you—you're gunning for a wealthy old man to feather your nest."

And there it was. Each time something went right between

them, he had to ruin it. "Why do you want me to be as dark and cynical as you? Why are you so determined to snuff out whatever light and goodness is in the world?"

"I guess it depends on what you call light and goodness. Think on it, Phoebe. Will it be all light and goodness to be Sarah Foulger's stepmother?"

Rather than answer Matthew, she looked over at the sun skimming the tops of the trees that lined the cemetery. In a moment of pure spite, she said, "Tales of thy misdeeds have spread far and wide. Let me not delay thy return home." She pivoted in the other direction. "Home for thee is closer, 'tis it not?" The gaol, she meant. The place for drunks. Well, perhaps that might be too harsh a word, but it was true Matthew drank too much. He was often involved in street brawls and charged to spend nights in the gaol, a cold and drafty place. He was permitted to leave the gaol and go to his workplace during the days and return each night—only because his coopering skills were desperately needed on the wharves and there wasn't much concern of a prisoner fleeing an island.

Instead of being insulted, Matthew burst out with a laugh. "You're right! Dinner will soon be served." He covered his mouth for a social cough. "Delivered, that is." He whipped off his hat and bowed down with a flourish. "Good day, Phoebe." Away to the gaol he strode, hands in pockets, whistling as he walked. Not a care in the world.

The very opposite of how Phoebe felt.

Matthew walked to the gaol in fine fettle, growing more pleased with himself with every step. As he passed Hannah

Mitchell and Eliza Pinkham gamming on the Pinkhams' friendship steps, he smiled warmly at the two portly matrons and they waved heartily back at him. The women of Nantucket—they were a special breed. Mayhap with the men so much gone, they had proven themselves to be flexible and strong.

As he let himself into the gaol, his thoughts kept returning to his encounter with Phoebe in the Founders' Burial Ground. Her remarks plagued him, though he took care that she would not discern as much. *Lost all ambition? Me?* 'Twas a sobering thought. He had always been an ambitious man.

"Why do you want me to be as dark and cynical as you?"

She was right. It shamed him, but he did indeed want to dim her happiness. How dare she be so happy when he was so . . . unhappy? He sent out arrows and barbs in her direction, testing to see when she would lose her temper and break.

She wasn't breaking.

Sometimes he wished he had an ounce of her steadfast faith. It would be nice to see the world through innocence and naïveté instead of his relentless skepticism.

The more he thought on it, the more surprised he was to realize he felt sorry about what he had said to her, how he had mocked her. Biting words came easily to Matthew. To humble himself and apologize was more difficult.

Phoebe had a way of keeping him off his soundings. She always had. He held his hand about an inch from his mouth and exhaled, then quickly inhaled. Ah no. No! She was right. Henry Coffin's brandy lingered still! He hadn't meant to have more than a glass with the old man after delivering the adze he'd repaired for him. Two glasses, at the most. But then Henry got talking about his theory as to why he'd been fired as warehouse security guard for Captain Phineas Foulger. A far-fetched theory, based only on something he thought he overheard. Henry kept pouring and Matthew kept drinking. And listening to the old codger's suspicions. And thinking on it.

There was no way it could be true—and no way such a secret could stay kept . . . not on this little island. Besides, Henry Coffin had weak hearing. And what did he really hear? A low exchange of male voices on a moonless night.

"Keep a good watch" and "I'll rest easier when we're unloaded."

What did that reveal? Nothing! And yet . . . he had a strange sense that something was amiss with the *Fortuna*. Something fishy. Baffling.

He sighed. More likely his jealous streak was heightening his natural wariness.

Phoebe Starbuck. He should be grateful to be cured of his dangerous boyhood fancy. Thankful that she had buckled and bowed to public opinion—by that he meant the stuffy elders of the Quaker meetinghouse—and had broken off their understanding. Never mind that their understanding was what kept him going during those three long years he was away at sea. Never mind that the thought of returning to Nantucket to marry her and start a life together kept him from despair after the sinking of the *Pearl*. After the untimely death of his father. Never mind all that.

He sighed again. That was the trouble with long nights in a cold, stinking gaol. Too much time to think. He needed more on his mind.

So here was a question that kept jabbing its sharp elbow at him: Why would the illustrious captain fancy Phoebe?

Perhaps the answer was as simple as attraction. Any man with blood pumping through his veins would find her comely. Some said Phoebe Starbuck to be the prettiest girl on the island. He would fall in that camp.

Ah, but those eyes of hers! Their shape, like two perfect almonds, colored like coffee. And a fine aristocratic nose. The Coffin nose. Thick hair, the color of mahogany. And those lips! Large and full. He gave his head a slight shake. Too much time to think.

There was something amiss here, like the *Fortuna*. And like the *Fortuna*, he could not put his finger on it.

Phoebe did not have a dowry to speak of, and while the captain was thought to be fabulously wealthy, he could be miserly with his pennies.

Could it be that Barnabas was in dire straits again?

The old fellow always seemed to find a willing investor or two for his ventures, and he must have some income from sheep. Mayhap not. Murmurs fluttered through the taverns of his latest fiasco: Barnabas had imported a ram and ewe from England to refresh the stock, convinced he could improve the quality of his flock's wool. Something went terribly wrong, as it often did with Barnabas's grand ideas. This spring's shearing was the worst ever for him—no one would buy his wool.

It's not that Barnabas's ideas were without merit; it was in their execution that things went awry. Still, Matthew had always had a fondness for him, partly because he had been his father's lifelong friend. Barnabas was a kindhearted man, loyal to a fault, devoted to the tending of his daughter . . . though it might be more accurate to say that it was Barnabas who needed tending to.

Matthew was never clear on the real reason as to why Barnabas chose not to pursue riches on a whaling ship, like nearly all of the men on this island did in their prime. He claimed he had no need for the world beyond the harbor. "Whales and wandering, what for?" Barnabas would oft declare. "There are voyages aplenty to be had right here."

That thinking never made much sense to Matthew, even though he did share a passion for this little island.

He stretched out on the hard wooden bunk and covered his eyes with his arm, wondering where the constable was. He had always been blessed with the gift of sleep—anywhere, anyplace, anytime. Thus, he didn't entirely mind sleeping in the dim Nantucket gaol, apart from the stench, though he would have much preferred a goosefeather mattress and a warm woolen blanket. There was a fireplace, but the constable, stingy about sharing wood, only provided peat to burn, and it stunk up the room. The food was entirely inedible. He planned to complain about it in the morning.

The constable, Zacchaeus Coleman, was Matthew's second cousin on his mother's side and accustomed to Matthew's candor, despite the fact that the cook of the inedible food happened to be his wife. A surly and sour woman on a good day. By contrast, Zacchaeus was jovial, with fuzzy muttonchops covering his round cheeks and a headful of frizzy gray curls, an effect like a halo.

Matthew's stomach growled. Where was Zacchaeus, anyway?

He jumped off the plank and went to peer out the window through the iron bars, though it wasn't much of a view from here. Not like his cooperage, right near the wharf, where he had a view of the world beyond the harbor.

Whaling—now that was where Matthew's heart had always lain. But that was where his heart had been lost. He let himself out of the gaol and walked to the end of the road, hands in his pockets, wondering if Phoebe might still be wandering around in the Founders' Burial Ground. And why? She never did say.

———

Phoebe walked around the grounds until she came to the live oak tree where she was convinced Great Mary had been buried. She had no reason to think so, but the thought pleased her. It was one of the only flourishing oak trees on the island and it never lost its leaves, even in winter. She often wondered how it had escaped the sharp saws of greedy settlers. It was surely safe now, providing shade to the final resting spot for those very settlers.

She plopped down to lean her back against the tree and pulled out the well-worn sheepskin journal. In all truth, she had not felt anything but a mild curiosity about the journal when her father presented it to her. Not until the captain showed interest in it, coupled with her father's strong reaction to resist him. Then Sarah Foulger also made reference to it as she was walking Phoebe to the door the other day—the very day she had relieved Phoebe of gainful employment—to ask if she'd had opportunity to read it.

"Nay," Phoebe said as she crossed the threshold. "I haven't had time yet."

Then Sarah made a remark about how unfortunate it was that Great Mary's greatness seemed to have skipped over certain generations . . . and closed the door in Phoebe's face. At first Phoebe didn't catch her meaning, but on the way home, as the remark rolled around in her mind, she realized that Sarah *meant* to insult her.

Phoebe opened the journal and gently stroked the first brittle page with her finger. Her first reading had been slightly disappointing and the fading ink made for slow going. Mostly, from the captain's reaction, she had gained an expectation for much more from her great-grandmother's journal. More of what, she wasn't sure. More wisdom, more insights, better guidance to navigate through life. Certainly, though, it wasn't fair to expect much from the thought life of a young girl, albeit a spunky and spirited one. Phoebe needed answers now.

She sighed. So what *had* she truly learned of her great-grandmother?

Well, one thing: Great Mary had been glad she was a girl.

Phoebe sat up and looked at the late afternoon sky, now streaked with clouds. She'd always wished she'd been born a man. Men seemed to have the best of it, of that truth there was not the smallest doubt in her mind. Traveling the seven seas, adventure, risk and danger. And riches too. Her male cousins were given full privileges from an early age, while Phoebe was expected to sit quietly in Meeting, to manage the household, to do good works, to hope for a husband and babies.

How she longed to be roaming the world, sailing on a whaling ship, hanging on for dear life on a Nantucket sleigh ride. She'd listened with bated breath to her uncles as they recounted their voyages, starting with "Thar she blows!" yelled by the lookout in the crow's nest, to "Fire in the chimney!" as blood spewed out of the whale's blowhole, a sign that death was imminent.

Phoebe straightened out a seam in her gray dress. It seemed as if gray was a metaphor for a woman's role. Not too loud, not too quiet. Not too bright, not too dim. The Friends of Nantucket seemed to be continually exploring the possibilities of the color gray. Gray, gray, gray! What if a person was born with a longing for blue skies, not gray fog? What if she felt she had a spark inside her, if there was a flint in her?

Her eyes shifted down to the sheepskin journal in her hand. Great Mary did not fit the metaphor of grayness. She was learned during a time when most girls weren't even taught to read and write and cipher.

Then it occurred to Phoebe that Great Mary was largely self-educated. Imagine that—teaching herself to read by borrowing her brothers' books. Imagine the mind of such a child. Imagine the determination of such a child.

Suddenly, the fog cleared in Phoebe's mind. She was *not* going to let her father be declared Town Poor. She wasn't quite sure how to manage her father, because even if she found a way to save their home from auction, he would find another way to risk everything. It was in his nature, that pride. A glimmer of good humor returned and she smiled. It was her father's "dreadful affliction."

The sun had dipped below the treetops, the wind had picked up, and Phoebe would be needed at home. As she hurried down Madaket Road, her spirits lifted as a plan began to stir in her mind. A *fine* plan . . . one that would solve everything!

And then she turned onto Centre Street and saw the constable standing outside of her house with the door flung open.

Mary Coffin

20 January 1659

This week has brought quite a shock.

A few days ago, Heppy's dear aunt did not come down the stairs for breakfast. When Heppy went to check on her, she found she had passed away during the night.

Heppy's father arrived for the funeral, and informed her that he wants to take her back to Newton with him. Heppy and I were both devasted by such an abrupt decision. Her father, who is not an amiable man, was unbending, even though I told him she could live with us. He said no child of his would live on charity. At this point, I wanted to ask what he thought great aunt Hepzibah had been providing Heppy these so many years, but Nathaniel Starbuck stepped in and mentioned that his cousin was looking for help with her new-born baby. She would provide board and lodging, he said, along with a small wage. Heppy watched her father carefully as he considered the option, then she offered to send him her wages. Heppy's father lit up at that offer, and quickly agreed.

Later, thinking back on the conversation, I thanked God I had held my tongue. What a child I'd have shown myself, and what a mess I might have made of Heppy's situation had I embarrassed her father and inspired his dreadful affliction to rear its head.

That very evening, Nathaniel helped Heppy and me to move her belongings to his cousin's house. Heppy will have to sleep on a pallet near the fire, a far cry from the private chamber she'd had in her great-aunt Hepzibah's house. She did not complain. Instead, she quoted me a Scripture: "Better is a dry morsel, and quietness therewith, than an house full of sacrifices and strife."

We said our goodbyes and Nathaniel accompanied me to my house, for the hour had grown late. He did not speak much on the way home, so I did the talking for both of us. He did not seem to mind.

8 February 1659

Another shock.

Lately, Heppy has been discouraging me from setting my heart on Nathaniel Starbuck. She reminds me that he is ten years older than I am, that the Starbucks are the quiet sort—unlike the Coffins, who are not at all quiet.

Today she told me news that she feared would hurt me, but she could not keep it from me any longer. She has learned from Nathaniel's cousin that he has been escorting Elizabeth Macy home from church for the last four Sundays, and there is rumor of an engagement soon to be published.

~~I know that Mother and God would not approve, but Elizabeth has no backbone, no vinegar in her blood.~~ If she is the kind of lifelong partner whom Nathaniel chooses, then I ~~fear he is woolywitted. He is a chowderhead! Weak-kneed. Spineless.~~ wish them all the best.

Mostly, I am brokenhearted.

5

The Starbuck house at 35 Centre Street was like most Nantucket lean-tos (though on the shabbier side)—two-storied in front, one-storied in back, covered in unpainted weathered gray shingles, anchored with a central chimney. And like most Nantucket lean-tos, the house faced south to catch the sun on its face. The sloping roof of the lean-to directed the wind right up and over the house. Inside was a tiny entry leading to small rooms, doors shut tight to keep rooms warm in the winter and cool in the summer. A narrow staircase led to two small bedrooms. And it was always tidy, for Phoebe had learned from her mother to keep house well.

The front door of the house was wide open, and the smell of simmering stew drifted out. As Phoebe crossed the threshold, she saw that everything in the house was all keeled over. The table was pushed over, the chairs were in disarray, the pantry shelves were emptied, everything tossed to the floor. Her father stood in the middle of the keeping room with the constable, turning in a circle with his hands on his hips, a stunned look on his face. When he saw Phoebe, he nearly sagged with relief.

"Daughter! Thank heavens! I knew not where thee had gone!" He lifted his palm in a wide arc. "Someone has ransacked the house!"

"What . . . in the world . . . has happened?" She peered into the back room and it too was topsy-turvy, with rusted pots and pans upended on the floor. She pressed a hand to her hammering heart and turned to Zacchaeus Coleman, the town constable. "Who might have done such a thing? What were they seeking?"

"Three ships came into port this week," Zacchaeus said in a helpless voice, "filled with sailors from foreign lands. The foreigners head for the taverns while the islanders head for home." He gazed around the room with a frown. "What is missing?"

What could they possibly have stolen? Phoebe was dumbfounded. The Barnabas Starbuck household had very little worth stealing. Anything left of value had been sold off to bury her mother.

Her father made his way around the table to the fireplace and turned a pewter mug upright. "A few coppers I had left on the mantel."

The constable scribbled it down on a piece of paper. "What else?"

Her father made a luffing sound and crossed the room to his desk. "My plans for a new enterprise!" He lifted the desk lid. "Ah, thank heavens. They are still here."

Phoebe took care not to exchange a look with the constable, but she knew what was rolling through his mind. Who would steal the business plans of Barnabas Starbuck? No one.

Phoebe hurried upstairs to find that the thief had entered the upstairs bedrooms as well. Her father's room was helter-skelter, her room had been turned upside down. Her wardrobe door was open, her dresses strewn on the floor. A silver hairbrush remained on the candlestand, one of the few items that had belonged to her mother.

A curious smell filled her bedroom. She sniffed the air. Musty, salty, smells of the sea. And what else? She noticed something on the rug and bent down to touch it. Tobacco ashes. She rubbed a finger in it and held it to her nose. Pokeweed, a cheap but common tobacco with its own stink. She closed her eyes. The thief could have been anyone. Anyone! She lifted the window sash to air out the room before she went downstairs.

"So then," Zacchaeus said when he saw her, "anything else amiss?"

"Not amiss," Phoebe said. "But much a mess." All was upset but the stew cooking in the pot—that remained untouched. She wasn't sure if she should be insulted or if the thief was simply not hungry. Too busy looking for something . . . but what?

"Nothing seems to be taken other than my coppers," her father said. "Five of them. Be sure to write that down. Five coppers. So, Zacchaeus, what are the chances of capturing the thief?"

The normally buoyant constable looked forlorn. "None."

After the constable left, Phoebe looked at her father. He still seemed befuddled.

"I am astonished, Phoebe. How could this be? We cause no one any harm. Why would God allow such a thing on us?"

Because God seems to favor some of his children above

71

others. It was a truth she was well acquainted with. But that was not how she answered her father. She took her time before she spoke, uprighting chairs, picking up broken pieces of pottery, sweeping up smaller shards. "I think it is simply what the constable said it to be. Sailors from foreign ports do not know us. They do not care whether we cause harm or not."

Her father sat down at the table and leaned on his elbows. "Tea, daughter. I need tea to calm my nerves."

A loose shutter banged against the house. The wind was rising. Phoebe drew the curtains, lit the candles, and added driftwood to the bed of coals. The sparks flew as she blew on the wood, and smoke became a small flame that caught and grew. She put a kettle of water on the crane to boil as she prepared two cups for tea. By the time the kettle whistled, the keeping room was tidied up. The rest of the house could wait. "Father, may we speak of something else?"

"Speak, daughter."

She handed a teacup to her father.

"I believe that Captain Foulger has . . . ," she kept her eyes on the tea, "taken a fancy to me."

Her father spewed out his sip of tea. "Phineas Foulger? Taken a fancy to thee?"

"Is that so hard to believe?"

"Nay, nay." His gray queue bounced upon his shoulder. "Yet thee is but a maid, he must be twice thy age!"

She gave him a look. "Father, thee was more than twenty years older than Mother. And thee has always said I am overly mature for my age and the captain is hale. Hale and hearty." And astonishingly handsome.

Barnabas set his teacup on the table. "This day continues to bring distressing surprises."

"The robbery was distressing, I agree. But why would it distress thee to hear of Captain Foulger's interest in me?"

"Has he spoken of such interest?"

She sipped thoughtfully on the hot tea. "No. Not yet. And he knows not my feelings for him. I wanted thy blessing first."

"Blessing? Blessing!" Her father's eyes went wide. "Phoebe, has he given any indication of . . . serious interest?"

She sighed. "Nay."

He seemed relieved. "Well, then, I shall cross that bridge when I come to it. If it comes at all."

She rubbed at a bit of candle wax that had dripped onto the tabletop. "What if that bridge is not far off?"

"The *Fortuna* is soon to set sail. He said so himself . . . standing right here in this keeping room."

She sighed again. How well she knew.

"I would not see thee harmed, daughter."

"Harmed?" She almost laughed. "Father, Captain Foulger would never hurt me. He is highly respected in the Society of Friends. He is . . . incorruptible."

"No man is incorruptible."

Mayhap. Except for Captain Foulger.

"Heed me, daughter. He needs an older woman to serve him well as wife."

"What if . . . he agreed to cover the defaulted loan on the house mortgage?" She dared not examine her father's face, but she could see his fingertips making a church steeple that opened and closed. That piece of information, she knew, made the entire subject another kettle of fish.

Barnabas reached out and put his hand over Phoebe's. "Tell me, daughter, why does thee think the captain is the man for thee? If I could get a satisfactory answer from thee, I will give the union my blessing. But I do not consider this temporary financial setback to be reason enough."

Phoebe rose and stood by the fire. How she longed for a sense of security, of solid footing. Was that so very wrong? Passion without substance led people astray, made an idol out of feelings. It seemed to be characteristic of her father—he followed his heart straight into poverty.

She knew how her father was perceived by others—she heard under-the-breath comments about his imprudent endeavors, about the stink of sheep on his clothes. It was ironic, in a way, because sheep raising had been the backbone of the island, up until England had discovered illumination by whale oil.

For a moment, Phoebe's thoughts traveled to her great-grandmother's journal. Mary Coffin knew what she wanted, even as a girl. It *was* possible to navigate one's own destiny. She swung around to face her father. "Captain Foulger is . . . Father, he's everything I want. Thee is just going to have to trust my judgment." She lowered her eyes to the rug, noticing a new hole worn through.

Then she looked up. Her father was staring at her as if her face had suddenly become unfamiliar to him. He did not smile. His eyes did not waver. His voice was steady, determined. "Thee has always had a strong will, Phoebe. Once thee sets thy mind on something, I have been unable to dissuade it. I fear this is the same situation. If the captain were to ask for thy hand, I will not withhold my blessing." He paused. "I just ask thee to remember that thy life is very precious. It is not to be wasted."

As Phoebe noticed her father's hands clasped together in

his lap, rivered with blue veins, dotted with age spots, she did not need reminding about the brevity of life.

The very next afternoon, Phoebe was sorting sheets for mending when a knock came at the door. When she opened the door, she suddenly felt as if all air had been sucked from her lungs. There stood Captain Foulger, smiling; his kind, intelligent eyes were tenderly searching her. "Phoebe, my dear, the afternoon is unseasonably warm. I hoped thee might like to take a turn with me."

She smiled. "I'll get my bonnet."

As they strolled toward town, Phoebe felt self-conscious from the stares of neighbors. At one point, at the bottom of Main Street, she nearly stumbled and the captain put his arm about her waist to steady her, letting it linger there for a moment longer than necessary. She felt a warm sensation spread from head to toe, like a snowflake melting beneath the warm rays of the sun.

Down by the water, they stood watching the ships rocking gently at their anchors, wrinkling the glassy surface of the water, their masts dark against the azure sky. The captain's eyes sought out and fixed on the *Fortuna*.

"Is all well?"

He startled as if he'd forgotten she was there. "I apologize, Phoebe. I fear my mind swam off to the ship." He turned to her, reaching down for her hand, lifting it, and to her great surprise, kissing it.

His mouth was soft and warm, and when he released her hand, his eyes met hers and she felt her knees begin to shake. She hid her flaming cheeks by dipping her chin and searched her mind for a question to distract him from her silly girlishness. One question had been circling her mind the last day or so. "Captain, I might ask a favor of thee. Does thee know of any employment opportunities?"

"For thee?" His hazel eyes were full of empathy. "Sarah told me that she had dismissed thee. I am sorry, Phoebe. It was not my intention. But a man cannot be faulted for spoiling his only daughter."

She felt her cheeks growing warm and gave a slight shake of her head. "Nay. Not for me. For my father."

He studied her face in such a way that she felt he understood all she did not say. "Perhaps thy father would consider signing on to a whaler. There is always need of crew. Alas, not the *Fortuna*. My loyal crew has signed on for the next voyage."

She shook her head. "My father would not leave the island."

"Ah, yes. Barnabas is a landlubber."

Ouch. There was no slight worse on Nantucket than calling someone a landlubber. But it was also true of her father, and she could take no offense.

"I'll give thought to the matter, Phoebe. Cheer up. Let's speak of happier things."

Two swans flew overhead, landing down the beach. "They are so lovely, graceful and elegant. 'Twould be wondrous, would it not, to live like a swan? To bring joy to all who gazed upon them."

The captain stared at Phoebe a moment. "Thee finds such pleasure in small things. I am surprised . . . given thy father's circumstances. I would expect thee to covet silver over swans."

Her lips tightened. "My father's circumstances do not make the swan any less lovely, nor the pleasures of nature any less sweet."

The captain's eyes shifted to the swans that stood at the edge of the gentle surf. Phoebe's gaze lighted on his hair, and she wondered if it was as wiry as it looked. Then, embarrassed by her silly mental ramblings, she whirled around to face the harbor.

"So how goes the journal reading?"

Great Mary's journal? It troubled her that the captain brought it up each time he was with her. Was she boring him? Saying stupid, infantile things? She hoped he realized she could discuss other things. "I have just begun to read it. The ink has faded. It is not easy to read more than a small portion at a time. It requires bright sunlight." And a great deal of squinting.

"And what wisdom does Great Mary have to impart?"

"So far, not much more than a girl's rambling thoughts."

"I am eager to see it."

A pair of screeching gulls flew overhead, but she kept her eyes on the water, watching it slosh around the wharf pilings. "If thee wants the journal, thee must be beholden to the journal's owner." Had those words truly just come from her mouth? How audacious! She felt her cheeks grow warm, then hot. A moment passed, then another. And still no response from the captain. She chanced a glance at him.

There was a quizzical half smile on the captain's face that she could not interpret. Startled? Pleased? Confused? Disdainful? She held her tongue, but her heart began to beat with an unpleasant heaviness.

"Well, then," he said at last, as he guided her elbow to

walk back toward Main Street. "I will see if I can find employment for thy father. Perhaps there is something Hiram Hoyt can find for him to do."

Oh. Oh dear. Oh dear me. She had been hinting at an altogether different kind of beholden.

Mary Coffin

28 February 1659

That day, that day, that day . . . I feel like such a fool.

I had refused to accept Heppy's rumor about the pending engagement between Nathaniel and Elizabeth until a few days ago, when I saw the two of them with my own eyes, strolling through the town with nary a care. Nathaniel's cheeks were red with cold, and he was laughing at something Elizabeth said. Elizabeth Macy! Who hardly says a word other than to answer a question with an aye or a nay, ~~and does not have an amusing bone in her body!~~

I considered ducking into the apothecary to avoid them, but it was too late for that. Nathaniel spotted me and lifted his hand in a friendly wave. I mustered my courage, straightened my back (Elizabeth is so tall!), and prepared to greet them politely despite the pain that was searing my heart. Suddenly, Elizabeth tightened her grip on my Nathaniel's elbow and turned him abruptly into the baker's shop so they would not cross my path. And he let her do it!

My stomach twisted into a tight knot and has not unraveled since.

That day, that day. How could I be so naïve?

7 March 1659

I have tried to not think of Nathaniel since that day. But that means I must not think of my future. Every dream, for as long as I can recall, has consisted of being alongside

Nathaniel. Heppy said that my wild imaginings are my undo-ings, and that I must face the situation hardheadedly.

She has not ever been in love.

17 March 1659

The General Court ordered the whipping of Ezra Win-chester for the crime of heresy. It was found out that Ezra hosted a secret meeting in his home with two Anabaptists to discuss the doctrine of infant baptism. Reverend Rodgers learned of the meeting and warned Ezra to repent. Ezra said he had nothing to repent of, for he was merely listening to the men. Reverend Rodgers said it grieved him deeply to turn Ezra in, but there was no other way to prevent the spread of erroneous beliefs.

Ezra was fined 20 shillings or 20 lashes. He refused to pay the fine, as he felt it would be an admission of guilt and he believed he had done nothing wrong. So he was marched over to the town square, near the stocks, and whipped in plain view, for all to see. Father and Nathaniel Starbuck made their way through the crowd to help Ezra when it was over, to get the poor man home. And for their trouble, the constable carried them off to spend the night in jail. Father and Nathaniel had not even attended the secret meeting held in Ezra's home!

As one can imagine, Father is furious, but it is a cold, si-lent fury. Most unlike him. Even Tristram Jr. is walking on eggshells, taking care not to provoke Father to annoyance with foolish antics as he normally does.

Something has changed in our town with the flogging of Ezra Winchester. It feels as if winter has descended.

6

In the cooperage, Matthew Macy sat on a wooden bench that he pulled next to the window to catch the full benefits of the slanting afternoon light. At his feet were curls of wood shavings. In front of him was a partially constructed barrel, with wooden staves that had soaked in a vat of water overnight to make them pliable, then he toasted them on a fire. The moisture and heat made the staves flexible enough to bend into a barrel shape, waiting to be fitted into a jig, a metal hoop that holds the staves fast. Barrels were constructed onshore, then dismantled and packed aboard ships to be reassembled as needed when whales were captured. An efficient use of space and time.

The door opened quietly and Matthew paused, listening for the familiar sound of his brother's light footsteps. He set the knife down that he'd been working with and braced himself for the loud "BOO!" that came from behind him.

It was their daily routine. After Jeremiah had been dismissed for the day from school (sprung from the cage, he called it), he would sneak into the cooperage and try to scare him. Matthew always played along, jumping or dropping tools in fright.

"Works every time," Jeremiah said proudly, as Matthew feigned a heart attack.

"What'd you learn in school today?"

"Absolutely nothing. A complete waste of time." His brother squinted and held a finger in the air. "Wait! I learned that Lillian Swain wears pink bloomers."

"Better not let Mother hear you." The boy's lightheartedness flooded Matthew with a sense of happiness.

Jeremiah grabbed an apple from the stoneware bowl, aimlessly polishing it on his coat. "Guess who I saw walking up Main Street?"

"Pretty much everybody."

"Phoebe Starbuck. She stopped me and gave me a horehound candy."

Phoebe. He had not seen her in three days. The admiration in the boy's voice was apparent. "Why do you like Phoebe so much?" he asked. Certainly, she was fetching, but Jeremiah was too young to notice such things. Mayhap not, though, if he was already observing pink bloomers.

His forehead wrinkled in concentration as he fiddled with a knife. When the boy finally spoke, his answer stunned him. "She listens to me like what I say matters."

Matthew's chest squeezed. "And I don't?"

"Thee is not home much."

Humbling. Matthew could guess what the boy did not say. He spent his evenings in the taverns, and that frequently led him to the unfortunate result of spending his nights in the gaol, arrested for public drunkenness. "What you say *does* matter to me, Jeremiah."

The boy shrugged but remained silent for a moment. "She was strolling with Captain Foulger."

Matthew dropped the croze he'd been using to cut grooves on the end of each barrel stave. "Jeremiah, I do not need to hear a detailed report on the activities of Phoebe Starbuck." His voice was harsher than it needed to be, and he was instantly sorry when he saw the hurt in Jeremiah's eyes.

"I'm not giving thee a report. I'm just getting to the good part."

"And what is that?"

"I heard Captain Foulger ask around town about thee. He will be coming to speak to thee this very afternoon. See if I'm wrong."

"What about?"

"That is the part I don't know."

Matthew picked up the croze and turned his attention back to the half-done barrel. "Well, he knows where to find me."

"Indeed I do."

Matthew whirled around at the sound of the captain's deep voice. Phineas Foulger stood imposingly at the threshold and Matthew wondered how much he had overheard. The captain took his hat off, tucked it under his arm, then strode into the cooperage, peering at the shelves of barrels along the walls, the tools carefully hanging on pegs, the curly wood shavings on the ground. "The very scent of raw wood—how I savor it." He pointed to one lone oval-shaped barrel. "I've seen plenty of flat-sided hogshead barrels, but never one like that."

"'Tis an experiment," Matthew said. "My thoughts are to keep it from rolling with the pitch of the ship."

The captain nodded approvingly, then glanced at Matthew's brother, whose eyes had been following him.

"Jeremiah, you'd better get on home," Matthew said, tipping his head toward the door. Frowning, his brother slowly ambled to the door.

After it shut, the captain lifted his chin. "I am in need of a cooper for the *Fortuna*'s next voyage."

"What happened to the *Fortuna*'s cooper?"

"His wife told him either he stays or she goes."

Matthew leaned against his plank. "I do not want to set sail again."

"I have heard it said that thee has an eye for pursuing sperm whales."

Matthew shrugged. It was true that he seemed to have a knack for locating the mighty beasts. "No doubt you're far more experienced than I." He gave the captain a direct gaze.

The captain picked up the croze and ran a hand along its smooth handle, then the blade where it made grooves in barrels. "Name thy price."

"Captain, I appreciate the offer and the interest, but there are other coopers on the island."

"None so skilled as thee."

"Not true. Many are better. I will give you a list."

"I did not ask for others. I am offering thee a position. A coveted position. Thee will receive a lay of one-fifteenth."

Matthew raised his head in surprise. A cooper's portion of the profits—his lay—was normally fourth to the captain's. Sizable, considerably more than the crew, but lower in rank to the captain and the first and second mates. One-fifteenth was nearly the second mate's portion. "But . . . Captain . . . I . . ."

He leaned toward Matthew. "Think of the greasy voyage we just experienced. Thee could be set up for life."

A cold spot started at the base of Matthew's spine and trickled upward like rivulets of ice water. All kinds of conflicting thoughts danced through his mind: *I will be rich!*

But I promised myself I'd never set sail again.

Set up for life!

But then I'd be leaving Jeremiah, and Mother.

And yet, after this voyage, I could amply provide for them. Mayhap retire the debt of the Pearl.

And then there is leaving Phoebe.

Would she reconsider me if I returned a wealthy man? She ended our relationship because I was disowned. Yet I've always wondered: if I were wealthy, would she have dropped me so readily?

Phoebe. Why should I bother myself about her?

The captain cleared his throat, waiting for his answer. "Is the offer not generous enough?"

"'Tis a very generous offer, Captain, and I am grateful, but I need time to consider it."

"Of course. A time of seasoning is always wise. Seek God's guidance. Pray on it before thee responds." As he walked toward the door, he spun around. "One more question. About Phoebe Starbuck."

Matthew stiffened. Phoebe *again.* "What about her?"

"My daughter, Sarah, seems to think there is something between the two of you."

"We were once childhood friends. Nothing more. I don't know why Sarah would entertain any other notion. As you recall, I am disowned."

The captain studied his face for a long moment. Then he smiled. "Excellent."

"Why? Why is that excellent?"

A flush started on the captain's cheekbones and spread down his cheeks, disappearing behind his sideburns. "I find myself quite . . . enamored with Phoebe. I have not met many women who have the purity of soul that she has." He put his gloves back on, one finger at a time. "'Tis a rare and lovely quality in a woman." He spoke softly, almost regretfully. As if he knew he didn't deserve Phoebe, and he didn't.

He adjusted his hat and turned all captain again. "I certainly wouldn't want to step on another man's toes. Especially my highly paid cooper."

"No toe stepping here."

The captain lowered his voice. "I trust this conversation, in its entirety, will remain between us."

"Naturally," Matthew said.

The captain opened the door and gave a parting sermon. "Whenever I think of Phoebe, this Bible verse comes to mind— 'Blessed are the pure in heart, for they shall see God.'"

"Right again," Matthew said flatly, but the captain had already gone.

23RD DAY OF THE NINTH MONTH IN THE YEAR 1767

To Phoebe's delight, the captain came round to 35 Centre Street regularly after the midday meal to take a turn. A routine had developed where they would walk to the harbor and sit on a bench in the afternoon sun, an ideal spot for the captain to keep one eye on the *Fortuna*. At the captain's request, Phoebe would read aloud an entry or two from Great Mary's journal.

Today, when she finished the section on the death of the Quaker lady, the captain seemed quite distressed.

"'Tis shocking, I agree," Phoebe said. "After all, this is our heritage. To think that a Friend was treated so violently, when she only wanted to share the Light with others."

He hesitated a moment before speaking. "Does Great Mary not ever write of Nantucket Island?"

"Not yet, but I admit I have not made much progress. 'Tis not easy reading, and not solely for the subject matter. I find I must read and reread, especially in sections where the ink has faded."

The captain glanced down at the journal in her lap, then squinted to try to cipher the wording. "Aye, I can see that."

"But, Captain, is it not a wonder? To enter into Great Mary's thought life, to grasp her spirit, to see what made her the woman she became." A seagull shrieked and Phoebe turned her head to follow its flight. "When my father first gave me the journal, I admit I felt a bit indifferent. But now"—she closed it and hugged it to her chest—"now I am relishing it. Savoring every entry. I feel I've been given a great gift. I look at it every chance I get."

He stared at her, his eyes bright, appreciative. "I look at thee, and I want to keep looking."

He smiled and she felt suffused in heat, head to toe. Whenever the captain spoke tenderly to her, she felt a rush of blood to her temples. He peered intently into her eyes for a very long time, his mouth so close his trimmed beard tickled her chin. She felt her thoughts grow dazzled and scattered.

In a low voice, he said, "Phoebe, my dearest, I am not

normally an impulsive man. And yet, there is something I'd like to ask you."

Phoebe's heart pounded in anticipation. *My dearest. He called me his dearest.* She had a premonition that this was a fulcrum point for her life, a before-and-after moment, and she would never be the same again.

Mary Coffin

1 May 1659

Tristram Jr. is courting Heppy! MY Heppy! I am flummoxed.

How did I miss this strange turn of events? And yet it never occurred to me that Tristram Jr. would appeal to her, ~~nor to any female in her right mind.~~

Heppy spends every Sabbath afternoon with our family. The last few Sundays have brought perfect spring weather, warm and gentle and sunny. Tristram Jr. and Heppy have taken long walks together. Each time, when they returned to the house, I thanked Heppy for minding Tristram Jr., as if he were a mischievous child to amuse! She would blush and I thought nothing of it. Oh, how blind I can be when I do not want to see something.

Last Sunday, I went outside to draw water from the well and spotted them coming through the woods into the clearing. Holding hands! My jaw dropped to the bottom of the well.

After supper, I confronted Heppy with this information and she burst into tears. She did not want to tell me of her growing fondness for Tristram Jr. for she feared I would disapprove. (I do!) She also said she was sensitive to my broken heart over Nathaniel, and did not want to rub salt in my open wound. (She did!)

But after we both had a good cry, I hugged her and told her I would give her my blessing to court Tristram Jr. ~~(though, for the life of me, I do not see what she finds attractive about~~

~~him).~~ I felt more cheered when I realized that my dearest Heppy might one day be my true sister.

That is, if Tristram Jr. doesn't botch this romance.

31 May 1659

Today Tristram Jr. is moving to Newbury to apprentice with a printer. He told Heppy that he will be too occupied with his work to continue their courtship. Heppy is heartbroken.

She says that now she understands why I have been so melancholy over losing Nathaniel to Elizabeth. She asked me to forgive her for a lack of empathy, and of course I did. I am somewhat shamed to enjoy that she feels a bit of the despair I have experienced these past few months.

But there is a difference. I have no doubt that Heppy was spared from a horrible life with my horrible brother. And I have no doubt that I might have missed a wonderful life with a wonderful man.

I **knew** Tristram Jr. would botch things up.

7

Phoebe found her father on his knees in the cellar, emptying barrels onto the dirt floor. "Daughter—I have thought of nothing else but candles since the captain's visit. Candles, candles, candles. They are calling to me. Where did thy mother keep her candle-making equipment?"

"In the back room." The obvious place. The place where household tools were always kept. Always, always, always.

When he heard the timbre of her voice, he stopped what he was doing to look at her. "What's happened? Thee looks like thee has had a fright!"

Her voice, when she spoke, was hoarse. "Nay, not a fright. A . . . surprise. A happy one. Come upstairs and I will put the teakettle on. I'll tell thee all about it."

In the keeping room, Phoebe took her time preparing the tea. Her father sat at the table, patiently waiting, until she set a cup of steaming tea in front of him. She swallowed. "Captain Foulger has asked me to marry him."

He raised his hand to his mouth and his eyes widened in shock. "And what did thee say to him?"

"I told him I would be honored to be his wife." Even as she said as much to the captain, she knew her heart was bolder than her words, for what she felt was far more than being honored. Jubilation filled her sails. *It's happened!* she thought. *Just as I had hoped and dreamed and planned.* She sighed, relieved.

Her father stirred sugar into his teacup, stirring and stirring, as Phoebe waited for his response. But there was no time for it.

Without even a knock, Sarah Foulger burst right into the Starbuck home and closed the door firmly behind her. Her black cloak doubled her size, giving her the appearance of a nearly man-size girth. Beneath her bonnet she glared at Phoebe.

"Thee!" Sarah's finger pointed at her, pinning her against the wall. "Thee has harpooned my poor, unsuspecting father!"

Phoebe bit her lip. Ah, so the captain told Sarah of their intentions to marry. It shouldn't have surprised her, yet it did. And then it warmed her heart, for it proved his proposal was not an impulsive one.

Sarah switched her gaze to Barnabas. "And thee! No doubt thee is partaking in this scheme! How trite a story. The quickest path to riches is on another's wake."

Barnabas blinked. And colored. And hung his head.

Sarah snapped her head toward Phoebe. "Hear me, girl! I am the mistress of Orange Street. It is my mother's home. She would never forgive me if I let a woman like thee take her place. I told my father that very thing."

Phoebe felt her cheeks grow warm. "And what did the captain have to say about thy declaration?"

"He said nothing to defend thee. Because he knows I am right." She marched to the door and spun around. "Do not think of installing thyself in my home. I will not allow it!" And with that, she pivoted and blew out of the house in the blustery style she entered, not even bothering to close the door behind her.

Barnabas got up from his seat and closed the door. "I daresay that woman can rankle the oysters in anyone's gullet. Small wonder the captain takes to sea so often."

"Indeed." Phoebe looked out the window and watched Sarah sweep down the street, her black cloak billowed like the sails of a ship.

"Phoebe, daughter, is there any truth in what she says?"

She turned back from the window to face him. "Does thee think I am so small a person as that?"

"Nay, of course not. But Sarah Foulger and her sharp tongue will be a permanent part of this marriage." When she had no response for him, he grabbed his coat and hat and said he was going out to check on the sheep.

Disappointed by the lack of enthusiasm her father showed for her betrothal, topped by Sarah's blatant rejection of her, Phoebe sat down in her chair and covered her face with her hands, trying to fight tears. This was not how she imagined news of her engagement to be received. Even her proposal was not how she had imagined. The captain had kissed her only on her forehead, like she was a small child. She had hoped he would truly kiss her, for it was the custom when a couple becomes beholden. She had imagined more passion, more fervor. Instead of embracing her, the captain took her hands and gently squeezed them, saying, "Well done."

Well done. What had she done?

Phoebe moved to the fireplace, took up a poker, and stabbed the logs, releasing a shower of sparks. She paced up and down in the keeping room. She had no illusions that Sarah would take joy in her father's betrothal, but she did not expect to be refused a place in the captain's house. A rightful place for his wife. How humiliating to be denied her husband's home by his daughter. All on the isle would wag their tongues at that.

Out of the corner of her eye, she saw her drawstring purse, left on the tabletop next to two abandoned cups of tea, now cold. She reached for the journal and sat down by the window, opening it to a random spot.

Little maids, do not let anyone snuff out your fire.

Phoebe read and reread that line. They were the first words Mary Coffin's tutor had said to her and her friend Heppy, when they were but young girls.

She closed the journal and put it back in her drawstring purse, grabbed her cloak and bonnet, and hurried up Centre Street to Main Street.

Do not let anyone snuff out your fire. Her step quickened, her spirits lightened. She called out greetings to neighbors who were closing up shop for the day. She was breathless, holding a stitch in her side, by the time she reached the harbor.

Boldly, Phoebe rapped on the warehouse door where she knew the captain had an office. No response. She tried the door, but it was locked. She knocked again, more persistently.

No response. She walked around to the side and saw the flickering of candlelight inside. Someone was inside. She went back to the door and knocked again, using the palms of both hands. Finally, she heard footsteps approach and the door opened a few inches. The first mate, Hiram Hoyt, poked his head out of the crack to greet her with his typically apologetic look and the perpetual pipe stem sticking out of his mouth. "I'm sorry it took so long to answer. What can I do for thee?"

Phoebe's confidence wavered. *Do not let anyone snuff out my fire.* She straightened up. "I would like to speak with the captain."

"I'm terribly sorry," the first mate said, sounding sincerely regretful. "He asked not to be disturbed." He took in a drag from his pipe and blew it out his lips.

She coughed and waved away the smoke. How she hated the smell of pokeweed tobacco! "Tell him Phoebe Starbuck must speak with him. 'Tis important."

Hiram Hoyt apologized again, before taking care to close and lock the warehouse door. Phoebe waited patiently outside, hoping the timid man could muster enough courage to interrupt the captain's important work and tell him she was outside. Surely he would come if he knew Phoebe waited on him, would he not? She tightened her fist on the edges of her cloak, thinking she might have skipped wearing it, for all the late afternoon chill it shut out. A storm was coming, dark gray clouds scudded across the sky.

At long last, the door opened and the captain appeared, Hiram Hoyt peering over his shoulder. "Phoebe. What brings thee to the docks at the hour of gloaming? 'Tis no time or place for a maid."

"Captain, I need to speak with thee."

"I am in the middle of writing a letter of negotiation to a French perfumery . . ." The determined expression on Phoebe's face must have made the captain realize there was a problem, but still he hesitated, as if reluctant to allow her into the warehouse.

Phoebe swept past him to go inside, leaned against a barrel, heaved an enormous sigh, and said in a shaky voice, "Thy daughter Sarah paid a visit to me. She said she will not permit me to live in thy house at Orange Street."

The captain's eyes remained fixed on the tops of his shiny boots. He motioned for Hiram Hoyt to stand by the door, before turning to Phoebe with a lowered voice. "I told her of our engagement earlier today. She did not take the news well." He glanced uneasily around the warehouse. "Perhaps I have made a mistake of letting her run the ship. 'Tis not easy to make changes to the crew, mid-ocean."

That was a ridiculous notion! They weren't talking about a ship in the ocean. They were talking about an overly coddled young woman who resented her father's choice of a bride.

"Phoebe, my dear, try to understand. The home on Orange Street belonged to my first wife. 'Twas her childhood home. Filled with memories." Pain darkened his eyes. "Sarah was very close to her mother."

How well Phoebe remembered. Sarah and her mother were mirror images, closer than sisters. Even their voices were similar—a sharp minor key.

He tapped her gently on the nose. "Thee can remain at thy father's home until I return again. Everyone understands that Barnabas needs tending to."

"I fear that is not possible. My father . . . mortgaged the

house and defaulted on the loan. If it is not taken care of, he will be evicted." *We will be evicted.*

The captain looked at her, expressionless. "Evicted," he repeated. He rubbed his forehead, folded his arms, then dropped them to his sides. "It might be prudent to allow Barnabas time to feel the consequences of his indebtedness. Look at Matthew Macy, town cooper. I daresay that time in the gaol has improved his sour disposition."

"Captain, 'tis a poor reflection on thee."

"Me? How so?"

"'Tis not fitting for a sea captain's wife to be kept from her husband's home. By his own daughter! People will . . . talk. And imagine what will be said when it is disclosed that the captain allowed his father-in-law to be declared Town Poor."

He frowned—the slightest crease of his forehead, his eyebrows tugging together briefly. "How much is the loan?"

"If thee could provide a hundred pounds on account for him, that would suffice."

A long moment passed without any response. Phoebe dared not look at him.

"Very well, my dear. Thy concern for thy father is admirable. And I will do anything to make thy lovely smile return again." He reached out and took both of her hands in his. "I will meet with the bank manager and pay off the mortgage on thy father's home." He squeezed her hands. "Give Sarah some time to get used to the idea, Phoebe. She'll come around. She had not expected this news today and she was in shock. Thy own father seems skeptical."

"My father? Thee has spoken to him?"

"He came to the warehouse. Not an hour ago."

Phoebe's heart sunk. "What did he have to say?"

"He wanted to be sure I am aware thee has no dowry."

Disappointed, she rocked back against the barrel. How could her father do such a thing? "Captain, has such resistance caused thee to change thy mind?" She glanced up at him. "Tell me, is thee wobbling?"

He laughed and her eyes flew to his. "Nay. I am not wobbling, Phoebe dear. I need no dowry to convince me to take thee as my bride."

Phoebe nearly sagged with relief.

"And thee? Has this resistance caused thee to wobble?"

"Not for a moment."

He gave her a warm smile. "Another quality to admire in thee, Phoebe Starbuck. Such courage and conviction. I look forward to discovering more and more fine qualities in thee."

She swallowed, wanting nothing so much as to fling her arms about his neck and kiss him right then and there, for all to see. But of course, her hands remained at her side. "And we will marry before thee sets sail?"

He laughed again and it broke the spell. He reached out for her hand and squeezed it, whispering, "Aye. And I will speak to Sarah about her . . . uncharitable behavior."

There now, he *did* love Phoebe. She knew he must! "I believe Sarah has inadvertently done us a great favor," she said, with an uncommon boldness. She inhaled a deep breath and looked him straight in the eye. "Captain, if go thee must, take me with thee."

At first the captain looked at her as if she'd offered to do cartwheels down Straight Wharf. Then his eyes widened in disbelief as he realized she was serious. And she was! "That is *not* possible."

"Other captains take their wives along."

He dropped her hand and tugged the hem of his waistcoat down. "Not many."

"But some do. I would like to start our marriage off right, Captain, and not be separated for a long duration."

His tanned skin became mottled. "Thee has no idea what thee is asking. The *Fortuna* is not outfitted for a woman."

"Oh, I don't need much." She smiled and gave a brief nod of her head. "My needs are simple, my wants are few."

"Phoebe . . . the crew . . . they are skittish with changes." His voice grew faint.

"There will be no need for any changes at all! They will hardly notice I am on the ship!" She gave him a beaming smile. "So then, we are in agreement. 'Tis a settled matter." And she swept toward the door before he could object. As Hiram Hoyt held it open for her, he puffed on his pipe and grunted, "Uh-oh!"

But as Phoebe left the captain's warehouse, she saw blue peeking through the clouds. It seemed the storm had changed its mind and shifted course.

Mary Coffin

20 June 1659

Thomas Macy, Edward Starbuck, and Father plan to sail to Nantucket Island to meet with Thomas Macy's cousin, Thomas Mayhew (from Martha's Vineyard). Thomas Macy has been considering a move there with his family for a long time, to start a new community outside of Puritan control. Father is going along to seek out business ventures. He wonders if settling the island might provide a fine opportunity to expand my brother Peter's lumber trade.

4 July 1659

Father returned from Nantucket today full of good cheer. He says they were able to purchase the west end of the island for 30 pounds and two beaver hats. He said there is no lack of fish, clams, scallops, and other seafood on this fine island. Father thinks we should move to the island too. He said he is tired of Puritan neighbors poking their long noses into everybody's business. "We will not go hungry," he told Mother. She did not look at all convinced.

"Did you see Indians?" she asked.

"Aye, a few. Peaceable ones. Thomas Mayhew assured me of that. Peter Foulger has Christianized many of them." He gave her a patronizing look. "'Tis not the howling wilderness of your imagination, Dionis."

"What would we live on? How would we survive?"

"Fish," he said. "We can harvest the sea. Plow the water rather than the land."

I wonder of that thinking. I do not think Father would last long on a seafood diet. He is fond of his jams and jellies and puddings.

18 September 1659

We are living in tumultuous times. That's what Edward Starbuck told Father last night and I believe he is right.

Thomas and Sarah Macy are in much trouble. First of all, a while back they joined the Anabaptists and were baptized again. They were fined for not attending the regular Sunday meetings and Thomas was charged with "disorderly" practice for holding meetings without hired clergy.

But it gets worse.

Not long ago, in a storm, four cold and wet people sought shelter from the rain and knocked on the Macys' door. Thomas took pity and let them in. The shower soon passed, and off they went with scarcely a word. But a neighbor had been watching. Reverend Rodgers.

Those four people were Quakers!

Reverend Rodgers went straight to the constable to make a report and soon Thomas was commanded to appear in court to face the criminal charge of harbouring Quakers. He was fined 30 shillings.

Father says it is the last feather that breaks the horse's neck. I am not sure what that will mean, but I think our family might be facing our own tumultuous times.

27 October 1659

This morning, Thomas and Sarah Macy left Salisbury

behind for Nantucket, taking their five children with them. The sky was blue as they filled the little boat in Great Harbour, but not long after they sailed out of sight of us, clouds darkened the sky, rain began to pound, and the wind whipped up the waves. I fear they will have a frightful sea journey.

Father is keen to move, as well. It is all he talks about.

4 November 1659

Mother is inconsolable. Father is adamant. He says we are moving to Nantucket.

Mother thinks Father will never be satisfied and will always believe happiness is in another place. First we leave England for the New World. After settling in Salisbury, Father moves us to Pentucket, then Newbury, and back again to Salisbury!

"You have itchy feet," Mother told him and, oh my!, he did not like that remark at all.

Father said it is God's will to move to the island and then he gave her a stern look and that just set off her crying jag all over again.

As for me, I am going to tell Father that I plan to live with my sister Abigail and her husband in Dover, or if they won't have me, I'll go to my sister Elizabeth. If I have to, I'll even live in Newbury with Tristram Jr., and I can't tolerate Newbury. Or Tristram Jr. I do not want to move to Nantucket and leave my dear friend Heppy. I see no good reason to move from civilization to a little island far out to sea that is filled with wild Indians.

Nay, I will not move.

Here is what I think: I wonder if all this tumult would be happening if Thomas and Sarah Macy would have just left those Quakers out in the rain.

31 December 1659

I am going to move to Nantucket. Edward Starbuck is moving there and taking his family. Nathaniel is going too.

Elizabeth Macy is not.

8

There are days in which nothing ever happens. One day looks like the day before, and the day after. And then there are days like today, a fulcrum day, on which the rest of life hinges.

Matthew's day started in the Nantucket gaol. Nothing unusual with that. Not until Barnabas Starbuck arrived with hot cross buns from Catherine Hussey's beehive ovens. He looked curiously at Matthew's face. "Thee looks like a man who has tangled with a nest of hornets."

He touched his split lip. "Had a little misunderstanding, 'tis all."

Barnabas gave him a sympathetic look. "Matthew, there is a favor I must ask of thee."

"And what is that?"

"To agree to sign on to the *Fortuna* as the cooper. I know the captain has asked thee to."

Matthew took a bite of the bun, chewed, swallowed. "That is impossible for two reasons. First, Phineas Foulger has plenty of coopers to chose from, ones who actually want

104

a chance to go to sea. Second, I vowed I would never set foot on another whale sloop. Never again."

"I understand all that. And yet . . . I'm asking thee to change thy mind. For my sake."

"Are you asking me to watch over Phoebe?"

"So thee has heard the news."

"Everyone has heard." He appeared nonchalant, but when his mother told him of Phoebe's engagement to the captain after Meeting last Sunday, when it was announced, the news disturbed and sickened him. When the elders asked if anyone objected to this union, how was it that no one stood up? He would have, were he allowed into Meeting, which he wasn't.

So disturbed was he that he went straight to the nearest tavern, had a few too many tankards of ale, had the brilliant idea of sneaking into Captain Foulger's warehouse to see if there be any truth in Henry Coffin's apple brandy–soaked hunches, was rudely turned away by a tetchy Portuguese guard, provoked him into a fight that did not turn out well for Matthew, and ended up with another sentence of fort-nights in gaol—doubled in length, for it was First Day—and a black-and-blue eye and split lip.

He reached for another bun. They were delicious—buttery, sweet, still warm—from the best bakery on the island. The only bakery on the island. "You could refuse to give your blessing on their union. Or is it just too tempting? 'Don't count the teeth of a rich bridegroom,' eh?"

That was uncalled for. As soon as Matthew said it, he regretted his words. He had no reason to hurt Barnabas, and indeed, the older man looked injured by his sharp insinua-tion. His mother was always warning him to weigh his words before he spewed them out.

"'Tisn't that at all. Phoebe fancies herself in love with him."

The very thought of it rankled Matthew. "Well, then, doesn't it all come together quite nicely."

Barnabas missed Matthew's sarcasm. "Mayhap, but I am perplexed by the urgency."

Matthew shrugged. "Perhaps the captain is concerned that if he waits, some lad might purloin his girl."

"Nay, nay. Not the marriage. 'Tis not unusual to marry quickly before a ship sets sail. What I wonder is why the *Fortuna* must set sail, so late in the season. Thee knows how sudden and dangerous storms arise at this time of year."

How well Matthew knew. An unexpected squall caused the demise of his father's beloved ship, the *Pearl*, after its fruitful years at sea. A powerful storm damaged both masts and sent the ship's keel straight into a coral reef. His thoughts traveled often to those dreadful few hours, reliving them, tormenting himself with questions. Could it have been averted? Barnabas coughed politely and Matthew realized he'd been waiting for an answer to his question.

"Competition, I suspect, is the reason for the urgency. The captain and his investors have a fondness for a chock-full hold. Same with his loyal crew."

"His crew? Thee hasn't heard? The loyal crew has abandoned him. And still, the captain insists on setting sail. He is signing a new crew as we speak."

"The entire crew? Walked off? What did he do to sour the crew?"

"Alas, 'tis word of Phoebe's presence on board. I overheard a sailor say it was tempting God's wrath. Something does not sit well with me." Barnabas walked to the window and peered over the sill at the captain's warehouse. "Thee spoke to Henry Coffin?"

"I did. Nothing to prove."

He turned. "Still, I am asking for thy help."

"To tag along the *Fortuna* as Phoebe's minder?"

"I need the help of someone who loves her. Thee loved her once. Mayhap thee loves her still."

Must he do everything? He refused to put himself in such a humiliating spot. "Barnabas, why would I put myself in such a position? Why would any man?"

Barnabas crossed his arms. "It shames me to use this, but do, I must. I am asking for thy help . . . because of the time I saved thy father's life."

Matthew's eyes squeezed shut. He knew well this story: Barnabas Starbuck and Isaac Macy were the best of friends. Isaac was born for the sea; Barnabas eschewed it. Isaac convinced Barnabas to go fishing with him early one morning. The weather shifted, as it could do, the wind whipped the waves, and the boat suddenly capsized. The mast hit Isaac on the head, knocking him unconscious. Barnabas held on to Isaac, turned the boat upright, somehow hauled Isaac into the boat, and rowed them to shore in the squall.

Matthew's father had knighted Barnabas Starbuck as his brother for that brave act, claiming he owed him his life. And he did, for Barnabas was brave—he could not swim.

Barnabas held the trump card and well he knew it. "Cheer up, Matthew. Knowing the savvy captain, thee will get wealthy in the process."

Savvy, indeed.

The day ended with Captain Foulger arriving in the cooperage, just as Barnabas predicted, and asking Matthew for his final decision. "I need to know now. The *Fortuna* sets sail tomorrow. I've had to sign on a new crew."

"So I heard. They all walked off?"

"All but my first mate and the mute cabin boy." He frowned. "Superstitious fools. Thee knows how skittish seamen can be about a woman on board."

"Why not tell Phoebe she must stay put?"

The captain whirled to face Matthew with a strange look in his eyes. "And let a crew know they can master the captain? Let all Nantucket wag their tongues over it?"

Ah, saving face. "Then, why not wait until spring to head out? That would allow time to find a worthy crew."

"Spoken like a man who has no shipowner investors to please. I have created a greedy monster in that syndicate. They are still licking their chops from the last greasy voyage. They want more of the same." The captain gazed around the cooperage before turning his attention back to Matthew. "The investors want thee as cooper. They are willing to increase thy lay to one-twelfth. Unheard of for a cooper." He pounded the tip of his finger against the top of the workbench. "Thee will return a wealthy man."

"Captain, even if I agreed, I still have a fortnight owed to the constable."

The captain waved it away. "I'll make it disappear. But since we're on that topic, I have one more term for thee. No imbibing while thee is in my employ. Even in port. The indulging stops." The captain walked over to the door. "Let me know thy decision by day's end or I'll find another cooper."

Even though Matthew was twenty-one years old, he had an overwhelming urge to seek advice from his mother. Libby Macy was an astute woman, solid and steady, who met life as it came to her. He found her in the small kitchen of the Macy home on Easy Street, the room filled with the woody scent of simmering bayberries. He stood by the open door, watching her for a moment as she carefully set a wick into each candle mold before pouring hot wax into the forms. She smiled when she noticed he was there. "Something's on thy mind. 'Tis written on thy face. Just like thy father. Everything churning in the mind is written on thy face." She set the pot of hot wax on the crane. "So sit down and spill."

He explained the captain's offer to her—of the overly generous lay of the profits, of the dismissal of the gaol sentence. He left out Barnabas's request to be Phoebe's minder.

"So what do you think? Would you be in favor of me heading out to sea? Could you manage?"

She had her eyes on the candle forms as the wax hardened. The frilled brim of her white cap shaded her forehead so that he couldn't read her expression. "We'll manage, Matthew. We'll always manage." She lifted her head. "But I'm not so blind I can't see what's behind this."

He studied the hearth's fire, flame licking the pot of wax. "I don't know what you mean."

"Oh, I think thee does. The entire island is abuzz with news that Phoebe Starbuck will be on the ship. Thee's been besotted by Phoebe for as long as I can remember."

Matthew turned to look at his mother. "Hold on. Phoebe and I . . . that's old history."

"I know, I know. But that hasn't stopped thee from wanting her." His mother could always size up the situation and read it correctly. To Matthew's further amazement, his mother said one more thing. "She's wrong."

"Who?"

"Phoebe Starbuck. Thinking thee has nothing to stand on in a gale."

"She's no longer of any concern to me. She's going to be another man's wife."

"She's marrying that man to save her father from ruin."

"She's a Starbuck. Hardly near ruin."

"She's a sheep-raising Starbuck, not a whaling Starbuck. There's a difference. Her father's always had a talent for betting on the wrong horse."

Matthew rose to his feet. "You're wrong about one thing. Phoebe loves Captain Foulger."

His mother scoffed at the thought. "If she thinks she loves him, then she doesn't know him."

"And you do?"

"I knew him when he was still in knee pants. I've always thought he loved himself best of all."

Matthew's mother had gone to school with Phineas Foulger. He'd learned from his aunt that there was a time when the two fancied each other, but Phineas ended up marrying Elizabeth Swain, an heiress. He was never quite sure what had soured between his mother and Phineas.

He heard the sound of his young brother, Jeremiah, running up the shelled path toward home. "Well, then, if I have your blessing, I'll tell the captain that I'll be going." He gave her a weak smile. "Off on the *Fortuna* to make my fortune."

"Keep thy suspicions from Phoebe. They would but trouble her and change nothing. Thee has no evidence from Henry Coffin. Merely grumblings from a disgruntled old man. No evidence to stand up in a court of law."

He could not deny that.

"Matthew. You'll not dishonor the captain in any way."

"O' course not."

"Mayhap thee should consider praying before thee gives the captain an answer."

Matthew felt the sting of her words, for he had not thought to pray. "There is always the difficult matter of discerning clarity from the Almighty."

"Aye, 'tis true."

His mother did not realize he was mocking, and he thought it best not to alert her. It would be nice to believe that there was something, some*one*, out there who responded to the questions of mere mortals. But now was not the time to rankle his mother. "The will of God, it seems, is often clouded and elusive."

"Sometimes," she added thoughtfully, "the Almighty does not answer us in full, but merely nudges us in the direction of his choosing."

He rubbed a hand along the tabletop. "The sole condition the captain put on me was that I'm to give up the drink."

A smile creased his mother's face. "In that case, son, I'll help thee pack."

Mary Coffin

9 February 1660

Peter Foulger is a surveyor as well as a missionary to the Indians. I have yet to make his acquaintance, but Father speaks of him with a great deal of respect.

Nathaniel Starbuck stopped by the house with a survey map of Nantucket Island that Edward and Peter Foulger had drawn up. His father, Nathaniel said, insisted that without Father's determination, negotiations would not have moved so quickly last July. Father seemed pleased by the praise. I was not at all surprised to hear that. My father is a determined man.

He unrolled the handwritten document and held it against the window. "Nathaniel, come and decipher your father's poor penmanship for me. I wonder who taught him to write? It looks like something the hens scratched."

It was like a cloud descended in the room. "I have no time to waste," Nathaniel said in a gruff way. He left without finishing his cup of mullein tea, which I know he finds dear.

Even Father, not the most sensitive of souls, noticed Nathaniel's coolness. "He's a tetchy one."

"You shouldn't have compared his father's handwriting to chicken scratch," Mother said.

"Oh bother," Father muttered. "'Twas a mild jest."

"Mother's right," I said. "Edward has worked hard to support this endeavor and Nathaniel has had to do the work of two men in his father's absence."

Then Father got huffy and rolled up the map, tucking it up on the hearth to be dealt with another time.

Later that night, Father asked me to stay downstairs after Mother and John and Stephen went to bed. He asked me to look over the survey and to help him seek out lots to lay claim for himself and for my brothers, including Peter.

I asked him to describe this land to me, as vividly as if I were sailing into the harbour.

"'Tis called Cappamet Harbour along the northern side of the island to the west. We chose it because the waters are deep, providing relatively deep anchorage for incoming ships."

"What is the shore like?"

"Steep, without sandy beaches and mucky marshes. That was my concern about the harbour to the east. I am considering this lot here." He pointed to the land that embraced the harbour. "Rolling hills surround it, which will protect the house and gardens from the sea's relentless winds."

I pointed to the lots on the other side of the harbour. "If Peter were to lay claim to this lot, Coffin land would ring the harbour."

Father looked up in delight. "And then Coffins would be at the very center of this new place."

He is an ambitious man, my father.

I was rather pleased with his confidence in my ability to read and reason. I took care as I read through each page and felt assured that all was within reason. Father describes this island as a Garden of Eden. A Paradise. I am most intrigued to see it for myself.

And I must say, Father's assessment of Edward Starbuck's

handwriting was accurate. It did look like a hen had scratched it out.

15 March 1660

'Tis a settled matter, Father said tonight. And so we are moving to this faraway island.

I find myself eager to see this place that will become home.

2 July 1660

I have counted over 100 men, women, and children who have chosen to relocate to Nantucket. Here is a list of the heads of family:

Tristram Coffin

Edward Starbuck and his son Nathaniel (Edward has remained on the island since last July)

Thomas Macy (relocated in October 1659)

Thomas Mayhew (from the Vineyard)

Richard Swain (son John is a Quaker)

Thomas Barnard

Christopher Hussey

John Swain (He insists on taking his elderly mother along.
Poor old Rachel Swain. Mother fears old Rachel's will
be the first grave to dig. A gruesome thought! I do not
want to think on first graves dug on the island. I want
to think on first babies to be born.)

William Pile

Thomas Coleman

Robert Barnard

Robert Pike

John Smith

Thomas Look

Stephen Greenleaf

Stephen Hussey (He is a Quaker who confirms to me that
  Quakers are not right in the head. This man will argue
  about anything and everything.)

Each family, I have discovered, has their own reasons to
leave their homes behind and seek out a new life, far away
from the mainland. Some, like Thomas Macy, to have distance from the invasive Puritans. Some, like Edward Starbuck,
to Christianize the Indians. Some, like my father, to seek economic success. Some for adventure.

May God bless each one of us.

9

Today was Phoebe's wedding day. She felt as if she were in a dream, one that delighted and surprised her, one from which she did not want to wake. After Meeting, on the afternoon tide, she would be sailing away from Nantucket Island. And as the wife of the whalemaster!

She remained in bed much longer than she should have, thinking of how few were the days in a woman's life in which she woke up as one person and would retire at day's end as another. Tonight she would be Mrs. Phineas Foulger. She was keyed up so tightly it was impossible to relax. She couldn't stop imagining the thrilling adventure she was soon to embark on. Imagining the joy of seeing Captain Foulger's charming smile each and every morning.

She must be packed and dressed and breakfasted in time for Meeting. When she rose, she was disappointed to look out the window to find that fog had moved in and settled low over the town, like a gray shroud. She couldn't even see the harbor from her window. What a gloomy start to her wedding day! Rain brought good luck, sun brought good tidings. But fog? It brought only dreariness.

She found herself continuously checking the clock, and finally, when it read eight o'clock, she combed and recombed her hair and twisted it into a knot. Her aunt Dorcas had loaned her daughter's wedding dress to her, made of silk. Beige, not gray! It was made in the fashion of the day, as Dorcas and her husband were well-to-do. A two-piece dress made of brocade, gathered in the front and very long in the back, with a blue silk cord laced across from side to side attaching the skirt to the bodice. Very elegant. And shoes! They were made of the same material as the dress, pointed at the toe and with very high heels. They were a size or two too small for Phoebe, but she did not mind.

After the ceremony at the meetinghouse, Captain Foulger planned a celebration meal at 28 Orange Street. Phoebe would don a white apron for the lunch, a thin gauzy material tied with a wide blue ribbon and a large bow in front. She felt rather . . . special, quite fashionable in these borrowed clothes.

As Phoebe modeled the dress to her father, his eyes grew misty. From paternal sentiment, she assumed at first, but she was wrong.

"Dearest Phoebe, I fear thee might be making a grave error."

Deeply shaken, Phoebe looked at her father. The possibility that she was about to commit a grave error was not one she dared to contemplate. She had set her foot on this path, and she could not, would not, turn back. "I know what I'm doing. Trust me on this."

Barnabas's eyes grew dim with sadness, as if a candle had suddenly been snuffed out. She wished to say something to ease her father's pain at her leaving but could think of no words that would serve.

As she walked down the stairs, she stopped on the last step to finger the small ivory-colored mortgage button with her hand. How well she remembered the day it had been drilled. Her mother had received a small inheritance from her mother and promptly took it to the bank to pay off the mortgage before her father could touch the money for his enterprises. Her mother had used an awl to make the hole in the newel post, carefully added the ashes of the house's papers, and topped it with a scrimshaw button. A tradition unique to Nantucket. "We'll never have to worry if we have a roof over our heads," she told Phoebe as she set the papers aflame with a lit torch.

Unless her father happened to mortgage the roof.

Phoebe wondered if her father's business ventures might have turned out differently had her mother not died. Would he have settled on one career and made some kind of success of himself? Mayhap. The women of Nantucket had the say of things. With husbands so much at sea, they were in charge of domestic affairs and money matters.

Today should be the happiest day of Phoebe's life, and yet she was suddenly filled with overwhelming and anxious thoughts. She realized she'd been holding her breath and exhaled, letting go of the mortgage button and continuing into the keeping room.

The captain was sending a servant to fetch her chest, and her father was still readying himself, so she pulled Great Mary's journal out of the trunk and sat by the window to read a scene or two, hoping it would settle her mind. It had a soothing effect and she often felt herself slipping into another world as she read. Slowly, Phoebe blew out a long breath. She thought she was starting to understand Mary Coffin. She was a girl who knew what she wanted in a man, and she was bound and determined to marry him. Was that so wrong? Phoebe thought not.

She closed her eyes and asked God's presence to fill her with the peace she so often received during Meetings. She should feel . . . blessed. Not anxious or troubled, nor burdened. Her father would be provided for, the house would remain his, and she would be having a sea adventure with a man she adored. Today was her wedding day!

A knock came at the door and there was the captain's cabin boy, Silo. Phoebe felt a tenderness for the boy as he lived in the shadows of Nantucket society (she understood *that*). This morning, surprised that he was the one sent to tote her trunk, as he was small and the chest was large, she hurried to slice a large slab of gingerbread cake for him. It was good to see the child's smile light up his usually serious face.

After the flurry of loading her chest onto the cart, the morning was gone and it was time to cast off to Meeting. Slowly.

Silo was not accustomed to horse and cart, and knew not when to ruffle the reins of the lagging horse. "Silo, keep thy rudder still!" her father cried, jostled from side to side in the back of the cart.

Nearly everyone stopped what they were doing and looked at Phoebe as Silo helped her climb down from the captain's wagon and turn to make her way toward the meetinghouse doors. She felt pinned in place, queasy under the gaze of so many observers. Somber elders stood clustered in their flat-crowned, broad-brimmed hats and long coats, bonneted matrons covered with black cloaks huddled in clumps, despite the warmth of the day.

Phoebe felt a hand on her elbow and realized the captain was beside her. She exhaled, relief flooding her body, anxiety evaporating. She tilted her head to get a look at him. How dashing he looked! How regal. A cardinal among sparrows.

"Thee looks frightened," he whispered.

"Yes," she said. "I believe I am. A little."

They began moving through the crowd, walking easily in step until they reached their rows. The captain dipped to the left while Phoebe took her place on the right, with the women.

The assembly began to settle as they parted. There was no need to look to know who was present. For all the talk of equality, the rows were filled from front to back in a quiet and tolerated hierarchy—it was something that had always rankled Matthew, she recalled. In the front were the Facing Benches, where the elders and ministers sat. At their feet sat the Coffin, Starbuck, Foulger, Hussey, and Macy clans, along with the rest of the original families, descendants of the first proprietors who sailed to Nantucket one hundred years earlier and never left. The captain took his place among them. It was said that everyone on Nantucket had one of those proprietor surnames, was married to one, or wanted to be one.

Behind them, the Gardners, Mitchells, Colemans, and their kin occupied two more benches, along with other captains and shipowners and their families, whose fortunes grew greater each evening as people in London depended on illumination by whale oil.

Farther back were those whose livelihood rested upon the

people in front: sailmakers, coopers, ship chandlers, black-smiths, mapmakers. Without the front rows filled, they would be out of work. Barnabas, he sat in the back row.

The actual wedding ceremony took place at the end of Meeting. It was simple and unadorned, as in the Quaker faith, marriage was not a sacrament but a covenant between man, woman, and God. Nearly every Quaker in Nantucket was there but for Matthew Macy, who stubbornly refused to apologize to the elders and thus remained disowned. Phoebe expected as much.

But Phoebe had not expected the absence of Sarah Foulger. Overcome by a dreadful headache, the captain had explained to Phoebe in a sorrowful whisper.

In a pig's eye, Phoebe thought, but she only smiled at the captain and told him she understood completely. He took her hands in his, and looked into her eyes in that way that made her heart race, and said, "I take thee to be my wife and promise with divine assistance to be unto thee a faithful and affectionate husband until death do us part." Phoebe then repeated the words to the captain.

Then—very suddenly, it seemed—the ceremony was over. Phoebe felt rooted to the wooden planks, as if glued to them, knowing beyond any doubt that this was the most important moment in her life, in any woman's life. All that ever happened was wedded forever to this place and moment.

After a lavish celebratory supper at the captain's house—in which Sarah remained sequestered in her chamber because of her dreadful headache—the captain rose to his feet, thanked everyone for coming, and said, "The tide waits for no man. Wife, we must make our goodbyes."

So the time had come.

Phoebe fought back a tear as she bid farewell to her father. As the captain helped her into the carriage, he said, "Thee remembered Great Mary's journal, did thee not?"

"Of course I packed it." She settled her skirts in the carriage and then remembered she had left the journal on the mantel. "Oh no! I took it out of the chest to read while I waited for Silo to come. He startled me with his knock and—"

Captain Foulger's face became suddenly solemn—an expression Phoebe found oddly chilling—perhaps because his charming smile disappeared so completely. "Stop the horse!" Eyes flashing, the captain shouted to the driver at the reins. "Stop! Turn the horse to Centre Street, 35 Centre Street. Make haste!"

He seemed so alarmed that she searched to find words to calm him. "Captain, the journal is over one hundred years old. It will be waiting for us when we return."

His hands were clenched, but his voice was studiously calm. "I have looked forward to quiet evenings at sea when thee can read sections aloud to me by candlelight in my cabin." The smile returned to his face. "Forgive me, my dear. *Our* cabin."

"'Tis a lovely vision." And it was that. She was grateful to be reminded of the journal, as she had fully intended to bring it for her own peace of mind, as well as interest. She had left off at the point where Mary Coffin was about to leave the mainland and move to Nantucket, and she was curious about what happened next.

The captain did not rest easy until Phoebe had gone into the house, retrieved the journal off the mantel, and returned to the carriage. At the captain's persistent urging, the driver drove the horse hard to arrive at the wharf to meet the dory that would row them to the *Fortuna*. The wind stirred strongly as they walked along the wharf, at one point whisking off Phoebe's bonnet and tearing at her heavy knot of hair.

"Prepare thyself, wife," the captain said, his eyes on the *Fortuna*, rocking with stiff-chopped waves, as he helped her into the dory. "A sailor must always keep a weather eye for shifting winds and rough water."

And it was on that short dory ride that Phoebe first felt her stomach began to churn. *Oh no. Not this.* She was sure she had outgrown the childhood malady. She had been raised on an island, for goodness' sake! Just an hour ago, she had been so eager to go on this voyage. But a sudden gloom spread over her. Her stomach clenched, her mouth started watering, her palms grew warm, she felt a bead of perspiration on her brow. *Oh no. Please, God, not this again. Let me not be seasick. Please, please, please!*

<hr />

The captain had signed on a motley crew. Mere boys it seemed; they were all running away from something, or someone. Because of that, they were willing to sign on to a ship rumored to be toting bad luck.

Matthew knew the reason—Phoebe Starbuck. Phoebe Starbuck *Foulger*.

For this very morning, she had married the captain.

The captain was true to his word. Matthew's gaol sentence was dismissed and he had been given freedom to spend his last night at his own home.

The most difficult goodbye for Matthew was to Jeremiah. They stayed up late last night talking as his young brother pelted him with one question after another. "Tell me again the story of Captain Hussey."

"Jeremiah, you've heard this story dozens of times."

"I need to remember it while thee is gone."

"The story, a legend, really, told the tale of the first sperm whale claimed by a Nantucket captain. In 1712, Captain Christopher Hussey was seeking right whales and his ship was blown off course."

"Right whales were named because they remained afloat after they've been killed. So they are the right whale."

Matthew smiled. "Good remembering."

"And whales have terrible eyesight."

"Aye. Terrible. Tiny little eyes. Big brains, though."

"And they can dive a mile below the sea surface."

"Aye."

"But they have excellent hearing."

"That they do. So Captain Hussey, he found himself surrounded by a pod of sperm whales. He laid chase to one and dragged it back to Nantucket Harbor, and the island went wild. In that one enormous beast—fifty to sixty tons, eighty feet long—and its cavernous head was something remarkable. Spermaceti oil."

"And suddenly the streets of London were lit by Nantucket whales."

"Nay, not so sudden, brother. Nor do I think the whales consider themselves as belonging to Nantucket Island. They consider themselves to be citizens of the seven seas. 'Tis true that London was enamored by the whale oil that came from Nantucket. And it did not take long for them to realize that the spermaceti oil could light their street lanterns."

"What happened next?"

"'Twas not so easy to find the sperm whales, not like Captain Hussey's good fortune. The Nantucket captains explored the North Atlantic to find them, and they did, but they also discovered that the blubber of the whales went rancid in six weeks."

"What does 'rancid' mean?"

"Spoilt. Soured. So they had to keep returning to harbor even if the hold wasn't full."

"Until someone invented the stove!"

"Aye, some smart fellow realized that a larger ship could have a stove built into it. They could process the whale and fill the barrels with oil. So now they can go out for longer durations. One day soon, they might even circumnavigate the world, from the Arctic to the Antarctic, searching for these giant whales."

"And that's what you're going to do on Captain Foulger's ship."

"That's my plan, Jeremiah."

"And thee will bring back enough of a lay to buy our own ship. Thee and me, brother."

It was Jeremiah's favorite dream. It used to be Matthew's dream too. And his father's. Tonight he would not squelch his brother's joy. "I will be captain, you will be cabin boy."

"First mate."

"In time, laddie. 'Til then you're a greenie."

"Matthew, will thee be gone a long time?"

"Aye. Until the hold is full."

"How many whales before the hold is full?"

"Usually, fifty to sixty whales." Jeremiah knew all this information. Matthew knew he just wanted to hear his voice, and he understood that. He had done the same thing to his father the night before he left on voyages. Clinging to their last moments together.

Jeremiah yawned once, then twice. "Then they break up the stove."

"Aye, when the hold is full, the tryworks is destroyed. The bricks are tossed overboard. 'Tis symbolic, and the crew delights in tossing the bricks overboard."

"Because then the captain cannot change his mind."

"He must pilot the ship back to Nantucket Island."

"Thee will make something for our mother from the scrimshaw?"

The scrimshaw was the lower jawbone of the whale. It had no commercial value, so the captain saved it for the crew. Scrimshaw carving became something of a maritime art for the sailors, something to pass the long, dull hours at sea. "I'll make you both something special."

"Thee will come back, won't thee, Matthew?"

His small voice seemed to come from a great distance, and Matthew took so long answering that Jeremiah sat up in bed, alarmed. Matthew shook off his dread. There were some things a man couldn't get out of, as much as he wanted to.

"'Tis my solemn promise, brother."

Phoebe's sea adventure had begun. She had looked forward so eagerly to setting sail, but the moment the anchor was hauled in, she was overcome with an ominous dread. She felt homesick, and seasick, and the ship hadn't even left the harbor yet.

Before she could say she'd changed her mind and thought it might be best if she remained in Nantucket, the sails were hoisted and the ship was under way. The weather had deteriorated ominously as dark clouds moved swiftly overhead, and the sky grew dark. A storm seemed imminent, but the captain seemed unconcerned. Phoebe, though, felt very concerned. She squeezed her eyes shut. *Diversion, diversion, diversion! Do not let my mind stay fixed on my churning stomach.*

The captain ordered Silo to lead Phoebe to his cabin, as his attention was required on deck. She stepped over the head of the companionway as if she were stepping over the threshold of a palace. The dark little chamber projected an authority that was at once royal, ecclesiastical. A sea king, that's whom she had married.

Silo lit a candle, set it in a candlestand, handed it to her with a shy smile, and left her alone. She walked around the cabin in utter amazement. It had rich walls of waxed teak and finely crafted fittings. A carved bedstead covered one end of the room. The center of the room was monopolized by a teak desk over which were strewn maps, ledgers, a brass sextant, and a compass. A logbook lay on the blotting pad with an inkwell and quill pen nearby.

The candlelight gleamed off the metal ornaments in the room. The teak desk had shiny brass pulls. The compass had been polished till it winked. She touched each thing, picked it up, put it down. The top drawer of his desk contained pipes and scrimshaw. His leather ship box was stored on the top of his desk. It was beautifully made, a foreign importation, the brass catch embossed with his initials. She tried the catch, wondering what it contained, but it was locked. Oh, it was wonderful to be in this cabin for the first time while the captain was not there to watch her appraise it. So many possessions of value. Treasures.

On a shelf affixed to the wall stood thick volumes with names on their spines tooled in gold leaf. Mathematics. Sermons. Philosophy. She was awed by the concentration of so much wisdom in one place. What a fine man she had married.

Married! She was *married* to Captain Phineas Foulger. *Me!*

Moving forward in a trance, she saw her reflection in the mahogany-framed mirror above the pitcher. Her hair was windblown, her cheeks aflame, her eyes luminous. Who was this girl? Could it be, she, here at last?

Phoebe busied herself by unpacking her trunk, then she picked up Great Mary's journal to distract herself. She hoped her churning stomach had more to do with the uncertainties of what activities lay ahead in the wedding bed than with seasickness.

She put a hand to her stomach, feeling increasingly nauseated. A jagged streak of lightning lit the small window, casting eerie shadows on the ground. Almost immediately, thunder boomed. Following the thunder was a strange quiet. The rap of knuckles on the cabin door made her jump. And in walked the captain with a gleam in his eye. He blew out the candle and she lost her breath.

Mary Coffin

5 July 1660

The day of our departure finally arrived. After a great deal of packing, of deciding what to bring and what to sell, we set out in an open sloop for Nantucket Island. It was a fine day for sailing, and we were all of good cheer, even Mother, who has reluctantly acquiesced to Father's decision.

The only moment that caused me pain was when I said goodbye to my dear Heppy. She promised to visit, but I think it unlikely. I wonder if our paths will cross again. I must put those thoughts out of my head, for who knows what the future holds but God?

All was fine as we crossed Massachusetts Bay to round the Cape, as we were always within sight of land. But then we were covered in fog, out in the choppy sound, and Mother grew fretful. Father was aggrieved with her for having such little faith in God, but I think Mother's doubt was not in the Almighty but in her husband.

Father remained determined, and told her to try to sleep. "The next island will be Nantucket Island," he told her.

But he was incorrect.

In the morning, the first land sighted was a small island. Father had gone off course toward the east and had to correct the course. Rather than admit as much, he only said, "Look, Dionis! This is Tuckernuck Island! I **own** this island!" as if this had been his plan all along to get lost.

A few hours later, we came to the northern shore at Capaum Harbour. The men dropped anchor and set out in the dory to go ashore, rowing through the narrow inlet, a bay with an extremely narrow mouth opening to the sea. They were hardly through the inlet when I could see the outlines of a structure down at the far right end of the harbour. As we drew closer, I could see our new home more clearly. The side frames were in place, built by my brother James earlier this summer.

The day was spent unloading the boat and ferrying the things in on the dory. We slept in a little covered lean-to that James had constructed for us. Stephen slept soundly next to me, as he is filled with a sense of adventure. But as I tried to sleep that night, I could hear the waves lap the shore. I could hear an owl hoot, and another hoot back in reply. We are living in utter barrenness.

And so, this lonely place is home.

10

Rain had started, a light tapping on the cabin ceiling turned into a steady pounding. As Phoebe's eyes adjusted to the darkened room, she saw the captain's gaze remain fixed on her as he started to unbutton his coat. She didn't move, but felt her heart race and her stomach twist. *Not now. Not now. Not now. Please, God, don't let me be sick in front of him.*

He took a step closer to her. "What thinks thee of thy new home?"

"Oh, quite lovely." She cleared the hoarseness from her throat. "Fit for a queen."

He bowed his head modestly, but she knew her words had pleased him. He tossed his coat on the floor and loosened the buttons of his shirt, pulled the tails from his trousers.

"Captain, I was hoping we could talk a little," she started timidly, but he put a finger to her lips and stopped her words with a shake of his head.

She wondered if he could hear the thudding of her heart over the sound of the drumming rain on the ceiling. Just as he leaned down to kiss her, so close she could feel his breath, an urgent knock came on the door. The captain froze. The knock came again, louder.

"Avast! I'm not deaf."

He yanked open the door to find the first mate, Hiram Hoyt, standing in his customary sailor stance with legs braced, a troubled look on his regretful face. He spoke in a low voice to the captain, who mumbled something back to him, then shut the door abruptly. The captain swore once, then twice more, then dropped to his knees and pulled out his sea chest from under the bed.

Such profanity mortified Phoebe. It was the language of the docks, not the Friends' meetinghouse. Of course, she realized, he must be tense with the start of the voyage.

The captain opened his chest and rummaged through it, yanking out his rain gear. "Phoebe, my dear," he said as he buttoned the wax-coated overcoat, "I am sorry to disappoint thee on our wedding night, but I fear we have sailed straight into a tempest. In the face of the approaching squall, I will need to be alongside my men tonight."

Daggers of lightning slashed the small windows, thunder rumbled, then boomed like a cannonball.

As soon as he left the room, Phoebe heaved over the side of the bed, right into the chamber pot.

Huddled in the captain's bed, Phoebe lay wide awake, sick to her stomach, frightened and dizzy from the wild pitching and swaying and rolling of the ship, like a child's toy in a bathtub. It would skim the crest of a wave, only to plunge into a watery trough. She was sure the ship was soon to sink.

Sometime during the second watch, the captain came into the cabin, threw off his rain gear, flopped on his back on the bed, told her he was going to sleep for one hour, and covered his eyes with his arm.

"Captain Foulger, could the ship capsize?" Above the roaring wind, she could barely hear her own voice.

He lifted his arm and peered at her, annoyed. "Would I be trying to sleep if my ship was soon to founder?" Another clap of thunder boomed, but it sounded more distant now. "The storm is passing," he said sleepily. Then he rolled over to face the wall.

So much for her wedding night. Not a foretaste of what married life would be, she was certain. It could go no lower, so she had high hopes it could only improve from this point.

Long after his breathing had become regular, Phoebe still could not fall asleep. Perhaps she had expected too much, but it seemed that now that they were married and alone and sleeping in the same bed, he might have told her to call him by his Christian name.

<hr />

Phoebe woke from a fitful sleep. She reached a hand out and felt emptiness on the captain's side of the bed. Empty and cold.

She lay on her back, eyes closed tight, trying to assess the storm outside, the storm within. There was less wind, less rain lashing the ceiling, less tossing of the ship from side to side. She heard sailors shout to each other, and the sound of feet run along the deck.

If only the storm would pass in her stomach. It was churning and twisting, every bit as much as last night, though it was thoroughly empty. Surely, this seasickness would pass as the storm had passed. She tried to sit up but felt dizzy. She tried again, more slowly this time. Once upright, she tried to stand, not at all certain her trembling legs would support her. A wave of nausea overcame her, and mercifully, she reached the chamber pot in time. What more could her stomach have hidden within? She had hardly eaten yesterday, so nervous about her wedding.

She wiped her lips, swished her mouth with watered essence of peppermint, washed her face, and slowly dressed. She heard more loud shouts and clanging sounds outside. What was happening? Something was going on.

She looked in the mirror. Oh . . . she looked awful. Green. She took a deep breath. *Never mind that now. Get thy mind on something besides thy stomach, Phoebe Starbuck!*

Phoebe Starbuck Foulger.

The name seemed strange to her. Strange and wonderful, both. She combed her hair, twisted it into a knot, pinned it, and covered it with her lace cap. Then she steeled herself, pulled the door handle, stepped over the companionway.

And cringed!

She shrank from the naked sunlight. Her eyes hurt, her stomach flipped, the cold sea air stung her face like needles. She leaned her forehead against the cabin door, trying to compose herself. The relentless wind had stopped, the air was clean, the sky was blue. She took deep breaths, squeezed her eyes tight, and distracted herself by listening to the crew as they shouted to each other on the masts and upper deck. From what she could gather, a whale had been sighted.

A *whale*.

Her eyes popped open. She turned, took two steps, and

nearly fell over on the unsteady deck, so she grabbed the railing.

"Ah! Finding your sea legs, I see."

Phoebe opened one eye, hoping the voice didn't belong to the man she thought it might. It did. She lifted her chin to look up at Matthew Macy. He nodded and moved to let her pass at the same moment she moved to proceed, and they found themselves face-to-face. It was an awkward impasse, even more so after she sidestepped, only to find that he, too, had decided to move sideways.

She frowned. "It appears we are destined to oppose each other."

"Perhaps one of us should wait while the other passes."

"Why is thee on this ship?" *Why, why, why?* Of all people!

"Captain Foulger asked me to sign on. Begged, actually."

"I still don't understand. He had a cooper."

"Apparently, due to seamen's assumption that the *Fortuna*'s luck had run out, his entire crew bailed on him."

She had heard such rumblings. "And thee?"

"Me? The captain offered a lay of the profits I could not refuse." He looked straight at her then, directly into her eyes. "Are you all right? You don't look at all well. Your face is a funny color."

Phoebe turned abruptly and walked to the railing. "Matthew, what time is it?"

"Did you not hear the bells? They sound every hour. They just rang twelve times."

"Twelve?"

"'Tis the noon hour."

How long had she slept? Or tried to sleep? She felt exhausted.

135

He leaned his elbows against the ship's railing. "Phoebe, you don't have the glow I would expect from a new bride. Don't tell me you've got a touch of mal de mer?"

"More than a touch." She scowled at him. "How long does it last?"

He shrugged. "It's different for everyone. I'll grant you this, it's a doozy of a storm." He peered up at the blue sky.

Something in his words alarmed her. "Present tense. Why did thee use present tense?"

"Because we're in the eye of it now. The dirty side is coming soon. Far worse than what we've endured."

"That can't be possible!" She looked around at the upper deck. "The whale! They lowered one of the whaleboats. I heard the shouting."

"Aye. A stray whale, separated from its pod. They're trying to reach it while we are still in the eye. If they can catch it, they'll drag it to the ship and tie it to the side until the squall passes. Then they'll start the flensing." He shielded his eyes from the sun and scanned the sky. "So far, so good. 'Tis a slow-moving squall with an extremely dry eye. They might have luck."

"Isn't that a dangerous undertaking for the crew? Surely the captain wouldn't expect his men to risk their lives during a storm. Even for a whale."

A laugh burst out of him. "Welcome to the whaling life, Phoebe. High risk. High rewards." He turned at the sound of one deckhand calling to another. "Actually, 'tis good practice for them. I highly doubt they'll catch the beast. This crew is unseasoned."

A wave of dizziness swept over her and she grabbed the railing.

"Phoebe, how long has the seasickness lasted for you on prior sailings?"

She fixed her gaze on the still water. Eerily still, like shimmering ice. "I don't know," she said, keeping her voice steady.

"Surely you've set sail to the mainland. Even . . . the cape?"

She gave a quick shake of her head. "Once. I was horribly ill. But the water was choppy."

"Ocean water is far choppier than Nantucket Sound." He crossed his arms against his chest. "Are you telling me that the captain agreed to take you on a whaling voyage when you had never been on a ship? He has taken on a greenhand bride?"

She let out a deep sigh. "He did not know."

"Oh, Phoebe. Did you assume you'd be immune to many a sailor's malady?"

She frowned at him. "I'm sure I'll grow accustomed to the pitching of the waves soon." She ignored the sentiment that flickered in its wake: Some never do.

He snorted at that, but she was too miserable to care. "I'll see if there's something in the galley that might help."

While Matthew was in the galley, the sky faded, slightly at first, then it was more obvious, changing from a bright blue to a steel gray, reminiscent of Nantucket's persistent fog. She heard a commotion on the starboard side and made her way over to see what it was about. The whaleboat had returned and the crew was climbing the rigging back into the ship. She watched the captain stand at the side of the ship, shouting down to his crew.

"Why have you returned without the whale?"

"We need to hunker down, Captain," one called up. "The skies are darkening."

Another shouted, "It's the boatsteerer, Captain! He sent

his harpoon sailing into the whale . . . but forgot to tie the other end of his rope!" The crew laughed, but not in a kind way.

The captain glared at the boatsteerer. "What did you do, Obadiah?"

"The harpoon was tied before we left—I know 'twas. The whale disappeared under water, dragging the harpoon and rope with it." Not much more than a boy, Obadiah looked like he was about to cry. "'Twas m' father's harpoon!"

Even Phoebe could see the crew was casting anxious glances toward the darkening sky. A gray mist had descended, and the wind had started up again.

Obadiah climbed aboard, a dark look on his face, and then he caught sight of Phoebe. "There! It be that one!" he said to all seamen standing by.

Shivers began prickling down Phoebe's spine like icicles dripping from the roof, and she began to slowly back away.

Obadiah pointed a finger in her direction. "I say it be her doing. She's brought a curse from the devil himself on this voyage."

All eyes turned to Phoebe.

As the dark side of the storm passed over the *Fortuna*, the next few hours were torturous for Phoebe. Matthew had brought her some hot tea made of steeped ginger root. The tea helped as long as she drank it, but as soon as she sipped the last drop, the clenching of her stomach returned. She tried to sleep, tried to distract herself, started a letter to her father but gave up when the ink spilled, reviewed memorized Bible verses, read Great Mary's journal though it was hard to stay focused. She had never felt so sick, nor felt so terrified, in all her life.

If the ship turned over, would drowning be quick? Merciful?

Oh, she hoped so.

Mary Coffin

8 July 1660

Father's judgment is of great concern to me.

Everything he described about the island has turned out to be incorrect. I don't know if he wanted so much to believe that Nantucket was his long-lost paradise that he could not see the island with clear eyes, or if he colored the facts to convince others to move. He is a highly persuasive man. Either way, this island is nothing like he described.

The wind on this island is relentless. I feel it everywhere I turn. I see it in how the trees have been shaped—short and bent, as if they have needed to brace themselves for daily assault. The soil is gray and sandy and salty, lacking in all the fertile ingredients necessary for successful cultivation. The moors are rugged and scrubby. The air is scented with salt. The small ponds that Father assumed to be sources of fresh water for our livestock are actually tidal ponds, rising and falling twice each day. It is a hostile place for farmers. It is a hostile place for ignorant settlers.

This island, I fear, is a poor choice.

15 July 1660

Father has hired Indians to help finish the construction of our house. They are very curious about our tools. They do not seem at all frightening, and it is amusing to try to communicate with them. They are enchanted with Stephen's blond hair, and reach out to touch it whenever he walks past them.

So far, he has not minded. I am glad to have dark hair, as I think I would mind greatly.

I offered one Indian a pewter trencher to scoop from the large pot of fish chowder I'd made for supper, and he tucked the trencher under his leather shirt. James thinks he thought it was a shield for stray arrows, not a dinnerplate for fish chowder. The Indian grabbed a wooden roof shingle to use for the fish chowder and would not relinquish the pewter trencher.

Mother thinks the Indians will scalp us in our sleep. They're not like the mainland Indians, Father reminds her. They are friendly. That is the beauty of Nantucket, the faraway island, he says. The Indians are not troubled by the same problems as those on the mainland.

I hope he is right. Mother is convinced he is wrong and cannot be dissuaded from her fears. "There is no place to hide on a sandy island," Mother said last evening as we sat around the fire.

"Why are we hiding at all?" Father said. "The Indians have given us no reason to think they are violent. Do you think the settlers would choose lots so far from each other if we had concern of violence? Nay, Dionis! You are letting your fears muddle your mind."

"Look at what is happening in Lancaster! You believe we will find a utopia on this island. No place is immune to violence."

Mother's worries matter little to Father. He has become quite short of patience. He used a sharp tone with her, a tone

he's never used with me or the boys. "These Indians have readily received the gospel and become Christians."

"All?"

"No. Not all. But many."

"Many?"

"Some."

Father's impatient responses fail to pacify Mother.

Wherever we go, it seems there is always something to be
afraid of.

25 July 1660

Steady rain today.

By evening, the exterior frame of the house was finished.
"It's so small," Mother said. And she was right. 'Tis much
smaller than our homes on the mainland.

"There are fewer of us now," I told her, trying to encourage
her. "Only you and Father, James, Stephen, and I. Plenty big
enough for the five of us." But she became so sullen that I see
now that was the wrong thing to say. It only reminded Mother
of those she left behind on the mainland.

Mother does not talk much. She feels weighed down, she
says, and cannot express what is dampening her spirits. She
thinks it is a demon, pinning her down.

I think I know what weighs on her. Sadness for what she
has lost by coming here (many of her children and all of her
grandchildren remain on the mainland). Fear of what life
will be like on this lonely place.

I do not think we will be much visited by mainlanders,
nor will we be able to visit much. The sea between us is rough,

and only slow-sailing vessels can navigate the open stretches where the ocean pours into the Sound. The weather has been so inclement lately that James and Stephen were unable to fish. We have eaten only hardtack and salt pork and cornmeal dumplings for two straight days. I happened upon a thorny thicket of blackberries, plump and shiny and smelling of summer, when I was out for a necessary and that was a joyful discovery for all.

5 August 1660

We have been busy in the daytime making our house walls strong and sturdy to endure against the fierce winter winds from the ocean that Edward Starbuck warned us about.

Today it was not Mother who was complaining, but Father. He is much concerned about the problem of farming, even an adequate vegetable garden for Mother's cooking. The soil is sandy, the wind is relentless, and although my brother James did plant early in the season, our harvest was meager. James has had to sail to the cape often for supplies.

14 August 1660

I was digging for carrots in the garden (the only vegetable that seems to appreciate this sandy soil) and looked up to find Nathaniel at the gate, holding a sack full of beach plum rosehips. "For you and your mother. For your doctoring," he said in his laconic way, then he turned and went on his way.

I near fainted.

22 *August 1660*

I had heard much mention of Peter Foulger but had no chance to meet him until today, when his sloop arrived in our small harbour from his home in Martha's Vineyard. He has been to Nantucket many times before. He was much help to Father and Thomas Macy last year as they surveyed the island. He knows the language of the Indians, and he brings Bibles to them translated in their own language by a man named John Eliot. Father had availed himself much of Peter Foulger, as he translated the talks between them and the Indians.

I have been much curious about this man, as he sounds quite remarkable, so when I heard his sloop had landed on the beach, I hurried to meet him.

For once Father did not exaggerate his assessment. Peter Foulger did not disappoint. Stephen hangs on to every word he says, as if the King himself has paid us a visit. I feel the same way.

Peter Foulger is tall, with broad shoulders and a firm abdomen, and he moves quickly in his stride, as if eager to find out what's around the corner. Although he is in no way handsome, his eyes have a penetrating quality that is both intriguing and unnerving. He has a boy's innocent manner and persuasive intensity. His eyes are bright and curious, and he has many accomplishments to his credit, though he is humble: he teaches school, he is a skilled carpenter and can build anything. And he is knowledgeable about milling, which is something our settlement dearly needs.

He is well learned, and knows surveying, and how to lay

out lots, and he is considered a friend by the Indians. Father said that he had known all along that the Indians would welcome us because they thought so highly of Peter Foulger. It is said that he seems able to turn his hand and mind to anything. He is a preacher, schoolmaster, blacksmith, author and poet, surveyor and record-keeper. He is interested in most everything.

As am I.

28 August 1660

Peter Foulger returned to the Vineyard yesterday. I was sorry to see him go.

Isolation is our customary condition. I suppose that will require us to become extremely self-sufficient.

Nathaniel Starbuck lives farther inland on the western side of Hummock Pond.

It is not such a long walk from the Starbucks' lot to the Coffins', but it seems too long for Nathaniel.

11

Growing up on Nantucket, Phoebe had heard her cousins speak of the zigzag course of whaling voyages. The ship was at the mercy of prevailing winds. She even knew the order of the winds: first came the westerlies, then the northeast trades, then the doldrums, then the southeast trades.

Having left Nantucket late in the season, Phoebe expected the captain to set full sail. She knew all this, but she did not expect to encounter so many squalls that knocked the ship back and forth, causing her to roll and tumble on deck, or in the captain's cabin. The *Fortuna* had barely had a break from one storm when the skies darkened and the wind increased, slapping the sails furiously. The waves were so high they broke over the ship; many times the crew had to take to the rigging to avoid a drenching.

Too weak to move about, too nauseated to keep down even water, Phoebe could only lie curled in the bed in the captain's cabin, curtains drawn over the small windows, a pillow over her head to muffle the sounds of the storm.

When the captain came in to change his clothing, drenched by the breaking waves, he told her that one of the crew fell off the masthead to his death below in the swirling sea.

"Who?"

"Obadiah, the boatsteerer."

Phoebe closed her eyes. She had known Obadiah all his life. His mother, Catherine, ran a bakery out of her home. The only bakery on the island.

"Can we not put in to land somewhere?" she asked. *Please, please, please!*

The captain looked at her as if she was barmy. "We are miles to the windward from the nearest land. We're much safer at sea in this churning cauldron than if we were to make for land." As he buttoned his coat, he patted her well-covered knee. "All storms eventually die out, lass."

But when? When, when, when? One storm passed and another came in its place. And Phoebe's seasickness remained. One afternoon, she heard a knock and Matthew entered her room. She grimaced. Every ounce of her body hurt, but he was the last person on earth she wanted to see.

"I thought I'd check in and see how you were faring." He looked at her with worried eyes. "No improvement?"

"None."

"Have you eaten today? You must eat, Phoebe."

"I feel too ill to eat," she said, pulling the sheets up to her chin. "I simply want to lie here and be left alone." Her seasickness was none of his business, and it was humiliating to be seen like this. "If you would please leave, I will be eternally grateful."

"I think you'll feel better if you eat something," Matthew said, sounding almost sincere, but she knew better. No doubt he enjoyed her suffering.

"I can't."

"You must. You must eat. Small meals, all the day long. And you must force yourself to go outside. Get some fresh air, some sunlight . . . if it ever shows itself again."

She felt tears well up. "I can't stand the sight of that ugly, chopping sea, heaving and pitching. When I go outside, I realize how small this vessel is, how vulnerable."

His eyes grew soft and his concern made her tears harder to blink back. She could handle his mockery, his sarcasm, but not his sweetness.

"Nonetheless, you must make yourself get out of this sour-smelling cabin and get some fresh air."

To her horror, her bottom lip began to shake. "For pity's sake, just leave," she managed to choke out.

"I'll be back with ginger tea."

She turned her face to the wall, finding it impossible to keep looking at the kindness in his face.

Matthew stood on the companionway of the galley, watching Cook flick his knife against a potato as a long strip of brown skin fell into a bowl. "Have you more ginger? The captain's wife needs it for seasickness." *The captain's wife.* It was the first time he had said it and it felt clumsy and awkward in his mouth. As if he had tasted something bitter.

"She don't belong here." He held a large, half-peeled potato in his left hand and tipped it back and forth as he spoke.

"Too late for that. So have you any ginger?"

The cook dug through a box, pulling up a knotty ginger root. "This is the last of it."

The cook would have nothing to do with helping Phoebe,

so Matthew boiled the water himself and steeped a few slices of ginger—coins, his mother called them—in the hot water. He carried the tea to Phoebe, glad to leave the rants of the cook about why the captain should not have brought a woman on board. "'Tis no place for a woman, this whaling ship. We don't want the captain distracted from his duties."

The captain, Matthew had observed, could not be faulted for being distracted from his duties. He constantly roamed the deck, ordering his young crew around. Now that Matthew saw the condition Phoebe was in, he could not pass blame. The window coverings on the captain's cabin were pulled tight, the small, cheerless room as dark as a pocket, the air rank and malodorous.

He knocked on the cabin door and entered without waiting for Phoebe to respond. She was curled up in the captain's bed. Ugh. There it was again, that bitter taste in his mouth. "Drink this. It will help."

She pulled herself up and took the hot cup from his hands. She took one sip, then another. "Matthew, why doesn't thee take a turn at watch?"

"I'm an idler."

"I am aware. I just wondered why thee doesn't take a turn at watch like the other crewmen."

He grinned. She hadn't lost her humor yet. "The idlers are the ones who work by day and sleep at night. Cook, cooper, steward."

"I don't see how it would matter—day or night, this ship is rocking and heaving."

"Oh, it matters plenty. The daylight is critical for our work."

She sipped more tea and he felt satisfied; a slightly pink

color was returning to her ashen face. He turned toward the door, but she stopped him with a question. "Matthew, why did thee leave Nantucket? Thy mother, thy brother, thy cooperage. I thought thee would never leave again."

He glanced over his shoulder at her. "I told you. I am seeking my fortune. Just like everyone else on this ship, from the cabin boy to the cook." *And that includes you, my dear little gold digger*, he thought but didn't say. He went to the window and pulled the covering open, letting light into the room. Phoebe squinted and moaned. "You need some fresh air in here. Some light."

"The light hurts my eyes. The salty smell in the wind sickens me."

That was almost laughable. The cabin smelled worse than salt air!

She opened one eye. "Is it the right wind to make port soon?"

He peered out the window and saw only churning waters, no land in sight. "When a sailor doesn't know what port he's heading for, any wind is the right wind."

She closed her eyes. "That's not how the saying goes."

He turned. "How does it go?"

"When a sailor doesn't know what port he's heading for, no wind is the right wind."

Ah. That felt a little too close to home.

The next morning, the violence of the storm had passed, though a strong wind and dark skies remained. Annoyed with Phoebe's lethargy, the captain said he did not coddle queasy crew and insisted that she get outside at twelve bells sharp to get some fresh air. So in the afternoon, she mustered herself and went outside.

Beyond the clouds were glimmers of blue sky. Phoebe forced herself to take a turn around the deck and breathe in the clean, biting air. She tried to keep her eyes fixed on her shoes and avoid the movement of the ship breaking through the water, and she actually felt a small measure of relief from the cold wind on her face. But as she walked along the upper deck, the crew stopped, stared, then scattered. She knew they considered her bad luck. Foolish boys! If she weren't feeling so poorly, she would tell them so herself. She hadn't eaten anything all day, yet her stomach heaved at the salty scent of the air. She went to the side of the ship, squeezed her eyes shut, and took in great gulps of air. She was so weak from vomiting that she barely had the strength to hold on to the railing.

Suddenly she heard shouts of "Fire! Fire!" and the deck-hands scurried to grab buckets of water, rushing to the galley. The captain and the first mate bolted down the steps toward the galley, just as Cook came through the door and spotted Phoebe. He pointed a long finger at her. "She is bad luck!" Cook yelled over the shriek of the wind. "She is the reason we are suffering such torment."

Phoebe felt the narrowed eyes of every deckhand fix on her. Fix and stay.

<hr />

Cook had taken an instant dislike to Phoebe. He was a vile man, coarse and vulgar, and sent out sprays of spittle as he cussed and complained at her. She reported his behavior to the captain and he told her he would speak to him about it, but she doubted he had done so because Cook continued with his uncouth attitude toward her. The next morning, she was hanging on to the rail, having lost her breakfast overboard, when he came beside her and spoke in a low voice. "I've got a surefire cure for seasickness."

She wiped her mouth and looked at him from the corner of her eyes. He grinned and pulled out a string that had a piece of pork fat dangling at the end. "Swallow it, and I will pull it up again. If the symptoms return, the process repeats." He leaned close to her ear. "Over and over and over."

"That's disgusting," Phoebe said.

Cook grinned. "I've been whaling long enough to know which greenies will recover from the seasickness and which ones won't." As he left her, he laughed and laughed.

Horrible man. *Horrible, horrible, horrible.*

Phoebe also saw that first mate Hiram Hoyt was harsh with sailors if they did not behave well. He had seemed like a perfectly reasonable young man on Nantucket, if not obsequious, and he was certainly fawning around the captain. Once on the ship, he turned into another man. He had no qualms about using force to obtain obedience. He swore and threatened them in a manner that shocked Phoebe. He would fetch them up for a slight infraction and order them to have ten stripes on their bare backs with a hideous-looking whip.

One rainy afternoon, Phoebe observed the first mate lashing the cabin boy, Silo, and objected. "What has he done to deserve such treatment?"

Hiram Hoyt gave her an apologetic look. "He stole a loaf of bread from Cook."

"He's only a boy. A growing boy! Hunger does not warrant a whipping! I insist thee stop this!"

"If it isn't dealt with now, it'll only encourage similar pilfering among the crew. Best to give troublemakers a taste of the cat."

Outraged, Phoebe went in search of the captain, but Matthew stopped her. "Who do you think is ordering such punishments?"

"Surely not the captain. He would never do such a thing."

He gave her that maddeningly patronizing look that usually accompanied his critiques of the Friends. "Surely you're mistaken, Phoebe."

The captain was working with a crew to master the dropping of the whaleboat—not a good time to interrupt him—so she went to rescue Silo and found him alone on the tween deck, sitting crouched on a coil of rope, with his hands dangling between his legs. As she drew closer, she saw that he was fashioning something in a piece of scrimshaw with a small knife. "There you are, Silo."

He deliberately avoided looking at her, though she knew he heard her by the restless tapping of his feet. Phoebe took in the slump of his shoulders—how cold and thin he looked!—and her heart felt tender toward him.

Phoebe put her hand on the boy's shoulder. He flinched, and she drew away her hand. "Silo, would thee let me put healing salve on thy back?"

He looked up at her with those large, round brown eyes, dropped his knife and scrimshaw, and peeled off his shirt. Phoebe's stomach twisted at the sight of his torn-up back, red welts and open sores. She collected her wits and opened the jar of salve she had found in the cabin.

"I'll be as gentle as possible," she said softly. "Let me know if I hurt thee."

Silo was utterly still as she put the salve onto the wounds. He remained so stoic it distressed her—he was but a child, and had no tears, no voice.

<hr>

Silo became devoted to Phoebe, waiting on her hand and foot, eager to do her bidding. Unfortunately, she had no bidding to do. She finally thought to ask if he could find her extra pots, and the dear boy had brought in every kind of pot or bucket that he could scavenge on the ship. That afternoon, when the captain came into the cabin, he stilled, waiting for his eyes to adjust to the dark.

"Captain, I'm glad thee is here. I have made a list of suggestions to help manage the crew."

The captain arched an eyebrow.

"I thought it might be wise to fine the sailors when they use foul language. After all, they are young and need shaping, and I do not think lashing or seizing is the answer. Nor does it seem to be effective. And then, there is First Day. I believe thee should hold regular Meetings. Thee has been neglectful of the Sabbath."

The captain looked at her as if a fish had spoken, then stumbled over a bucket, knocked over a pot, and swore like a . . . hardened sailor. Phoebe grimaced. Such language!

"I can't walk in m' own quarters!"

Phoebe started to explain, but the captain interrupted with an impatient wave of his hand. "Save your apology. I just need the logbook." He moved things around on the narrow desk, found the logbook, and strode out, slamming the door behind him.

Save your apology. Not "save thy apology." Not "how is thee faring today?"

She looked in the mirror. Her face no longer had the youthful glow she'd carried but was the pallor of snow. No wonder the captain wanted little to do with her.

And what did she want? She wanted to be safe and not seasick and on dry land. She wanted to be back on Nantucket, strolling along the shops of quaint Main Street, watching the fog clear as the sun warmed the air. Walking toward the beach, inhaling the heady scent of rugosa roses. She wanted to stand at the water's edge (not on it) and listen to the slosh and swoosh of the ocean. She wanted to have rose hip tea with her father in their keeping room, as was their habit each afternoon. She wanted the captain to look at her the way he used to, with warmth and appreciation in his eyes. And she wanted more from him . . . she wanted . . . she wanted . . . she did not rightly know.

Waves of sickness were crashing over her fast and hard today. Her stomach was empty, her head full of wool, her legs thick and heavy. She crawled back into bed, pulled her knees up and faced the wall, and pushed the wanting away.

Mary Coffin

3 September 1660

Mother and I spend much time searching for herbs to doctor us: feverfew, bayberry, nettles (how I despise them!), wormwood, horseradish, juniper berries, angelica, scurvy grass, dill, wild viburnum, cranberries. Then comes crushing, grinding, boiling, steeping, straining. 'Tis a great deal of labor for imagined illnesses.

I tell her that Coffins are a hearty lot, but Mother fears for winter, so far from civilization. I have a worse fear: Mother's vile concoctions might be a worse affliction than enduring the sickness.

Heppy once said her sister would take wild tansy and soak it in buttermilk, to make her complexion fair. If I can find wild tansy, I will try it.

4 September 1660

Wild tansy looks much like wild carrot, I have learned. Mother wondered why my face had an orange cast to it and did I have a rash and if so, did I need duck grease to rub on it? I did not, I told her. The last time I rubbed duck grease on a rash made by horrible nettles, the Indians' dogs followed me everywhere.

26 September 1660

I have never appreciated a hearth as much as the one Father built in our house, especially as the weather is turning cold. At night we gather around the warm hearth and watch the sparks rise up the chimney. The bright glow of the fire draws others. Now and then, neighbors lift the latch and take their place in our family circle for a quiet chat. On Sundays, Father will light a bayberry candle and read from his father's Bible.

I have seen little of Nathaniel.

3 October 1660

There was frost on the rooftop this morning. The water bucket on the bench outside the house had a layer of ice on top. James had to crack it to wash his hands and face. Wood is so valuable and so scarce on this island that Father refuses to heat the house during the night—he says any and all wood is needed for building, not for burning. There is little wood to be chopped. If a straight and tall tree is found, it is swiftly cut down and used for houses or fence posts.

14 October 1660

Today a damp cast to the air promised snow. Mud has frozen into hard, gray ridges that make walking treacherous. Clouds the color of oyster shells loom overhead and darker clouds crowd the sea's horizon. I dread winter.

15 October 1660

A freeze has trapped us inside and I am sorely restless.

The winds are so fierce and the dark is so very dark. And this is not yet wintertide! 'Tis so bitterly cold that I put on my dress and stockings while still under the covers when I woke this morning. Stephen laughed and said I was a poor excuse for a pioneer. Mayhap, I told him, but at least I will not freeze as I dress!

I wore my cloak all morning long, partially to keep warm, partially to tweak Father. He refuses to keep the fire banked in the night. Firewood is too dear, he says.

And what if his children freeze to death in their sleep? Are we not more dear than a few sticks of wood?

18 October 1660

Father found the ink in his inkpot had frozen solid this morning. He had to thaw it over the fire. With **that** inconvenience, he is willing to keep the hearth fire banked throughout the night if Stephen and I will scavenge the beaches daily for driftwood.

Life begins again!

22 October 1660

The strangest thing happened today. Stephen and I had taken the pony and cart down toward Tuckernuck Island (which Father owns, a fact that he feels bears repeating each time the island is brought up—but I digress, as I often do!) to gather driftwood for the kitchen fire.

Stephen spotted something jutting out on the horizon. Then we saw a flash of fire, and we knew it was a vessel in trouble. And if a ship was in trouble, it meant the lives of the sailors were in dire straits. Most sailors cannot swim; they just hold their breath and hope to drown quickly. I learned that fact from the men who rode Father's ferry back in Massachusetts.

Stephen unhooked the pony and jumped onto its back and rushed to find someone to help. He came across Nathaniel Starbuck. The two of them hurried home to fetch a dory and rowed in it to rescue the survivors. It was not easy rowing because the wind was blowing hard against them. But they reached the sloop, which had been stranded on the Tuckernuck shoal, and they brought back three wet and cold seamen. The poor men were half frozen, and unable to speak for the longest time. Mother made them sit huddled around the fire. As they warmed up, Mother fed them broth, and soon they were sufficiently warmed to tell their story.

They had sailed around the cape and got blown west by a strong wind, so strong it cracked their mast in two. They saw an island (Tuckernuck) and decided to make land, but didn't realize there were shallow sandbars. That was when their boat became stranded.

Suddenly, one of the seamen remembered his bird. Nathaniel had brought the cage into the dory and ran to the beach to bring it back up. It was a gray pigeon, and it too was nearly frozen. The seaman said it was a very special bird, his good-luck bird, and that it could recognize words. Father scoffed, so the seaman grabbed my slate and wrote out a few words. Would you believe that when he said a word, the pigeon pecked at it? I laughed at that. What a wonder! A reading bird.

"If a pigeon can read," I said, "surely there's no excuse for any human being to not be able to read." And then I clapped my hands over my mouth, for my own dear Granny Joan could not read! How addlebrained of me, how insensitive.

Nathaniel left the house without saying goodbye to anyone. Not even a backward look.

He makes me confused. My heart flutters around him like a moth to a candlelight, my cheeks grow warm, my stomach *goes swoony. But it seems he is either hot or cold to me. Most often, cold.*

28 October 1660

The weather was pleasant today, a reprieve, so I indulged in a long afternoon walk. I happened across a marvelous tree. Tall and straight, and it grows straight up in spite of the wind that forces most island trees to bend over. I believe it is an oak tree, and I suspect it is very old. I have decided not to let Father know of this tree. He would chop it down by nightfall. This tree has more of life ahead of it than being a beam to a house, as noble an end as that might be for most trees.

Not this tree.

30 October 1660

Edward and Nathaniel Starbuck brought four bagged geese to Mother and she was very pleased. She uses every bit of the goose, from feathers to feet. Goose grease is her favorite remedy for skin conditions.

As Father and Edward smoked a pipe, Nathaniel went outside to wash his hands of goose. I slipped out to take a clean towel to him. "Was not that reading pigeon a curious thing?"

He dipped his hands in the water. "Aye."

"I wonder if such a smart bird could also be taught to talk."

"Most people," he said, as he wiped his hands on the towel I had brought him, "think there is already more than enough talking in this world." He handed me the towel and went back inside to join the men.

Humph!

5 November 1660

The sun came out and warmed the world. Winter has been put off, at least for another day.

I went walking toward Hummock Pond today and happened upon Nathaniel Starbuck, chopping down scrub oak and loading it into his pony cart. He seemed pleased to see me and stopped his work. "What are you doing down this way, Mary Coffin?" he asked.

"We have been so busy that I have not had opportunity to venture out much. I could not bear to waste this glorious day indoors, so I allowed myself a little time to see more of this place."

Nathaniel seemed to not know what more to say and started to pick up his axe to return to his work, so I quickly spoke again. "How are you faring? Does this island suit you?"

He took his time answering, which is typical of Nathaniel, I have discovered. Unlike me, he thinks through his thoughts before releasing them. He turned in a slow circle, his hands on his hips, as he surveyed the flat, open moor filled with poverty grass and scrub oaks, then he slowly turned in the opposite direction, peering out at the gray sea. "Aye, 'tis a fine place. No better place on earth."

Then he dipped down and picked up his axe and returned to his wood chopping. I left him to his work and continued on my walk, pondering his assessment.

If I am going to marry Nathaniel Starbuck one day, it is plain to see that I must learn to love this island.

12

With a cup of ginger tea clutched in her hands, Phoebe walked away from the galley, down the upper deck, wondering why Cook must always be so surly toward her. She was grateful to him and expressed as much, and all he did was glare at her as if she had sprouted horns. These ignorant seamen! So superstitious. Everything that went wrong was blamed on Phoebe's presence on the ship. When this mal de mer passed—and surely it would soon pass—she would make more of an effort to befriend Cook, to win him over so that he would see she was not a hex but just a fellow traveler, sharing the adventure of whaling together.

Adventure. She puffed her cheeks and exhaled. There was no adventure to be found on this whaling ship—just water and waves in every direction. The only whale sighted had been the one they'd lost.

She opened the door to the captain's cabin to find the captain rifling through her chest. "Captain! What is thee looking for?"

He straightened, a mildly sheepish look on his finely chiseled face. "I had a rare surfeit of time and thought the time was right that I would read through Great Mary's journal. So . . . where is it?"

"It's here, with me." She lifted her drawstring purse. "Thee only needs to ask. Of course thee may read it."

He took it from her eagerly and sat at the teak desk. He flipped through pages, squinting as he read, holding it close to his eyes. Phoebe folded her clothes and put them back into her chest. She heard him grumble once or twice—"Blasted weak eyes!"—saw him light a candle and hold it close to the book.

After a long while, the captain slapped the cover shut. "'Tis impossible to decipher! The ink is too faint for my eyes."

"'Tis difficult reading for me as well. I'm making slow progress, but it does divert me."

He leaned back. "Phoebe, has Great Mary made mention of Eleazer Foulger?"

"She has only mentioned Peter Foulger, the surveyor of Nantucket Island. Why does thee ask?"

The captain lifted a shoulder nonchalantly. "I am a Foulger. I've heard many tales of my relations." He rose and took a step to the door. His hand was braced against the doorframe. "If Eleazer's name does get mentioned, I would ask thee to tell me. Straightaway."

"Of course." She smiled through a sudden wave of nausea.

He took a few steps toward her and reached out to her, a certain luster returning to his gaze. Thinking he meant to take her hand, she extended her own, but he ignored her gesture and placed his hands on her waist.

Oh dear. Not now. Not when she felt so sick. She was aware of her marital duties, but she could think of nothing else but mal de mer. Her stomach did a flip-flop as he touched her, and not in a good way.

He slipped his hands around her back, then frowned. "Thee has lost weight. Thee must eat, child."

She wondered where the nearest chamber pot was. Her stomach let out a loud gurgle. The captain seemed not to notice. He smiled a man's smile—secret and knowing. A chill rolled over her, in a long, slow wave, like the ocean in January. She smiled at him, a tight smile, icy as the frozen beach. "Captain," she managed to utter, knowing that she risked irritating him, but she could not swallow away how she felt. "Surely thee is aware that I have not yet turned the corner."

"Not aware. Don't care." He pulled her toward him and started fumbling with her laces. "You need something else to think about."

"I don't think so," she gasped, and it was a gasp, for she could hardly breathe.

It confounded her that he could think of marital duty while she felt as if she was barely functioning. Her heart beat in her chest like a trapped moth. She felt like a trapped moth! *Oh Lord God, please help!*

And then a hard knocking rapped on the door. "Captain? Captain, you're needed at the helm."

"Blast!" The captain released Phoebe, grabbed his hat, and stomped toward the door. "These imbeciles wouldn't know how to sail their way out of a wooden box."

She let out a sigh of relief; she had never known the Lord to work with such haste.

19TH DAY OF THE TENTH MONTH IN THE YEAR 1767

One of the first orders given to Matthew by Captain Foulger was to make two additional quarterboards. One with the words "British Queen" on it, and the other, "Freedom." Matthew did what he was told, though he was unsure why the captain wanted them.

On a sunny morning, rare and relished, he was up on the upper deck when the lookout spotted a ship on the horizon. The captain pulled out his scope to identify the other ship, then ordered sailors to switch the quarterboards and change the flag on the mast. Ten minutes passed, with the captain peering through his spyglass, before the other ship turned and went on its way.

Matthew watched the sailor lean over the side to swap out the quarterboard. "Ah, now I see," he told the captain. "You are playing with the king."

The captain's face turned as red as an autumn apple. "You're paid well to keep your mouth shut."

Matthew's smile faded. The remark made to the captain was not one any Nantucketer would take offense to. The island juts out into the sea, and tension was brewing on both sides of the Atlantic. Nantucket must remain neutral in the conflict between England and the colonies, or it would be surrounded by danger. Matthew thought playing with the king was a clever ruse, wise and judicious during this dangerous period. And yet the captain's rage was that of a thief caught in the act of looting.

And this was the man his Phoebe had married.

That evening, the captain entered the cabin, moved to the bed, and slowly lowered himself so that he was sitting, facing Phoebe. He pressed his palms together, then separated them and splayed them on his knees. The slight smile that usually graced his face was gone.

A trickle of unease curled through her.

The captain's voice was low, a thick rumble in his chest. "Phoebe, I think thee has forgotten thee is a wife."

She felt the weight of his disapproval pressing against her. And she felt indignation rise in response, rise and release. She stiffened in anger. "I have not forgotten. How could I forget! Thee reminds me each night the sea is calm!" She did not mind the lack of physical intimacy between them since she was so thoroughly seasick. A look of surprise at her sudden outrage crossed his face, but she did not back down. "Thee doesn't need to lecture me on my duty as thy wife. I know my duty and will perform it when I am able. The sea has troubled my stomach no little bit."

"If I am unwelcome—" he paused, all trace of warmth gone from his voice—"I will not press myself on thee. There are other options."

Phoebe winced. "Other options," she said dully. She was quiet for a long while, so long that he went to the door. Before he closed the door behind him, she asked, "Captain Foulger, dost thou love me?"

A terrible stillness seemed to suck the air out of the room. She ought not have asked, for he did not answer.

After that conversation, Phoebe marked a change in how the captain treated her. A chill descended like a cloak of dark clouds. He complained continually. First about her need for the window curtains to be drawn. "I require the cleansing breeze from the sea to sleep," he told her. But the breeze brought in a heavy, nose-curling, salty scent with it, coating the room with a layer of humidity, as well as the sound of churning, churning, churning waves.

He complained of the aroma of the room. What could she do but send for Silo to bring her new pots?

And then he complained about the crew's complaints of her. "Cook needs his pots!"

Then the captain stopped complaining to her or about her altogether. He rarely spoke to her, only out of necessity. When he did speak, there was inexplicable annoyance in his voice. He no longer asked after her health. She longed for his companionship, his devotion and empathy, and yet she only received disapproval in his scowling glances and a tart condescension in his tone of voice.

Her father was right. She had made a grave error.

Mary Coffin

1 January 1661

Christmas came quietly. James shot a goose so that was a fine feast for our dinner. Mother appreciated the gift of its feathers, though Stephen and I did the plucking.

And now a new year has arrived. Tonight Father thanked God for seeing us through another year, a very significant year, and asked for safekeeping in the next one. I wonder, what will this year be like? Mayhap it is better not to know.

10 January 1661

We would not be able to survive through the winter without the help of the Indians, who have provided us with dried corn and smoked meat stored in underground baskets. The Indians have taken a few men out to sea to catch fish. They know of places where schools gather. Nathaniel has become quite friendly with them. He has learned some of their language and accompanies his father to the other side of the island quite often.

12 January 1661

In Siasconset today, a dead whale drifted up to the beach and everyone got all excited. They raced ponies and carts over to Siasconset with barrels and buckets, to beat the Indians from getting first crack at it. Father said it is a gift from the sea.

Now drift whaling is all Nathaniel talks about, if he does indeed utter more than a word of greeting to me. He spends an inordinate amount of time building himself a birch bark canoe so that he can go hunting after whales, the way the Indians do.

Sometimes I think Nathaniel has the sea in his blood. He dreams about a seafaring life, he studies it, he absorbs information about it. He has cold saltwater in his veins instead of warm blood.

31 January 1661

The day dawned, a cold fog rolled in from the north, and beneath the fog, the morning was chilly and gray. Mother and I were kneading bread when we heard the sound of men calling out. We grabbed our shawls and hurried outside. Down on the shore were three men, cold and wet. We helped them up to the house and fueled the banked fire, giving them warm clothing and hot tea to fight the chill.

Their sloop had been blown off course in yesterday's storm, and they were forced to do what no seamen ever wanted to do: abandon their ship.

Somehow word got around and soon neighbors made their way to the house to hear the sailors' story. The fog started to clear, and Nathaniel asked if I wanted to go down to the shore to see if we could see their ship. Of course! I said, of course! I grabbed my shawl before he could change his mind.

As the fog cleared, we were able to see the ship out in the harbour, lying eerily on its side. As we watched, the tide came in and the ship slipped under. Nathaniel and I remained on the beach to watch the ship go down. Down, down, down.

"It's sad," Nathaniel said, "when a boat dies."

"'Tis sadder when living beings go down in the ship."

He turned to me with such a solemn look in his eyes. "But Mary," he said, with sorrow in his voice, "a boat IS a living thing."

Each time I think Nathaniel is silent with me because he has nothing to say, then out he comes with something like that. Something so beautiful it makes my heart hurt.

2 February 1661

I went walking this afternoon, and stopped on a high bank where sea oats drooped, laden with heavy water droplets. The fog swirled about my knees and obscured the distant view of the shore. I knew the sea was there, though, because of the eternal sound of incoming waves that floats in the air.

A great loneliness overwhelmed me. I moved on through the marshes, wondering what Nathaniel was doing at this very moment. And does he ever think of me as I so often think of him?

I kept walking and thinking. About Nathaniel, about how exasperating his silent ways are when I know there are wonderfully wise and sweet thoughts rolling around in that comely head of his. I walked on and on and on, puzzling over it until my mind finally wandered to other things. It occurred to me that I was lost. But in my aimless wanderings, I had an epiphany.

This island is not meant for farming, not with those wide, open moors and the sandy soil. But it is meant for something else. Something that might be a perfect solution to provide for the settlers' well-being and sustenance.

I will have to bring this idea up carefully, so that Father will think it is his idea. That is the way to work with men. That is something else I have discovered lately.

5 February 1661

Just the right opportunity arose last evening to bring up my idea: raising sheep on the island. Father was in a state because we had run low on onions and his gout was flaring up. Mother makes a poultice for him of onions that is very curative. He had been looking forward to putting his gouty foot up, puffing on his pipe, before a quiet fire. Instead, he sat with his foot in a pail of cold water, trying to reduce the swelling, and railed on about the poor soil. I brought him a tot of brandy and sat beside him.

"Interesting to think about, isn't it, Father?"

He looked up at me from rubbing his sore toe. "What?"

"Farming is such a toil here. Other things might be better suited for island life."

He gave me a curious look.

"Think of all you've discovered about this island. 'Tis free of wolves and other natural predators."

"Aye, I did just remark on that the other day."

"Did not James comment on the price of wool when he was on the cape last week?"

"Sky high."

"Did he say why?"

"Flocks have been ravaged by wolves."

I kept my eyes on my hands in my lap, waiting to see if the spark would ignite.

"Sheep!" Father jumped up, knocking over the bucket. "The moors and meadows are ideal for sheep to graze! There is adequate room for grazing . . . and good undergrowth. Why did I not think of this sooner!" He grabbed his sock and jammed it on his sore foot. "I must go run this venture past Edward." He grabbed his hat and coat from the back of his chair. "Mayhap goats, as well."

As the door slammed shut, Mother came to me and wrapped her arms around me, just for a moment. "What would we do without you, daughter?" It was a rare moment of affection from her, and I did not take it for granted.

7 February 1661

Some of the men came by this afternoon (this time, Nathaniel was among them) at Father and Edward's invitation. They sat by the fire, drinking mugs of mullein tea, considering options of economy on the island. "I know that most of you are looking to the sea for the harvest," Father said. "I think this island might provide another possibility. Not just making an adequate living, but that we might thrive."

The men turned to look at him. "Speak up, Tristram."

"Sheep. Their needs are well suited to this land. There is a steady demand for wool on the mainland."

"'Tis an interesting notion," Edward Starbuck said. "Sheep would provide a necessary source of income through the sale of wool. We certainly need a source of steady income."

"And the meat, Edward," Father said. "Do not forget that they would provide us with meat."

Stephen Hussey looked skeptical. "How will we keep them

penned in? We have barely enough imported wood to build our houses."

Father looked to me to respond.

"Let them roam," I said. "There is plenty of common land for grazing sheep. Then we can round them up in the spring for a shearing. We could all help each other. Make it a . . . community gathering." I looked out the small window and saw the little pond out there. "We could do it here. Wash them in that pond, shear them in the pen. Sack the wool and take it to the mainland. Or better still"—my mind was reeling with ideas—"better still, we could start a fulming process right here, on the island. Boil the wool down and send it to England. It could be an economic foundation for the proprietors."

There was murmuring among the men, then Christopher said, "How would we know whose sheep is whose?"

Father looked baffled, then turned to me.

I tugged on my earlobes. "Earmarks. I have read of it. It's a little like . . . well, almost like branding cattle."

"Bah!" Thomas Macy said. "Too easy to alter."

"Calm down, Thomas," Edward said. "We can make it illegal to alter an earmark. There can be fines attached."

"I have a concern, though." Peter Foulger leaned back in the stiff wooden chair. "Sheep are well suited for those open moors, I agree. But we only own a small portion of the island. The Indians plant their crops on much of the land. They will not permit us to graze cattle or sheep to ruin their crops."

Such a thoughtful comment was typical of Peter Foulger. He says that the Indians are very peaceful, and he hopes they will be given no cause to change. He often reminds everyone to treat the Indians fairly, and not to try to cheat them. He wants to do everything in his power to insure that English-Indian relations continue in a mutually beneficial manner.

"Peter's concern bears listening to," Edward said. "We must appease the Indians and make genuine efforts to show that we are willing to cooperate."

Again, Father looked to me to respond, as if he knew I had already considered an answer. And I had! "We could tell them we will let the sheep graze only after the Indian harvest has ended until planting time. See if the settlers might be free to use the entire island as common land from October until May."

Edward and Father, all the men, in fact, seemed quite satisfied by my suggestions, and Peter Foulger even praised me.

My knees went weak when I saw Nathaniel watching me. Then he bent his tall, lean figure over the hearth, carefully stoking the fire with long pieces of driftwood that I had gathered on the beaches. He drained his cup of mullein tea, ran the back of his hand across his lips, and left the house without a word.

20 February 1661

On the doorstep this morning, Stephen found a quill pen, made of a swan feather!, and a small pot of indigo ink alongside it. 'Tis my birthday today, and Nathaniel left me a gift. I know 'twas him because I had happened to see that his fingertips were blackened, and noticed he had left inky smudges on his cup of mullein tea.

My heart is singing.

13

Numerous times each day, Silo popped into the captain's cabin to bring Phoebe peppermint candies or lemon drops to help settle her stomach. It never occurred to her that he had stolen these delicacies from other crew members. It should have.

Someone saw Silo rummaging in the forecastle and turned him over to Hiram Hoyt. Phoebe heard the commotion and went outside to see poor Silo tied to the main mast like an animal. His large eyes pleaded with her.

Phoebe tried to untie the boy, but Hiram Hoyt stopped her, grabbing her arm. "I'm sorry, but he's been seen stealing from the crew."

She shrugged her arm away from the first mate and sought out the captain. He was in the cabin, changing clothes. He stood by the window with his back to her, unbuttoning his coat.

Phoebe explained what she had just seen. "How could this be? He's merely a boy."

"He's twelve. Hardly a boy. You distress yourself unnecessarily, Phoebe." He slid his arm from his left sleeve and turned to look at her. "A crew requires severe discipline. The success of a voyage depends on the crew."

"I believe Silo was trying to help by bringing me things to ease my suffering."

He rolled his eyes when she used the word "suffering," as if he was tired of it. "The first mate is making an example of the boy. Better to instill respect for the ship's authority now, when the barrels are empty, than to face a mutiny when the barrels are full."

"Captain Foulger, a crew would not mutiny a captain they respect."

He narrowed his eyes. "Phoebe, your naïveté was once charming but has already worn thin. A whaling captain bears a heavy weight of responsibility. I not only have to train and manage my crew, but I must answer back to the owners of the ship with a full hold of oil." He buttoned each button of his jacket. "If you plan to continue this journey, you will keep silent about things that you know nothing about."

She stared at him. It suddenly dawned on her why he had never requested that she call him by his Christian name, only by his formal title. She was nothing more than a crew member to him, a disappointing one at that. "Or what?"

"Or you will be put off at the next harbor, to return to Nantucket on a ship that is homebound."

"Thee would put me off?"

"I have considered it. You're not well. 'Suffering' was the word you just used."

She couldn't argue that. Her seasickness had not alleviated, and she was losing weight she did not have to lose. But to be put off ship by her husband, to return to Nantucket . . . how *utterly* humiliating.

"Don't," she begged in a tiny voice.

"Don't?" he repeated, a hard edge to the word.

"Don't put me off the ship."

He looked at her directly, frowning. "Come," he said.

She followed him as he moved to his shipbox and watched him unlock it. The captain's shipbox was considered indispensable by seamen. She'd seen him open it once, to fetch something for an ill sailor, then he locked it up again and slipped the key into his coat pocket. Each compartment was fitted with a corked glass bottle and each bottle was marked with a sticker, its contents named in the captain's neat handwriting.

He took out a small vial, uncorked it, measured one grain, and mixed it into a cup of grog.

"What is it?"

"A wonder drug called Sea Calm." When she objected, he said, "Drink it. It will chase away the sea devils. 'Tis harmless. Not like rum, which addles the mind."

She took a few sips, nearly gagged at the bitter taste—both grog and drug, but the captain insisted she finish.

By the time the cup was empty, she found the drug to be effective. He helped her into bed. Drowsing, drifting, she murmured, "Ah, blessed relief. The sea has finally calmed."

The captain laughed. "Not hardly."

Her eyes popped open. "Silo! He must be unseized."

"I'll see to it." He knelt beside her. "Phoebe," he said, "where did you put Great Mary's journal? 'Tis not in your purse."

The journal? Where *had* she put it? When had she last read it?

"Phoebe? The journal? I have looked high and low for it."

Her mind was floating, and before she could grasp words to answer him, she fell into a deep sleep.

<hr />

The door to Matthew's cooperage opened behind him, and he immediately knew it was Phoebe by the swish of her skirts accompanied by a slight hint in the air of lavender oil. That and the smile on Silo's face—much like Jeremiah's moonstruck look whenever he encountered Phoebe. "Hello, Phoebe." He turned, the hammer still in his hand. She hadn't yet found the seaman's stance—legs sprawled for balance. She held onto the doorjamb with both hands. "Feeling any better?"

"The captain gave me something to sleep away the cover of darkness." She dipped her head. "But then I woke again to the pangs of seasickness."

Matthew's curiosity was piqued. "The captain gave you something to help you sleep?" He put a hand on Silo's thin shoulder. "There's the bells. You'd better see if Cook is looking for you to deliver the captain's tea."

Silo had come by the cooperage and held a barrel steady while Matthew tapped the bottom into it. As soon as the boy disappeared through the door, he turned to Phoebe. "What did the captain give you?" The ginger root was long gone. Cook had given him a few stale horehound candies; Matthew smashed them and steeped them to make a tea for her. But there was not much else he could think to do to ease her symptoms.

"I . . . don't remember." She blinked. "'Tis harmless, he said. I was finally able to sleep. And at least until I woke this morning, I was not seasick."

Matthew leaned back against a barrel. "Are you feeling better today?"

"I was." She seemed so hopeful. "It should improve soon, doesn't thee think? How long does it usually take?"

"Usually? Just a few days. It's been nearly three weeks since we left Nantucket."

"Only three weeks? It feels like months." Her face clouded over. "Shouldn't we be reaching a port soon? Any . . . port?"

"It usually takes three weeks to cross the Atlantic, but that's with fair winds. We've had nothing but storm after storm."

Frankly, he wasn't quite sure where the ship currently was, nor which port the captain was aiming for. When he'd asked the first mate, he'd responded in his usual apologetic way. "I'm sorry," Hiram had said, "but you'll have to ask the captain for specifics."

That answer annoyed Matthew, particularly because he took care to avoid the captain. He was afraid he would say something he would regret . . . and get put off the ship. And how would he face Barnabas if he returned to Nantucket without his daughter? He couldn't. A promise was a promise. Barnabas was right too. Phoebe did need someone to look after her. The captain certainly didn't. She'd been naught but a shiny new toy to him, exciting at first but soon forgotten.

She cleared her throat and he realized he had forgotten she was standing right there. "Need something else?"

"Nay." Again Phoebe cleared her throat. "Aye."

His hand holding the hammer tightened upon its handle.

Phoebe's eyes shifted downward nervously, then back up. "I wonder if thee knows where the captain holds services for First Day. It wouldn't do to miss a meeting."

Matthew gave her a sharp look. "Why'd you say it that way?"

"Well . . . because that's what we do. We go to Meeting."

"Why?"

"Is thee being contrary? Or does thee truly not know?"

"I'm not being ornery. Not intentionally, anyway. Tell me why."

"I haven't missed a First Day Meeting since I was born. Until now."

"You think God is keeping track in his big black book up there in heaven? He's going to mark you absent?" He grinned, and she snapped that now he *was* being ornery, so she would leave him to his work. It pleased him, to see a spark ignite. He feared she was losing hope as she was losing color. "Phoebe, wait. I'm sorry. Tell me why you go to Meeting. I truly want to know."

"So thee can mock me?"

"I'll not mock you."

"We are supposed to take a day off from work and go to church on First Day."

"So that's why you go? Because you're supposed to?"

"Of course. Why else would people go?"

"To worship God."

"Well, of course to worship God. That goes without saying."

"No, it doesn't. I think it should be said. Otherwise, if people go to Meeting because that's what they always do on First Day, or because they think they're supposed to go, then they're going for the wrong reasons. And most do. That's why the church is full of hypocrites."

She looked at him for a long while. He knew what she was thinking—that he was a hopeless skeptic, faithless and futile. She dropped her head with a sigh and left him alone with his barrel staves.

As Phoebe left Matthew's workroom, she didn't know why, but she felt like crying. The feeling began as she arrived at the cooperage to find Matthew carefully explaining to Silo the intricacies of barrel making. She froze, bewildered by the poignant sight, by the way it triggered a wellspring of deep longing and unfulfilled dreams. Silo looked up, sending her a wide smile, so she swallowed hard and tried to tamp down this strange sense of yearning. She could smother it only for so long, despite Matthew's best efforts.

She couldn't tell if Matthew was trying to aggravate her about being Quaker or if he was sincere, but she didn't have the emotional stamina to find out. This kind of frustrating stalemate was always where their discussions of faith took them, even before he had left on the *Pearl*. Had it been nearly four years now?

The memories came flooding back to her of the time when they were together, so young, thinking they were head over heels in love . . . walking along Madaket beach after a storm, gathering driftwood together, sitting on the water's edge at Sankaty Head to watch for ships so they would be the first to see whalers return to port. And then his father bought an old sloop, the *Pearl*, and had it overhauled to serve as a whaler. It was a dream his father always had—to captain his own ship. She thought her heart would break when Matthew sailed away on the *Pearl*. She thought her life was over, at the tender age of fourteen.

But life went on.

No word came from Matthew. That was not unusual, she had expected as much. Voyages were long, destinies uncertain. Mail was passed when ships gammed together.

With both Matthew and her mother gone, Phoebe began to feel overwhelmed by anxiety: fear that Matthew would die at sea, fear that her father's futile ventures would take them under. Captain Foulger was on island at the time. He was particularly attentive to Phoebe whenever she visited Sarah at 40 Orange Street, or when he saw her at Meeting. Once, he'd even given her a small trinket from his travels.

A letter finally arrived from Matthew, full of news and stories, but it did not fill the growing void in her heart. The sense of complete helplessness. She was helpless to keep Matthew safe. She was helpless to fix her father's poor judgment.

A visiting minister spoke at the Quaker meetinghouse and made a comment that pierced Phoebe's heart: "The Spirit of God is always present, waiting to be noticed. Has thee minded the Light? Gained an awareness of the Light within? If thee is living in the dark, how can thee mind the Light? The Light brings peace to thy heart, regardless of circumstances."

Thunderstruck, Phoebe could barely hold back tears.

Later that afternoon, something happened to her that she would never forget. It was a typical July day, hot and humid in the morning; in the afternoon, rain clouds gathered to cool things down. The rain had come and gone, but clouds still filled the sky. Phoebe walked along the beach in a melancholy mood, watching the seagulls soar back and forth across the surf. And then the clouds started to lighten and separate, limned by the sun. Beams of light cast down on the shoreline, the lapping waves, the shrieking gulls, and on Phoebe. It seemed as if someone up above was shining a light behind the clouds down onto the earth. Suddenly a strange and wonderful feeling had come over her.

She couldn't find the right words to describe it, but it seemed as though she was there and she was not there. She soaked up the beautiful scene, filled with peace as she had never felt before. Her heart seemed to be telling her something she could not understand, or put in words. *This*, this peace, this sense that she was not alone, this was what had been lacking in her life. There it was: she understood what it meant to mind the Light.

After a few minutes, the clouds gathered again and dimmed the sun behind them, covering the light; that special feeling was gone, but she was still so close to it, remembering it, that the peace of that moment stayed with her a long while.

A change came over Phoebe. She attended Meetings on First Day to seek that peace that she had found on the beach. And then she attended other Meetings during the week, and her faith deepened and grew. In it she found great sustenance. She wrote to Matthew of her newfound faith, but wasn't sure if her letter would ever reach him. Knowing Matthew as she did, he would scoff. He found more amusement with the Society of Friends than sincerity.

To her surprise, a letter arrived from Matthew to his mother, with a note enclosed within for Phoebe. In the letter, he told of the *Pearl*'s encounter with a coral reef, its subsequent sinking with a full hold, of his father's death. To Phoebe, he added that he had decided God was either a cruel despot, or there was no God. Either way, he wrote, he wanted nothing to do with him. He said he did not intend to pass through the doors of Meeting again. *Not until pigs grow wings,* he wrote.

Phoebe found herself caught in a terrible position. Sorrow for the Macy family, compassion for Matthew, coupled with concern for his soul, and concern for her own soul. The elders continually impressed on everyone the importance to stay close to the Light, and to not allow others to sway one from the Light. Phoebe felt herself struck, as if they were speaking straight to her heart. By the time Matthew was due to return, she had painfully sorted it out by "holding it to the Light," a Quaker phrase for praying for discernment. She knew she could not marry him, as long as he felt the way he did. But it didn't mean it was an easy decision. It didn't mean she had stopped loving him.

As the memories came tumbling forth—recollections she'd always tried to keep tamped down—tears started to fall down her face, so she hurried to the captain's cabin to seek solace. The captain and Hiram Hoyt sat at the teak desk with grim expressions on their faces, poring over maps. The air was thick with swirls of tobacco smoke. The captain waved her away with a flick of his wrist. Her ever-present nausea worsened and she spun around on the companionway. Where could she go on this ship to be alone? Nowhere!

Matthew was impressed that Phoebe would care about First Day Meeting when she could barely stand straight or have a conversation without fleeing off to find the nearest empty bucket. She looked awful. Dark circles under her eyes, a greenish cast to her skin. Why would she care about Meeting?

The Friends had set Matthew aside when he was only sixteen for laughing out loud one too many times in Meeting. Irreverent, they called him. He minded not at all. Religion had become distasteful to him. It smacked of rules and regulations and hypocrisy.

In truth, he was delighted to be set aside. He'd never liked Meeting—the solemn faces, the interminable silence during which he had to sit still, hands folded in his lap, waiting until someone felt moved to speak. And then he or she would stand and drone on and on and on. What a waste of a beautiful morning.

Phoebe assumed that if he did not make some effort to reconcile his disownment, then surely he was a pagan. Or worse still, an atheist.

He set down his tools and stretched his back, then went outside for fresh air. As he walked up to the forecastle deck, he mulled over Phoebe's assumptions.

The truth was, he did believe in God. How much nearer God seemed on the open sea than in a stuffy meetinghouse filled with hypocrites. Here was mystery, beauty, a sense of God's infiniteness and man's finiteness. But he did not understand God's ways.

Phoebe did not allow room to question. Not in her world. He had to hand it to her—whatever she set her mind to, she did with her whole heart. Quakerism. Marrying the pompous captain. And now . . . seasickness.

By now, Matthew was fairly confident that she was not going to be able to shake the mal de mer. She reminded him of a story he'd heard from his father. He had sailed with a greenie who'd been affected by seasickness to this degree—it was thought to be an inner ear balance gone out of whack. It wasn't as simple as mind over matter. The greenie nearly died. Nearly.

Matthew's head jerked up. He remembered what his father

had done to help that greenie. Mayhap there was something more he could do to help Phoebe.

He followed voices to the propped-open door of the captain's cabin, but drew up short, stunned at the conversation he overheard. The captain was puzzling over maps with the first mate. They could not discern where the *Fortuna* was currently positioned. The onslaught of storms had blown the ship off course, and the sky was seldom cleared of clouds, making it difficult to fix the quadrant on the horizon to measure a reading. Matthew shielded his eyes and looked up at the leaden sky. Somewhere, up there, was a fixed North Star. Once that could be seen, they could position the *Fortuna*. And then he heard his named mentioned.

"I thought bringing Macy along would help us locate sperm whales."

"I'm sorry, sir. I thought so too. His father was known for it."

"Indeed. Better still, ambergris."

Then there was silence.

"Who goes there?"

Matthew jerked his head down and realized the captain had spotted him. He moved into the open threshold. "I want your permission to build something that might help Ph—the captain's wife—with her mal de mer."

"God be praised." The captain inhaled his pipe and blew smoke out. "What have you in mind?"

"With the captain's permission, I want to fashion a cuddy and use a small portion of the upper deck. I've heard of one ship outfitted with such a cuddy, with small windows on each side to allow for fresh air. It helped a seaman afflicted with chronic seasickness."

"Cured it?"

"Not sure. Helped it, that I recall."

"Where would it sit?"

Matthew pointed through the door. "In the middle. Out of the way."

"Build it. Today." The captain sighed. "I cannot tolerate another day."

"Aye, she has been quite ill."

"It's not her I'm concerned about. It's the gripes from the entire crew. Especially from the cook. He is running out of clean pots. She keeps using them to retch into." The captain glanced at Matthew. "Don't misunderstand. I but wish my wife well."

Sure you do. Matthew tried not to dwell on the noticeable lack of empathy the captain revealed about his bride.

It took the better part of the day to create the little place of solace, but when he had finished the cuddy, he was pleased. He'd even fashioned a bunk for her to rest in, low to the ground for when waves rocked the ship.

When he showed Phoebe what he had made for her, she burst into tears. "A place of my own!" she kept repeating, as if he had built her a fine palace.

Mary Coffin

28 February 1661

Late most afternoons, if the chilly gray fog doesn't creep in, I have made a habit of walking along the beach. I listen to the waves lap softly on the shore, and watch the birds seek their evening meal.

After a squall, interesting flotsam and jetsam often appear on the shore. The sea floor gets churned up, and releases its treasures from old shipwrecks. My afternoon walks after a squall are especially enjoyable.

I feel a twinge of conscience at benefiting from someone's misfortune, but such is the plight of island living. All kinds of things float up and we use every bit of whatever happens to land on or off our shores. Many's the story of who got what from which wreck around Nantucket, from coconut oil to brass fittings to army boots to bottles of whiskey to compasses. If it isn't used up, it would go to waste.

And the island rule is that he (or she) who sees it first lays claim to it.

1 March 1661

Peter Foulger has come to make a home on Nantucket Island and I am greatly cheered by this news. He is a fine man and provides wise counsel to the other proprietors.

12 March 1661

I have not seen Nathaniel in a month's time. He spends all his spare time with the Indians, learning how to go whale hunting.

15 March 1661

I had an interesting conversation with Peter Foulger today. He came to the house seeking Father, but as he had gone fishing with James, I encouraged Peter to come inside and wait for their return. I wanted to make the most of the rare opportunity to speak with him, to ask questions that have been swirling in my mind. He does not seem to mind conversation.

Peter welcomed the invitation to stay for a spell, so I made him mullein tea and served him a ginger cake, and then I peppered him with questions. "What are they like? The Indians, I mean. They come to our settlement as hired workers, but what are they like in their own village?" I am aware of some characteristics of the Indians. They are very curious about us English settlers. But they are quiet people, or perhaps they fear my father and are quiet around him.

"They are God's children," Peter said, "as are you and I."

"You consider them to be Christians?"

Peter's bushy eyebrows lifted. "What is a real Christian, Mary?"

"A real Christian attends church and obeys rules. Oh . . . and reads Scripture."

Peter looked at me with such sadness in his eyes. "Oh, Mary, Mary. There's much more to the Christian life than obeying rules and going to church and reading the Bible. So much more."

What more is there? I felt a burning in my heart to find out more from this wise man, but Father and James appeared at the open door, holding up three large fish, and our conversation came to an abrupt halt.

The unanswered question continues to burn in my heart.

25 March 1661

I have discovered something else about Peter Foulger. He considers each person as an individual. He looks me right in the eye, and he asks me questions about what I think of living in Nantucket. He listens carefully to my answers. 'Tis a wonderment!

I find myself wondering what Peter Foulger's wife is like. How fortunate she is to be married to a man who sees her as a whole person, with thoughts and feelings that are valuable and worth listening to.

That is the kind of marriage I want to have. That is the only kind of marriage I will consider.

28 March 1661

Peter Foulger is teaching me some Algonquin greetings to say to the Indians who are helping Father build fences. They seem pleased when I use their words instead of ours.

Peter told Mother and me a charming story about the local Indians: Many years ago, there was an Indian girl named Wonoma. She was the daughter of the sachem of the Squam tribe, which lived at the eastern end of the island. Wonoma was wise and beautiful and kind, and she was a skilled medicine woman. One day, a runner came from another sachem, named Autopscot, the chief of a tribe to the west, near Miacomet Pond. Many of his people had fallen ill and their medicine men could not cure them. They knew of Wonoma's skill, and begged her to come and help them.

But there had been conflicts between the two tribes. Wonoma's father called his council together. They decided to allow Wonoma to go to Miacomet with the runner. Indeed, she cured the sick ones in Autopscot's tribe.

Sachem Autopscot was a young man, wise and handsome, and he and Wonoma fell in love and wanted to marry. They knew their love would not sit well with the Squam Indians, so they kept their love a secret.

And then, one day, some men from the western tribe were found hunting on the eastern lands. This was a serious offense. Sachem Wauwinet, Wonoma's father, called a council of war, and made plans to attack the Miacomet tribe. Wonoma could not bear the thought of her tribe going to war against her beloved Autopscot. She hurried to warn Autopscot. Alarmed by her news, Autopscot made a plan. With Wonoma's help to seek out her father, he would offer to punish the two young braves who had trespassed on the Squam tribe's lands. And then Autopscot told of his love for Wonoma and asked permission to marry her. Wonoma's father looked at her, astounded. "Father," she said, "it is my wish."

The courage and love of the two young people were enough to overcome the reluctance of Wonoma's father to forgive the trespassing and to enter into friendly relations with the Miacomet tribe. The two were happily married, and since then the tribes have lived in peace with each other.

I got teary at this story. Mother thought I was being overly sentimental. "They are only heathens," she scolded. But that's not why I was crying. I cried because Sachem Autopscot was so brave and willing to risk everything because he loved Wonoma. And because Nathaniel Starbuck does not love me like that.

14

Matthew scanned the sky. Gray clouds lay heavily, threatening rain. Captain Foulger had set a southerly course, hoping to avoid the thick band of storms they'd sailed straight into. The captain was tense, distracted, and the crew unsettled. Under normal conditions, days at sea were long and monotonous. The idle crew had time to practice whaling drills when the sea was quiet, as well as keep the ship cleaned and repaired. Unfortunately, the *Fortuna* had not faced normal conditions but one squall after another. The ship grew filthy, maintenance and repairs went untended, and the inexperienced crew remained unseasoned.

The captain was the one to blame. The *Fortuna* had left Nantucket too late in the season.

Matthew walked around the bulky tryworks and up the steps to the forecastle. Silo was tucked into a corner where he was out of the wind, scraping into a large whale's tooth with a sail needle. An ink-stained rag sat beside him. The art of scrimshaw, a pastime of sailors.

"Can I see what you're working on?" Matthew crouched down beside him and held out his palm.

Silo held up the large tooth, bigger than a man's hand. He had scratched out a picture of a woman and rubbed black ink into the engravings, so that the picture appeared in outline form. It was remarkably true to life.

"Why, 'tis Phoebe. Well done, Silo. You've quite a skill in the making."

Silo smiled.

Lowering his voice, Matthew added, "Better not let the captain see it."

Silo nodded.

Speaking of Phoebe, he saw her walking along the deck toward the forecastle, hand over hand on the railing. He studied her face while she was concentrating so intently. Poor girl. Her cheeks were flushed and her eyes were bright. Too bright. And she was thin! So thin. Was she not able to keep anything down?

Yet despite her frailty, he still recognized the vigor, that inner steel and determination, that had always captivated him. Even now, here she was, forcing herself to take a turn on deck for fresh air when he knew what the sight of the endlessly churning waves did to her spirits. And her stomach.

"Thar she blows! Thar she blows!"

Matthew craned his neck and shielded his eyes to look up at the crow's nest, as did Silo. The sailor in the crow's nest was pointing to the eastern horizon, hollering the same words over and over. Deckhands appeared out of nowhere and were suddenly crawling all over the ship—some up the rigging, some lowering the boats, grabbing harpoons and hooks, ropes and oars, tripping over cleats, pulling off their shoes and tossing them on the deck.

"It's too soon," Matthew said to himself as he watched their clumsy efforts. "It's too soon. They aren't ready." On his father's ship, the *Pearl*, preparing for a chase was like watching a finely tuned mechanism. Each part knew its role. This was like watching a riot take shape.

Matthew jumped off the forecastle deck in one leap and reached Phoebe, pulling her out of the way of two rushing sailors. "Get back inside the cuddy and stay there."

She yanked her arm out of his grasp. "I'm not afraid of the chase."

He forced her to turn and face him. "Do as I say, Phoebe. It's for your own good." He practically shoved her into the cuddy and slid the door shut. As cooper, he would remain aboard as a shipkeeper, along with the captain, Cook, and the cabin boy, but he knew to get out of the way when the chase was on.

It was great fun to watch. Matthew went to the forecastle deck and leaned over the railing to watch the crew climb down the rigging and into the three whaleboats, arguing over who sat where, clasping oars, dropping them in the water, retrieving them—finally, organized enough to row hard out to where the whale had last broken the surface. He hoped it was a sperm whale, the most valuable of all whales, but he doubted it. Most likely, in these warm waters, it would be a right whale, slow and easy to catch, rich in blubber and baleen.

An experienced sailor in the crow's nest could have identified the whale by its spout. Each species had a unique size and shape of the spout. A sperm whale's had a single blowhole, spouting forward and to the left. A right whale had two blowholes and a V-shaped spout. But the sailor in the crow's nest was a fifteen-year-old boy whose experience in whaling had been limited to gathering scallops from the shore.

Matthew watched until the boats were nothing more than dots on the horizon. He would need a spyglass to see anything more. He walked down to where the captain stood with one eye peeled to a spyglass. "Any sign?"

The captain handed him the spyglass. "Have a look. 'Tis a sperm?"

Matthew focused and refocused, surprised the captain would have even thought it a sperm whale. "Nay." Clearly not. "Nearly flat." He handed the spyglass back.

"Blast. The elusive sperm whale."

"Unlikely in these waters." But the captain should know that. Sperm whales gathered near the Azores, off the coast of Portugal.

This blowhole indicated a minke whale, the smallest of the baleen whales, with a spout that is low and barely visible. "A minke will give the crew needed experience."

The captain lowered his spyglass and sighed, passing it to Matthew for another look. "A man gains experience through experience."

Matthew doubted it. He'd never seen such a skittish, immature crew. On a daily basis, fights broke out; Hiram ordered an overuse of the cat-o'-nine in an effort to subdue them. They alternated between being frightened of Phoebe or provoking her—either way, they did not show proper respect due the captain's wife.

Then again, neither did the captain.

***

Phoebe thought she had grown accustomed to the smell of rendering whale oil in Nantucket, but nothing compared to this stench. The decomposing whale fastened alongside the ship worsened her seasickness. How was it possible to get any worse? She tried to stay in the cuddy that Matthew built for her, but it was too close to the cutting. Even if she could avoid the sight, the sounds and smells overwhelmed her.

Matthew brought a sack of coffee and opened the top of it. "A barrel broke open. I thought the smell of coffee might wipe out the stink of blubber."

"How long will it take to . . . butcher . . . the whale?"

"'Tis called 'flensing.' It should take all day. Then starts the trying out of the blubber. The smell will get worse, especially with the heat from the fire. You might be better off in the captain's cabin."

The sight of his deep-blue eyes, brows knitted with concern, overwhelmed her. Against her will, tears sprang up and spilled over.

"Ah, Phoebe. I'm sorry this voyage has been such a trial for you."

She wiped away her tears and managed a weak smile. "'Tis not the adventure I had expected."

After he left her, she put a cloth around her face and went to the captain's cabin to lie down. As she walked down the deck, she slipped on a puddle of whale blood. She stood, her hands covered in blood, and rushed to the side of the ship to empty her stomach of its meager breakfast. As she leaned over the ship's railing, she saw a sight that made her legs go weak. She felt her head start to spin, as if she might faint. Far below, tied to the ship, was what remained of the whale, and shark fins circling the carcass.

A taunting voice came behind her. "I'll be serving up greasy whale blubber soup for midday meal." She turned to face Cook, a sour smile on his leathered face. And worse still . . .

there were two of him! Double vision. Phoebe walked away from Cook—both Cooks, each one vile—to make her way to the captain's cabin. She looked for a towel or rag to wipe her hands of the whale's blood, and saw one lying under the captain's outer coat on the teak desk. He was a surprisingly untidy man, the captain. He regularly threw his discarded clothing about the cabin. Using her elbow, she moved his coat to grab the towel, and the coat slipped to the ground. She wiped her hands and reached down to pick up the captain's coat, remembering the key to the shipbox was in the pocket. Perhaps just a grain of Sea Calm could help her cope with her nausea. She felt inordinately weakened, shivering and sweating, after experiencing the flensing of the whale.

She stuck her hand into each pocket and found the key in the last one. She locked the door behind her—the captain had a temper; he would be outraged if he happened upon her in his shipbox—and sat at the small table, fitting the key into the lock. A small corner of paper caught her eye and she realized there was yet another compartment in the shipbox, below the vials of medicine. Curious, she carefully lifted the box and found an envelope addressed to the captain, its seal broken. She opened the envelope, struck a match to light a candle, and held the letter up to read it. The script went steeply uphill, the hand studiously rounded.

Nassau
Bahamas
1 August, anno domini, 1767

My dearest Husband,
I am praying each day, that you be safe and you return

soon to me. I am imploring you return before year's end,
as another Child will be born to us. Also, I am in need
of more Provisions. What remains is running fast out.

I am thinking you bring Quiet with you.

If you do not come soon, then I am thinking I will
come to Nantucket in the springtime. I will bring our
baby to meet your beloved Sarah.

I am longing for you.

Your loving wife, Lindeza

Phoebe let the letter flutter down from her hands.

Her heart began to thud and then to pound and then to palpitate so wildly she could think of nothing else. She felt no pain, mental or physical, merely intense surprise. No, not surprise. Shock.

How foolish the captain must find her, he with a life she knew nothing of!

She paced, she bit her nails, she prayed. Her eyes kept returning to the shipbox. She pulled out the vial of Sea Calm but kept the letter. She locked the shipbox and returned the key to the captain's overcoat pocket.

She sat at the chair of his teak desk, waiting for the captain to return. And then she would . . . she would . . . she did not know precisely what she would do, but she was naïve no longer.

When he finally came into the cabin, he startled to see her waiting for him. "I thought you'd be long asleep by now."

She stood and held up the letter to the candlelight. "Who is Lindeza?"

The captain didn't flinch, but she saw the color drain from his cheeks. The captain took a long draw on his pipe.

The sweetness of the smoke burned the back of her throat. That infernal smoking! It made her nausea worsen and he knew it. "I asked thee a question."

"*Lindeza* is a word for 'beautiful woman.'"

She looked directly at him. "She signed the letter as 'your loving wife.'"

The captain merely puffed on his pipe.

"Thee has another wife? Other children besides Sarah?"

Still, he did not respond to her.

"Thee cannot have two wives."

"Under English law, mayhap. Yet it is a custom among other countries. The Bahamas is a crown colony."

"What about God's laws?" she asked more softly.

"What of King David, of King Solomon?" He moved toward her, rounding the desk, and plucked the letter from her hand. "God seems to understand the needs of men. I certainly have gained no husbandly comfort from sharing a bed with you."

That wasn't fair! She'd been overwhelmed with seasickness from the start. "Thee is twisting God's words to suit thy own purposes." Phoebe ground her heels into the wooden planks, put her hands on her hips. "Thee has read from the Bible about the sins of hypocrisy. I have heard thee read in church!" She gripped his arm. "Thee can't be one man at sea and another man at Nantucket."

He shook her off. "Unhand me."

"Why did thee marry me?"

He narrowed his eyes into a piercing stare. "Out of pity." He lifted his eyebrows. "How could God possibly frown on that?"

"'Tis dangerous to mock God."

His eyes—those hazel eyes that had once seemed so warm—they narrowed as beady as a snake's, as cold as ice. "Who are you to censor me?"

She used every ounce of her will to keep the tears back and to appear calm. "Thy daughter Sarah does not know of thy secret life, does she?"

She had never seen the color wash out of a person's face as if lifting a drain stopper. "Hear me, girl." He grabbed her wrist, twisted it. "*No* one threatens Captain Phineas Foulger."

She glared at him, tears filling her eyes, though he was not hurting her that much.

He flung her wrist down, and rubbing it, she thought of her father's counsel, that he was worried the captain might harm her. How right he was!

"Do you really think Sarah would believe *you?* She wouldn't. Don't underestimate my daughter. She's just like her mother. She will make your life miserable."

"This dual life must not continue."

"I am not the first man to have women in other ports, nor will I be the last."

He had no intention to quit this! "I shall have to—"

"What? What shall you do? Divorce me? Finish your words, girl. Or better still, allow me to finish them for you. You shall run back to your father's drab house. Back to your former life—filled with ridicule and humiliation. Oh, don't look so shocked. Surely you're aware of how people speak of you, think of you. Do you really think anyone will believe you chose to divorce me? *You?*"

She flinched as if he was striking her with his hateful words.

He touched her chin as if it were made of spun sugar, but though gentle, it was as unloving a touch as that of sprinkling salt on an open wound. "Your face might be the comeliest on Nantucket Island, but it doesn't change the fact that you're the daughter of Barnabas Starbuck—the biggest fool on the island." He dropped his hand, stuffed the letter back into the hidden compartment of the shipbox, and closed it tight, locking it with the key. He strode toward the door, picked up his hat, and reached for the handle, then turned his head slightly. "You're not so different from me, Phoebe. You want the admiration of others as much as I do. Maybe even more so." The door closed firmly behind him.

Oh, but this man was strangely mixed; she knew him not.

She pulled out her chest, packed all her belongings, and called for Silo to carry the chest to her cuddy on the upper deck. Flensing or no flensing, she could not stay in the captain's cabin. She paced the small cabin as she waited for Silo, and noticed a little brass key near the threshold. In his haste, the captain had dropped the key. She picked it up and put it on his desk, then thought twice. Silo's familiar knock rapped on the door, and she slipped the key into her drawstring purse.

After Silo left her in the cuddy, she sat on the small bunk, head in her hands, utterly distraught, and wept. She had brought this on herself, plotted and planned to coax the captain to marry her, used Sarah's rejection of her to box him in so that he had no choice but to let her accompany him on the *Fortuna*. *"Be careful what thee prays for,"* her mother used to say.

When she was emptied of tears, she took the vial of Sea Calm out of Great Mary's journal. She measured out one grain. Then one more grain, and stirred it in a cup of luke-warm tea. Just to sleep tonight, to find relief from nausea, from despair, from all-around misery.

She curled up into the bunk Matthew had made her, rolling her cloak into a pillow. She did not know what hurt her most—her aching belly or her troubled heart. As she covered herself with a blanket from the captain's bed—let him be cold!—the last thought that floated through her mind was, *What have I done? What have I done?*

Mary Coffin

30 March 1661

Peter Foulger came to the house today and stood just inside the open door. He asked for Mother, but she has gone to sit with old Rachel Swain today. He seemed quite concerned, so I asked him if I could help. He wondered if I knew how to stitch a bad cut. "You are hurt?" I asked. I did not see any blood.

"No, there's an Indian outside who cut himself while scalloping."

If the Indian were scalloping this close to our English settlement, I knew my father would send him away without getting stitched up, no matter the risk of infection. He would consider it a just consequence for crossing the lines. The natives felt differently about the island. They do not understand that there are invisible lines all around the island that are not to be crossed. They do not understand that they sold their rights to own the land, because they never believed they owned the land. They believed they were stewards of the land while they were alive. I like their way of thinking, but I know it won't work in the white man's world. We want to own land, and give it to our children, and to their children. It's just part of our blood, and the Indian's way of thinking is part of theirs.

I looked into Peter Foulger's gentle brown eyes that droop charmingly at the edges, and I made a decision. "Let me get my sewing basket and I'll go with you." He gave me a warm smile and I knew I made a good choice, even if Father gets bothered.

I followed Peter down to the beach and saw the Indian. He was just a boy, not much bigger than my brother, and the cut on his foot was quite severe. He turned his head to look at me and I saw the fear in his eyes. Everyone knows that these kinds of cuts can carry you to the grave.

Peter sat behind the boy and held him tight, but I don't think the boy would've twitched a muscle. He was frozen like a statue, and I must have hurt him with that needle. I cleaned out the cut and stitched him up as neat and tidy as if I were making a buttonhole. It was the first time I felt grateful to have learned to sew.

Peter could talk to the Indian in his own language, which I admired.

After I had finished, Peter said that perhaps others need not know of this surgery. He was saying that to protect me from my father's strong opinions about trespassing Indians. "I will tell my father," I told him. "I would rather he know of it from me than hear about it from another."

"He will not be pleased."

"Nay," I said, as I packed up my sewing kit. "But that doesn't mean it wasn't the right thing to do. Some things are worth the fuss."

I thought of the tender way Peter Foulger soothed the boy, how he tried to protect him from consequences. He's a kind man, and I told him so. I do not think most men are particularly kind. My father is many things: strong, courageous, determined, often reckless, sometimes ruthless, but kindness is not in his nature.

Peter put out his hand and helped me to my feet. "You are a special one, Mary Coffin." I have to say that my heart warmed to those words. And I have been feeling very guilty about that. Because Peter Foulger is a married man, and for one fleeting moment, I wished he wasn't.

15

Phoebe felt as if she had turned into another person, like someone else walked around in her shoes and she didn't know who she was before, or who she was now.

She was indulging in Sea Calm each day now, morning by her own volition. Evening, by the captain's. He brought her a cup of grog each night to help her sleep, and if she refused, he picked her head up, pinched her cheeks together, and poured into her mouth little by little the contents of the cup. She hated it, she loved it.

As her tolerance to the drug increased, the benefits lessened. She doubled the dose and from double, triple was not far away. She had little appetite to speak of, as all manner of food upset her touchy stomach, so she hardly ate. She spent most of the day drowsily curled up in the cuddy Matthew had built for her, not caring about anything or anyone.

A joyous scream from the crow's nest shouted the news that every sailor lived to hear: land was sighted! At daybreak

205

the next morning, the captain put the ship into a deep water cove in Abacos, one of the northern islands in the Bahamas chain, to provision the ship with fresh water, fruits, and vegetables. Matthew hadn't seen Phoebe for a day or two and knocked on the door of the cuddy. Silo sat outside the door, scratching on his scrimshaw. "Silo, has Phoebe heard the news of the island stop?"

Silo shook his head, his eyes grave.

"She's in there, is she not?"

Silo nodded.

Matthew knocked again, heard no answer, so he slid open the door and peered in. "Phoebe?"

As his eyes adapted to the darkness, he saw her tucked in the bunk, breathing shallowly. "Phoebe?" She did not respond. He touched her forehead and felt fever. Alarmed by her weakened physical state, he sent Silo to fetch the captain. When they returned, the captain peered inside the cuddy.

"Phoebe is ill," Matthew said. "She needs a doctor. Can you send someone to fetch one?"

"Fetch a doctor? From this island?" He scoffed. "Certainly not an English-trained doctor. Most likely a witch doctor. Even they won't come on ship. Too superstitious. They fear we'll abscond with them."

"Surely there's someone who could help."

"I'll have Mr. Hoyt ask around when he is in the village for supplies."

Hours later, Hiram Hoyt rowed back to the ship with a midwife, a large dark-haired woman who held herself like a queen. Matthew waited anxiously on the upper deck with the captain while the midwife went into the cuddy to check on Phoebe. The first mate interrupted once to ask when the captain wanted to push off.

"One day to water the ship."

"One day?" Matthew was shocked. "Captain, you're pushing Phoebe too hard. There's a long voyage ahead. She needs time to regain her strength. A few days, at the very least."

The captain dug in his heels. "I cannot—will not—delay departure. We will be here until tomorrow's high tide."

"She will need more time than one day."

The captain's eyes turned flinty. "Impossible. We're already delayed from the storms."

Matthew was outraged. "What is the purpose for haste? Especially if it means—"

But before Matthew could finish, the midwife came out of the little room, shaking her head. "She die soon."

Matthew stared at her. "You can't be serious! She's seasick, 'tis all."

The woman shook her head. "Not seasick." She rapped her chest. "Heart is sick." She tapped on her head. "Head is sick. She in perilous waters. She want to die."

Stunned silence settled over the small group. The captain paced the deck, dragging an agitated hand through his hair.

"I won't accept that," Matthew insisted. "Phoebe is young, she's stronger than anyone thinks. She'll turn the corner, especially if she can get off the ship for a bit."

The captain looked to the midwife. "Is there a place in the village where she can be cared for?"

The midwife hesitated.

"I will pay."

The midwife smiled, revealing a gold tooth. "My house."

The captain nodded at the first mate. "See to it."

Matthew felt relieved that the captain was bending to accommodate Phoebe's serious condition. He wrapped Phoebe in a blanket and carried her out to the side of the ship, where he, Hiram, and Silo carefully lowered her down the rigging to the whaleboat, then he held her as they rowed to shore. She seemed hardly aware that she was being moved. The midwife's house was more of a shanty, but there was a small clean cot for Phoebe to lie on. She was warm, dry, and off the churning sea. Matthew stayed by her side, wiping her feverish brow with a cool rag, giving her sips of water.

The captain remained on the ship.

The following morning, the captain appeared at the door of the midwife's small house. "How does she fare? Any better?"

Hiram Hoyt stood behind the captain, Silo behind both men, lugging Phoebe's chest in his small arms.

"Nay. Much worse. See for yourself." Matthew feared for her life.

The captain did not enter the house, but turned to look at the shoreline. "The tide returns in a few hours."

"Phoebe's gone as far as she can go. Have you no eyes in your head?"

"I'll make arrangements with the midwife."

And then it dawned on Matthew what the captain intended to do. "You what?" he growled, taking a step toward the captain. "You would leave Phoebe here? On a strange island where she knows no one?"

"She is near death. You heard the midwife. I've seen the look of it before."

"Even more of a reason to wait!" What kind of monster

was this man? Matthew looked to the first mate, the only one here likely to have influence to countermand the captain. Hiram Hoyt shifted his weight, beads of perspiration trickled down his face, his eyes remained fixed on the captain. He said nothing.

The captain seemed resolved. "'Tis unfortunate circumstances, I admit. Phoebe knew the risks. She was the one who insisted on coming on board. It was a poor decision on my part to agree. Even if she were not ill, I would send her back to Nantucket. She is not suited to a seafaring life." He glanced at weak Hiram and silent Silo. "And then there is the crew. The men have rebelled against her presence."

Matthew's fist clenched. Men? There were no men among the crew, only juveniles. He was well aware of how they perceived Phoebe. She was a hex, a witch, a demon in a skirt. They believed she put a curse on the ship. Any bit of misfortune on the *Fortuna*—and there had been plenty of it—was blamed on Phoebe. Barnabas had been so right—Phoebe needed minding. "I'm going to stay here. Someone needs to tend to her."

A knowing glint came into the captain's eyes. "Still fancy her, eh?"

"Nay. I told you before. We were—we are—childhood friends."

The captain waved his hand away. "Matters not to me. If you feel obligated to remain, so be it." He looked at Matthew. "There are other coopers. You can be easily replaced."

How well Matthew knew that.

The captain held out a brown envelope.

Matthew took it. "What is this?"

"After Phoebe . . . passes on . . . I would ask that you see to

the disposal of her . . . remains. A proper burial. No grave-
stone, of course. That would not be proper."

The air seemed to crackle in the silence before a storm.

Matthew looked at the captain for a long moment. A grave-
stone would not be proper in the eyes of the Quaker captain,
but leaving his bride to die alone on a foreign island—with
that he saw no moral conflict. He tucked the envelope inside
his jacket pocket. "I'll see to her."

"Come to the ship to receive your portion of the lay of
the one measly whale the crew brought in. It will tide you
over to find another ship to sign on, or to hitch a ride back
to Nantucket."

The two men stared at each other. It occurred to Matthew
that the captain was waiting to be thanked.

When pigs grow wings.

"You, Captain Foulger, need to be the one to tell your wife
you are leaving her behind."

A muscle jerked in the captain's jaw and his eyes darkened.
"Fine!" he said in exasperation.

In that instant, Matthew felt the bitterness of sheer, abject hatred for the captain. He felt suddenly bloodless and
cold. His fists clenched and his heart started pounding. *I
will make him sorry.*

Mary Coffin

8 April 1661

Granny Joan has come! Brother Peter brought her for a visit when he delivered a load of lumber. When I saw Peter carry her up the beach, I felt momentarily saddened. She looks much older.

But my sadness quickly evaporated. She is as spirited as ever! She said she refused to die until she saw this faraway island that has claimed her favorite son.

Father is her only son.

9 April 1661

Peter Foulger came over from Martha's Vineyard and brought his son Eleazer to be the island's shoemaker. He is tall like his father, but gangly and awkward. He has bright blue eyes, fringed with black lashes, bluer eyes than I have ever seen before. He stared right at me from the minute he walked in the door. It was like he'd never seen a girl before. Even his father noticed and gave him a jab with his elbow.

I offered them supper and they accepted. Father did most of the talking while they ate. (No surprise with that!) But Eleazer had much to say as well, and Granny Joan was very impressed with him because he offered to scour the beach to fill the empty woodbox. After they left, Mother said she thinks he is more comely than Nathaniel Starbuck and didn't Granny Joan agree? Mother wants me to stop pining after Nathaniel.

Granny Joan did not answer.

12 April 1661

Peter Foulger is a Baptist, I learned today. I asked him what that meant and he said that our Lord and Savior, Jesus Christ, was baptized as an adult and that was reason enough for him. He says he is an Anabaptist, which means that he got baptized again as an adult.

The Puritans do not like Baptists. They think Peter Foulger is a heretic. I do not know what to think, other than I do not understand how the Puritans left England because they felt oppressed, and they turned right around and started oppressing Quakers and Baptists.

People oppress people. It is in their nature.

16 April 1661

Nathaniel returned a tool to Father. I invited him in for tea and, to my delight, he said yes. He sat with Granny Joan and was very polite to her, asking after her health. I remembered that James brought a newspaper from Boston and thought to show it to Nathaniel. I pointed to an article about the hanging of two Quaker boys. "How can that be? They were just boys."

Nathaniel jumped up so fast he spilled his tea. "I'd better be off before the rain starts."

There was not a cloud in the sky.

"What do you make of that?" I asked Granny Joan, as I watched Nathaniel hurry down the lane.

"Remember, little Mary, why God provided Eve to Adam in the Garden. She was to be his partner, not his superior."

Superior? When have I ever thought Nathaniel to be lesser than me? Never!

I told her as much, of my heart's longing for Nathaniel, yet how frustrating and exasperating he could be. "Like just now!"

She smiled then, a lovely smile, warm and kind. "God made you the way you are for a reason, my dear," she added, "but you must learn to to bridle your mouth."

And then, before I could ask what she meant, in walked Father and James and Mother, the table was laid for supper, and my opportunity was lost.

17 April 1661

Granny Joan's words have rankled me, for I think I know what she was aiming at.

How can I survive if I am not myself?

22 April 1661

I took Granny Joan on a long walk today, as the weather is fine and fair. She says she will return to Boston soon with Peter. I showed her my favorite tree, the one that does not lose its leaves, even in the midst of a bitter cold winter. We sat under it for a long while, enjoying its shade. I told her to savor it, because when Father finds this tree, he will cut it down by sunset. And that will break my heart.

"Well, Mary Coffin," she said in her matter-of-fact way. "You'd better think of some way to dissuade him. For this is no ordinary tree and you are no ordinary girl."

25 April 1661

There is some talk among the Swains and Husseys of bringing a permanent minister to Nantucket Island. They fancy themselves to be the religious leaders on the island, which I find amusing because they are the most argumentative, literal-minded ones.

Every now and then, an itinerant minister sails in and tries to establish a ministry here, but he does not last long. I am hopeful the Swain and Hussey faction will not persuade a minister to move here. I have no patience for paid clergy. They might start their preaching with the best of intentions, but it will not be long before they demand obedience to their rules and regulations. And then they will pass out fines for disobedience, and stocks will be built for public humiliation. And it will start all over again.

This is why Father left England, why he left Massachusetts and came to Nantucket Island. If this island turns into those other places, I fear there is no place left for us to go.

I said as much to Peter Foulger and he said, "There is always Rhode Island." That is a colony tolerant of dissenters. There was a time when he fled there with his family because he was under scrutiny by the Court of Law.

Peter Foulger is quite knowledgeable about all things, including matters of religion. I find myself often saving up questions to ask him when he stops by the house. We have very stimulating discussions about religion, and others listen carefully. If Peter Foulger were to establish a church here, I might be persuaded to attend even though he has radical views.

11 May 1661

I have not written in a long while. Preparing the garden for summer has taken all our time. I went out to tend to the sheep this afternoon. The stark beauty of this wonderful, fierce island overwhelmed me, and I stopped by my beautiful tree to soak it all in.

As I stood under the tree, gazing upward, my mind aflame with wonder, I heard a voice call out, "Is something amiss, miss?"

Startled by such an odd greeting, I turned to see a stranger loping toward me. Despite the brisk wind, he wore no hat and his jacket looked uncomfortably thin. His gait was so rhythmic that it was oddly graceful. As he drew near, I recognized him as Peter Foulger's son.

"Good morning," I said. "Eleazer, isn't it?"

"The very one," he said cheerfully. "And you are Mary Coffin." He glanced up at the tree. "Is there something up in the tree that you've lost? Something that needs fetching?"

I laughed. "Nay. Just the opposite. I am intrigued that it does not lose its leaves."

"A live oak."

"The only one on the island that I've encountered so far."

"All the more rare and remarkable," he said, smiling warmly at me.

I felt a flush suffuse my cheeks as I realized, by his steady gaze, that he was no longer speaking of the tree.

12 May 1661

Eleazer Foulger joined me down on the beach this afternoon, when I was gathering driftwood. "Finding anything special?" he asked me.

"Anything and everything," I told him. "I'm interested in most things."

Turns out, so is Eleazer.

24 May 1661

Eleazer joins me most every afternoon, as I go beachcombing. We get along very well, the two of us. We both like to read and learn about new things, and he isn't afraid of a woman with a mind of her own, unlike a Certain Someone.

16 June 1661

Today was a day I will never forget.

Let me start at the beginning.

All around the island of Nantucket are treacherous shoals, churning, shallow waters. Heavy fog makes those shoals particularly hazardous, causing ships to run afoul. Usually, fishing ships.

There had been a wreck in the Tuckernuck shoals during a bad storm a few weeks past and odd things were still appearing on the shore.

The flotsam and jetsam on the beach looked like they came from an old ship, not a fishing boat. On the beach, I started a pile of peculiar finds, and then I heard someone call out to me. I looked up and there was Eleazer Foulger, waving at me, his face wreathed in his big grin.

I was glad he had come down to the beach. I'd been watching a shimmering object stuck between two rocks, bobbing up each time the waves hit it. I pointed it out to Eleazer and he went wading out after it and brought it back. It took him a long time and he was soaked through when he got back to the beach, carrying the box in his arms. It was about the size of a loaf of bread and made of dark wood, but silvery flashes indicated it was inlaid with some special material. Despite gentle prying, the lid refused to open. Eleazer created a make-shift lever out of two iron pieces from the shipwreck, which I thought was rather clever of him. When he was finally able to pry open the lid, inside were silver coins. We both gasped, as if struck by lightning!

He held one up and squinted to read the Spanish inscription. "Well . . . I'll be . . ." He looked at me with eyes widened in disbelief. "Mary, this is Spanish treasure!" Laughing, he sunk his hands down into the coins and lifted them up, palms full of wet, slippery, tarnished coins. "Spanish pieces of eight!"

I was glad Eleazer could laugh over it, because my thoughts were troubled ones. Who did this chest belong to? Pirates? Was it stolen treasure? Would the owners return for it? Or mayhap they had drowned in the shipwreck. "Eleazer, what should we do with it?"

"Scavenger rule is such that whoever finds it, gets it." He looked up at me. "You found it, Mary. 'Tis all yours."

That didn't seem right. "You're the one who went out for it."

"I wouldn't have even seen it. It belongs to you, Mary Coffin."

"Should we report it? Show it to our fathers?"

"Nay! If I did, people would come to Nantucket for all the wrong reasons. They'd be after my father too. He's already got the Puritans hounding after him. The last thing he needs is to wave around pirate's booty."

So he had the same thought. I, too, thought it was silver from pirates. "My father would be under similar scrutiny."

After a long moment, Eleazer lifted his head. "Let's bury it, then. And if one or the other of us has need for it, then we will dig it up."

So we did. We buried the treasure, Eleazer and I. We buried it under my special tree, so we would always know where it was. I walked six paces from the trunk, to the farthest branch, to not disturb its roots. And we made a promise to each other not to tell anyone else about those Spanish silver coins.

There aren't many men (or women, for that matter) who could refuse riches. I felt rather impressed with Eleazer for suggesting it.

It was the right decision, and I feel good, deep in my soul, knowing that there is treasure if ever I need it. Or if he needs it. Or better still, that it is waiting for someone worthy. I told him so, and he said, "Mary, I think you are the only treasure a man needs."

He is starting to remind me of his father.

16

Phoebe thought she heard rumblings of male voices, rising and dropping in vehemence, outside the window of the house where she was staying. When her eyes flickered open, she realized that the captain was here. He had come into the room. Silo followed him in, his large brown eyes fixed on Phoebe, filled with worry.

The captain stood by the side of her cot, feet spraddled, the palm of one hand clasping the back of the other over his lower abdomen. "'Tis so peaceful here. Phoebe, my child, I think it best if you recuperate here, on this lovely, tranquil island."

Her mind felt filled with cotton. Slowly, the intent of the captain sunk in. Did he truly mean to leave her on this island to fend for herself?

He pressed a small vial into her palm and closed her hand around it, kissing it. "I wish thee safe harbor, my dear."

She stared at him, shocked by the look that came into the captain's eyes. A look of sheer relief. Tears tore at her throat, but she remained silent. How she longed for him to apologize, to express regret, to plead for her forgiveness. But instead he turned and left without bothering to close the door behind him, barking an order at Silo to follow. The boy slowly obeyed with his chin hanging against his chest. The front door slammed abruptly, leaving an absence so profound it seemed about to swallow her. It took several minutes before she believed he was actually gone.

She had ceased to exist for the captain.

After the captain and Silo and the first mate returned to the *Fortuna*, Matthew went into the room and sat in a chair beside Phoebe. She leaned upon an elbow and handed him a vial of medicine.

He held it up and read the small label. "Sea Calm? Phoebe, this is laudanum. Opium." Taking laudanum was not uncommon, thought by many to be harmless, but he had seen many a man bound to it, a costly habit, unable to live without it. In London it was fed to the workers to keep them at their benches. "Is . . . this what's making you so sick? Oh Phoebe, have you become dependent on it?"

"I fear I have," she whispered. "At first, it gave me such relief from seasickness. I thought it was harmless. He promised me it was harmless." She swallowed. "I needed more and more of it to get the same relief, to sleep away the seasickness. And then the vial ran out. I realized I had become dependent on it."

"When did you run out?" He had to repeat the question, for her eyes closed and he thought she had fallen asleep.

Her eyes blinked open. "Not yesterday, but the day before."

"Did you not think to ask the captain for more?"

"He said he had no more to give."

Something was starting to click in Matthew's mind. "Did the captain leave this vial with you just now?"

She gave a brief nod.

"How many days have you abstained?" Again, she took such a long time to answer that he thought she had nodded off, but now he realized she was thinking, sorting through the fogginess in her mind.

"One day. No . . . one day plus one half day."

Just before the captain decided to make land. The ship did not need to be watered. Matthew, as cooper, knew exactly how much water remained in the barrels. Cook did not yet need provisions. "He did this to you."

She took a deep breath. "I am aware what he has done. At first, I believe he was trying to help my seasickness. And then, when I found out about his deception . . ." She closed her eyes. "The Sea Calm seemed so harmless at first, so helpful. And before I knew it, it was my master." Her eyes opened again, and he saw a bit of the old Phoebe in them. "I am determined to break free of its hold on me."

"Phoebe, this is going to worsen before it gets better. I've seen men try to withdraw from poppy sauce. 'Tis ghastly symptoms."

"Take it away from me. Throw it in the sea. I do not want to die beholden to it."

There. There was his Phoebe. Strong, courageous, determined. "All right, then."

"Does thee promise?"

"I promise." He stroked hair off her forehead. "I won't leave your side."

"Thee should go, Matthew. Go join the *Fortuna* before it sets sail."

"I'll jump on board when it returns for you."

She turned her head toward the wall. "The ship will not be returning for me."

What could he say to that? She was right. "Phoebe . . . what did you mean when you said you had found out a deception? Did it have to do with the *Pearl*? With my father?"

Slowly, she turned to face him. "The *Pearl*? Thy *Pearl*? Nay, I know nothing of that. Nor of thy father."

Matthew was quiet for a while. "Then what deception did you mean?"

She closed her eyes and turned away. "The captain has another wife, Matthew. A woman in the Bahamas. She is soon to give birth to his child. That is how I know he will not be returning for me."

Another wife! Matthew rocked back in his chair. He felt enraged. Look at what that man had done to Phoebe. She lay at death's door. He clenched his fists.

Phoebe's eyes flew open, as if a thought had just flown into her fuzzy mind and landed. "Matthew, I need thy help. Please go to the ship and find Great Mary's journal." Her voice was stronger than he had heard it in days. "'Tis hidden in the cuddy. There's a floorboard that I have worked loose. Under the bunk. Lift it and thee will find the journal. It is imperative that the captain not see thee."

"I'll go. I'll go right now."

She took his hand and held it in a bone-crushing grip, stronger than he thought her capable. "If anything happens to me, thee must promise that the journal be returned to my father."

"Why is it so important?"

"I read something in it recently that I don't want the captain to discover. He would benefit unjustly from the knowledge."

"In that case, I give you my solemn promise. Anything that benefits Captain Foulger is an anathema to me." He cupped their joined hands with his other hand. "And I also promise that nothing is going to happen to you. You will survive this."

She dropped back onto the cot, as if she had used all the energy she had. "How does thee know that?"

"Because you're far too bullheaded to die. Look at this situation . . . giving me orders from your deathbed." He squeezed her hand. "Don't you dare die on me, Phoebe Starbuck."

As he closed the door, he leaned his head against it. He wasn't at all sure she would be alive when he returned.

Momentarily, Phoebe felt bolstered by Matthew's certainty. Normally, he was the skeptic and she was the one who never wavered. They had flip-flopped. Now, she was the one filled with doubts and he was the one who sounded so sure.

Her throat ached. Her head pounded. Her stomach cramped. Her teeth clenched. Her legs twitched.

"I won't leave your side." Matthew didn't say more but his meaning was clear. It was more touching than any words of love.

She had fully expected to see contempt in Matthew's eyes when she confessed she'd grown dependent on the Sea Calm. Instead, he was compassionate, nonjudgmental. She was the one who judged herself, who loathed what she'd become. Stupid, stupid girl! How foolish she was. She had fallen for the captain for all the wrong reasons. She dashed headlong into a loveless marriage without ever letting God's Light guide her. Had she ever once stopped to hold the question of marriage to the Light? To allow time for seasoning? Nay! She'd been so certain, so captivated, so headstrong . . . she never once bothered to ask the Lord God for guidance. And in doing so, she'd walked right into a trap of her own making.

When would she ever learn? She kept exchanging one set of problems for another.

*A few hours later, Matthew stood on the beach, watching the *Fortuna*'s sails hoist as the ship glided out of the harbor. He hurried down the narrow lane to the midwife's house. Carefully, he opened the door to Phoebe's room and breathed a sigh of relief when he saw her struggling to lift her head.

"Did thee find it?"

He pulled it from under his shirt. "Here it is."

"Matthew, thee is bleeding."

He held out his hand and looked at it. He had wrapped a rag around it to stop the bleeding, but it had seeped through the rag as well as his shirt. He hadn't wanted her to see his cuts. He had done what he had to do. "Ah, it's nothing. I scraped myself on the board as I pulled it up."

Worry creased her forehead. "And the captain did not see thee?"

"He did not see me search for the journal."

"But he saw thee?"

"I spoke to him in his cabin. I received my lay. And then I . . . told him exactly what I thought of him."

It was the first genuine smile he had seen on Phoebe's face

in nigh two months. She reached out to squeeze his forearm. "Dearest Matthew. Go to the *Fortuna*. Sail on with them and return to Nantucket. This is not thy trial."

"Mayhap not, but thee is my trial." Besides, that ship had sailed in more ways than one.

"Matthew Macy, did thee just hear thyself?" Her eyelids slid closed. "Thee is still a Friend to God."

He walked to the small window and saw the masts of the *Fortuna* slant in the water to round the bend of the small harbor. A heavy feeling descended over him. He turned to look at Phoebe, limp as a rag doll. He turned back to the window to see the *Fortuna*'s mast sail out of sight. Was he still a friend of God?

"What in the world have I done?" he whispered. "What have I just done?"

Mary Coffin

20 June 1661

I went to the commons today to bring the sheep down to prepare for Washing Day. 'Tis finally warm enough to shear the poor woolies! The sheep were milling all about, the herds all mixed up. Along came Peter Foulger and his son Eleazer. Peter cupped his mouth with his hands and let out a long, solemn call. Dozens of sheep lifted their heads at the sound of his voice, and as he called them gently to him, they made their way through the clumps of grazing sheep. 'Twasn't long until they were all crowded near him. His entire herd! I knew it to be true because Eleazer counted them. Thirty-five sheep, all accounted for. There was no need to check earmarks. As Peter walked by me, he said, "Does it not remind you of the Holy Scriptures?"

"How so?" I asked him.

"'My sheep will know my voice,' sayeth the Lord."

After Peter and Eleazer left the commons with their sheep trailing behind them, Peter up front, calling and calling, Eleazer coming from behind, I pondered his remark. I am none too fond of sheep, for they are fearful of everything yet have not the sense to avoid trouble. I do like baby lambs, so sweet and soft.

I tried to call my father's sheep with a similar call as Peter's, but no sheep lifted its head at the sound. Not a single one. They did not know me. I did not know them.

Peter Foulger knew his sheep, knew them intimately. And the sheep loved him, if it was possible for a dumb beast to love a master.

"My sheep will know my voice," sayeth the Lord. The intimacy of that bond was what struck my heart. This is not the kind of Lord that the Puritan clergy speak of (gloomy Reverend Rodgers comes to mind!), a Lord full of wrath and rules and displeasure.

Could it be . . . that this Lord, this loving Good Shepherd, is calling me to follow him? And I have not ever heard his voice, for it had been drowned out by the clanging sounds of scolding clergy.

The thought makes me shudder.

22 June 1661

A few days ago Peter Foulger asked if I might be interested in getting baptized. He is planning to baptize some Indians in the Waqutaquaib Pond in a fortnight. The pond is one of the boundary markers in the original Indian deed. "But I already was baptized," I told him. "When I was just a few weeks old. Why should I be baptized again?"

"But Mary," he said in that particular voice where I knew I was about to learn a lesson. "You did not make that decision. Your parents made it for you. Each adult must come to a point in his or her own life in which he professes his, or her, own faith. That is the example our Lord Jesus Christ made for us, when he was baptized by John the Baptist in the Jordan River."

24 June 1661

I cannot stop thinking about this notion of getting baptized again. Peter says it comes from the Holy Spirit, stirring my heart.

In the afternoon, I walked along the shore, pondering Peter's words. I stopped to listen to the sound of the waves pounding on the beach, the eternal sound of them.

Something strange and wonderful happened to me at that moment. I heard a deep and beautiful voice in those waves, and this was what it said: "I am with you. I am with you. I am with you."

26 June 1661

I have decided to be baptized. My father thinks it utter non-sense. My mother has remained silent, but I think that is because she has sensitivity to spiritual matters. My father, less so.

Nathaniel Starbuck came to me in the carrot patch in the garden behind the house. I was sweaty, my bonnet was askew, and my hands were deep in the mud. "I hear you are getting baptized." It was not a question he posed. It sounded like an accusation.

"You heard correctly."

"Is Eleazer also getting baptized?"

"Nay, not that I know of." I leaned back on my heels. "Why would you ask such a thing?"

"Because those Foulgers seem to have a strong influence over you."

"I seek baptism for my own spiritual need, Nathaniel."

He frowned. "I don't understand you, Mary. I never have." And then he turned and left through the garden gate.

I sat back on my knees and watched him through the fence posts. He does not say much, but when he does speak, he says the truth. He does not understand me. I fear he never will.

26 June 1661

After supper, Mother found me out with the sheep. Each day, I have been calling and calling to them, so that they will know me. So far, it has not been effective.

"Nathaniel came looking for you today," Mother said.

I told her what he had said to me in the garden. "He seemed quite distressed that I want to get baptized."

"You're independent, Mary. Most men find a woman who has her own thoughts to be threatening to them. They don't know how to manage such a woman."

Ah, yes. "Their dreadful affliction."

Mother smiled. "Aye, so true. 'Tis their pride."

"I want to get baptized, Mother. I've thought it all through and I truly want to do this."

"I'm not discouraging you. But you might have told Nathaniel your plans, rather than let him find out from others."

"Why should that matter?"

Mother sighed. "Did you not hear the jealousy in his question to you, Mary? He is troubled by the time you spend with Eleazer Foulger."

I had not considered such an insight. Eleazer and I are great friends, but Nathaniel has no cause to be jealous of him. My feelings for Eleazer are friendly. My feelings for Nathaniel are mixed-up and uncertain and cause my stomach to spin in circles.

"Mary, are you truly not aware that Eleazer has grown exceedingly fond of you?"

"We are but friends."

"I sense his feelings for you are more than friendship. If you don't share his feelings, perhaps you should be cautious about spending time with him. 'Tis not fair to mislead him."

Mislead him? I have never given Eleazer reason to believe that we were anything but friends. Yet I am fond of him, and growing fonder all the time. It is hard to separate Eleazer from his father; they are similar in so many ways.

Now I am thoroughly confused.

17

During the night, Phoebe suffered cramps in her arms and legs that created excruciating pain. The following day, she grew worse. She shivered and sweat and felt pain in her bones. Under the blankets, chills racked her body till her teeth chattered. She twitched, jerked, kicked involuntarily.

She had no fear of dying, nor of death, only a disappointment that she had not done much with the life God had given her. Was it not meant more for others? She had made such a mess of things, dashing headlong toward her goals instead of letting God set the pace. She'd forgotten God's sovereignty.

Give up. Rest.

As promised, Matthew stayed by her side. He wiped Phoebe's hot face with a wrung-out cloth, changed her soaked bedding, piled blankets on her, fed her tiny sips of sugared tea. She closed her lips, turned her head away from the liquid he offered.

"You must eat and drink some."

But why? She had not the strength to survive. Malaise poured through her, wave after wave.

Let it come. Surrender.

She felt her life-force ebbing.

━━━━━━━━━━━━━━

Matthew sat utterly still, resigned, watching life seep out of Phoebe. Her face was pinched from dehydration, her lips a husky blue, her eyes dull in color—when had Phoebe's eyes done anything but sparkle? He felt a great distress, an agony at her suffering.

Out of the blue, she opened her eyes and spoke clearly. "Matthew, I have one more thing to ask of thee. Nay, two."

He studied her face. It frightened him to see her so suddenly lucid. He'd heard of such moments coming right before death. "Anything."

"First, would thee say a prayer?"

"I don't know any."

"Thee spent thy childhood in Meeting."

"Aye, but not listening."

"Think, and it will come."

A prayer. What prayer? "Hold on . . . something is coming to me." So Matthew recited the Lord's Prayer, which he knew but did not know how he knew.

Phoebe gave a nod when he finished, as if she had expected it all along. "Matthew, one more thing I ask of thee. Walk in the Light of God."

Bewildered, he blurted out, "How do I walk in the Light when I only see darkness?"

She gave him a soft smile before her eyes fluttered shut. "Then trust God in the dark."

When the midwife came in, she nudged him and he did not resist. "I sit. I watch. You go," she said. So he wandered outside, blinking against the bright tropical sun, and headed toward the cove. Above his head came the honking of geese. He looked up and watched their graceful, determined flight, arranged in a V formation—whether by instinct or wisdom, they knew their destination.

He'd had glimpses into Phoebe's confident faith. It had been during those moments when he wanted to be reunited with something from which he'd severed himself long ago.

All his life he'd been driven by a nagging discontent—even before his father's death—a sense that there was something missing. He felt a void. He rubbed his chest, the hollow emptiness beginning to ache. How odd that the pain of separation from God, from the community of Friends, had never bothered him until now.

He struggled to find the words to offer a prayer, but they came straight from his heart. "Lord, let her live and I will make my peace with you, whatever the cost." He sighed and corrected himself. "With thee."

What else was one supposed to say in a prayer? His was clumsy and short, nothing like the long-winded ministers at the Friends' Meeting. But then, he was a hard, unforgiving, sinful man who didn't deserve an answered prayer. Would a prayer like his even work? Probably not.

Later that evening, Phoebe's fever broke. The midwife walked straight into the room and bent over to peer intently at her. After a long while she straightened her back and turned to Matthew, clutching her elbows. "She not die," she announced, as if the decision were hers to make. "Not her time."

━━━━━━━━━━━━━━━━━━

Phoebe woke in the night from a dream she couldn't remember, but the dream's feeling remained—a sweet, sweet relief. She listened to a night bird sing and thought it was the loveliest sound she'd ever heard.

Her eyes flickered open. Was it possible that she was over the worst of it?

She pulled herself up to lean on one elbow and saw Matthew asleep in the chair in the corner. Her heart went out to him. She leaned back down, looking out the window at the bright stars. She'd been given another chance. She was going to live. She could feel it, and sense it. Oh, sweet, sweet relief!

She thought of waking Matthew, but then decided against it. Let him rest. He deserved it.

She felt strength return to her, ever so slightly, and she saw her life differently, with new eyes. She'd had everything upside down. The captain, for example. He was the most selfish man God ever made; he loved only himself.

And then there was God. Phoebe was every bit as proud as the captain, thinking she could manage her life by her own wits, her strength. How foolish she was!

And then there was Matthew. How often had she woken to find him looking at her with his dark brows creased with worry. She choked up with grief over the hard things she had thought and said about Matthew. She had wounded him so needlessly—convinced he was cynical and faithless. Wrong again! There was no man more faithful. She had told him she could not love him. The truth was, she had never stopped.

She squeezed her eyes shut as a memory flooded her mind, the day she had told Matthew she could not marry him . . .

The bells tolled and she knew a ship had come into Nantucket Harbor. As she had hurried down to the wharf to join the excitement, she quickly realized something was amiss. She expected to see the typical throng of runners rushing to the wharf—wives, children, mothers, and fathers. There was not the usual joy that accompanied the return of a ship. And then she saw the reason. 'Twas not a ship returning, but a schooner, filled with a crew whose heads hung low.

"What's happened?" she asked an old fisherman, as word trickled through the crowd. "What's wrong?"

"The crew of the *Pearl* has come in. Who's left, that is."

Phoebe's heart started racing. She ran to the wharf, breathing hard, searching the outlines of the crew for the familiar shape of Matthew. She waited near the wharf for Matthew, and when he finally alighted to climb on the dock, she saw him scan the crowd to find faces he recognized. She quietly moved toward him and stopped when he spotted her.

He took the first step, slow at first, then another and another, coming toward her deliberately through the crowd, eyes never wavering from her. Matthew had filled out to manhood, thicker of face and waist, with long L-shaped side-whiskers framing his cheekbones. His thick dark hair was sun-streaked, his tanned skin the color of copper. And he seemed . . . what was it? Weary. Sad. He looked cheerless.

When he stood close, so close she could smell the damp wool of his pea jacket, he drank in her face for a long, silent moment, gazing down into her eyes as if she were a precious treasure he had hunted for.

Unsmiling, she touched his cheek, studying his beloved face—long, lean, handsome. But then her eyes dropped down, and Matthew was astute enough to surmise something was amiss. He tipped her chin to make her look at him, but she avoided his questioning glance. She felt the blood leap to her cheeks and opened her mouth to tell him the truth, then closed it again. She had dreaded this moment.

"Something has changed."

From low in her throat came a single, strained word. "Aye."

"Out with it," he said.

"We were but children when thee left. Time has changed us both."

His shoulders stiffened. "There's someone else?"

The image of Captain Foulger had popped into her mind, of the fireside chats they'd had at his house while she sewed for Sarah. Of the way he'd speak in Meeting, so confident and full of faith. Of how sorrowful she felt when his ship set sail, as if the sun had dimmed. Aye, there was someone else who had begun to steal her heart, but Captain Foulger was not the main reason she needed to end the understanding she'd had with Matthew. She shook her head. "No. But I cannot be with thee."

"Can't be with me," he repeated flatly.

She remembered watching a single white cloud drift along in the sky as she pulled her courage together to tell him the reason. She was a Quaker. He was disowned.

She had put a hand on his arm and felt the muscles tense beneath her touch. He shook off her touch and passed around her to head toward his home. She had hurt him deeply.

Matthew stirred in the chair and she lifted her head to look at him. If only one could live life backward.

236

16TH DAY OF THE ELEVENTH MONTH IN THE YEAR 1767

Little by little, Matthew could see Phoebe's health being re-
stored. Five days after the *Fortuna* had set sail on high tide,
she felt well enough to sit outdoors, three days after that
she was able to walk to the road and back without stopping
to rest.

Matthew brought her soup and biscuits and she drank
and ate all. It pleased him to see her appetite return.

"Matthew, I thank thee. 'Twas just the thing. Delicious."

"I have some news."

She pointed to the chair. "Come in for a moment. Please."
When he sat down, he stretched his long legs in front of him
and crossed one ankle over the other.

"I found a ship that sails for Boston on the morrow." He
had heard of a ship that was on its way to Boston, and spent
most of the morning tracking down the captain. "He'll carry
us to Boston and it's nothing to hitch a ride home from there.
If we miss this, it might be a long wait for the next ship."

"Will not this captain be loathe to take a woman aboard?"

"'Tis a merchant ship, not a whaler. The whalers are the
skittish ones."

"I don't know if I'm saddened or relieved by the news.
Would be a nice life here on this little island."

Indeed. One fellow stopped him this morning and asked
if he might be willing to show his men how to hunt whales.
In return, he would give him land. Servants. Whatever he
wanted.

Truth be told, Matthew had rolled the notion around in
his mind, more than a little tempted. But he was no hunter
of whales, nor did he want to be. He'd had enough of the

whaling life. He wanted to return to the island he loved. He wanted to make barrels and get rich on other men's risks and dangers. "Then, I'll make the arrangements with the merchant ship?"

She nodded. "I thank thee, Matthew."

"For what?"

"For remaining with me. I'm sure I would have died otherwise. Thee had faith in me."

"I doubt that. You're much stronger than you think, Phoebe."

"I have no doubt that thee gave me strength."

That was the wonder of Phoebe Starbuck. She had no doubts.

Mary Coffin

30 June 1661

I was baptized yesterday in a pond on the eastern side of the island, by Peter Foulger, along with two Indian men and one squaw. I waded into the pond as one person, I emerged as another.

It was a holy moment.

1 July 1661

Elizabeth Macy is visiting her aunt Sarah and uncle Thomas, and it seems she is here to visit Nathaniel too. I have seen them together walking down by Capaum Harbour, and another time, I saw Nathaniel head toward the Macys' house at suppertime.

Elizabeth came to the house yesterday to share a basket of berries she had picked. "Did you pick these last evening with Nathaniel?" I asked, out of pure spite.

"Why, in fact, yes," she said, a surprised look on her tiny mouse-like face. And then she hurried home.

My stomach did a cartwheel and I felt color surge to my face. Pure jealousy! One of the worst sins.

But I was outraged that Miss Mouse had made a claim on the man I'd considered to be mine most of my life.

5 July 1661

Another shearing took place yesterday at Washing Pond. It was called by the Hussey clan who asked for help to fleece their flocks. Later in the summer than we would like, but we have had a cold spring and summer. Hopefully, we will have a late-coming autumn so the poor woolies have plenty of time to grow their fleece before wintertide.

Earmarks were the only dispute, as the earmarks were not easy to identify after a hard winter's exposure. I will have to think on that.

The day turned out to be a perfect day. Clear, calm, blue sky, water the same, and full of sunshine, with a lady's wind blowing through the reeds, wafting wild rose petals and perfume. Soap seethed up in the pond, bubbles caught in the gentle wind and floated over the men's heads as they scrubbed the lowing sheep. It was enchanting.

After a supper served by the women, the men participated in games. They threw the bar, hurled stones, had footraces, and threw the discus by using Mother's wooden chargers for disks (when she realized **whose** chargers they were using, she was **not** happy). Folks cheered their favorites, laughter sang through the air, and it was all such good fun!

Nathaniel Starbuck came off the hero of the day, winning all but the footrace, which went to Eleazer Foulger, who is lean and lanky, swift and long legged. Nathaniel is strong muscled with fine shoulders, and not so tall. Just tall enough.

I congratulated Eleazer and brought him a mug of mint water sweetened with honey. He smiled warmly at me. As I returned to the table, Nathaniel locked eyes with me. "Must you seek the attention of every man on the island?"

Humph! "Eleazer Foulger is a newcomer to the island. I was being sociable. I try to be a friend to all." And then I added

something I shouldn't have. "Mayhap you should try being sociable sometime!"

Nathaniel turned away without reply. I looked after him,
biting my lip, astonished by his insult to my character. Down-
right unmannerly! But on top of that came anger with myself
for lashing out. I leaned my back against the tabletop. Mother
sidled up to me. "He has won every single race," I told her.
"Was that not enough?"

"Jealousy, Mary. That is what makes him speak to you that
way."

"Jealousy? Of Eleazer?"

"Not just Eleazer. Of all the men on the island. They notice
you and they like what they see. Mind you, I do not mean
to make you proud. But you should know that you have blos-
somed fully into womanhood, and men take notice of such
things."

I am not entirely unaware of how men act around me.
Boasting, talking overloud when I am near, stealing looks to
see if I see them. And yet, I do NOT seek out the attention of
men. Nathaniel offended me greatly by such a remark. "What
of his dalliance with the fair Elizabeth Macy?"

"She might be fair, but she does not have your fire."

I wasn't at all sure Nathaniel liked my fire. And I wasn't at
all sure I could be tied to a man who tried to douse it.

6 July 1661

When Nathaniel dropped by today to borrow Father's plow,
I told myself not to say a word about it. To be wise, for once,
Mary Coffin. That's what I told myself.

Instead I said, "You've been seeing Elizabeth Macy."

His face was somber, and he studied me as if he was trying to decide how to answer. "I have . . . a few times."

My heart raced, and I could not stop myself from asking, "Do you enjoy being with her?"

He shot me a sharp look. "What makes you ask such a thing?"

I knew he was courting Elizabeth, and he need not say another word for me to know why he was. Elizabeth Macy is meek and mild and a fair lady.

So I told Nathaniel that I was not destined to be a meek and quiet fine lady. If he is wanting a fine and meek and quiet lady, then he should just go off and spend all his time with Elizabeth Macy because I will be an endless disappointment to him. I have a fire inside me and I have a hunger inside me and I know it. I told him God made me the way I was for a reason. I can't help it. But I know I want a man who is not trying to continually extinguish the fire inside me. I would rather not ever get married than have a man always trying to shush me or look embarrassed for the woman he married. Or worse, disappointed, the way Nathaniel looks sometimes when I speak my mind.

The most mournful look came over him and his eyes grew ever-so-slightly watery. "Mary, 'tis not you I'm disappointed in."

He wouldn't explain what he meant by that. He just left. Good riddance to him. I hope I never see him again, as long as I do live.

I don't mean it. I've been crying all afternoon.

18

From Boston, Matthew found a schooner that was setting sail for Martha's Vineyard, then Nantucket. As the ship rounded Tuckernuck Island, Matthew and Phoebe stood side by side on the bow. Her seasickness had returned with a vengeance as the merchant ship sailed in open seas, though it was a blessedly squall-free sailing. These shorter trips, from Boston to the Vineyard, from the Vineyard to Nantucket, made it slightly more manageable. A little. Her skin still had a greenish-gray hue and he hadn't seen a smile from her since they left Abacos. But she was determined to get home, and that gave her the stamina she needed to endure the voyage.

"There she is," he said quietly.

The midday sun was casting her light over Nantucket, dissolving the fog that hovered so restlessly over the island.

Ah, Nantucket. How Matthew loved this island.

"Home." Relief covered Phoebe's face. "As soon as my feet touch Nantucket, that blessed, beloved island, I will never leave its sandy soil again. I will never, ever step foot in another boat. I never want to hear the words 'hunker down' again."

He laughed.

"Matthew, I thank thee for all thee has done for me. Were it not for thee, I don't know what would have become of me."

He returned his gaze to the approaching island. Here and there, he could see smoke wisping out of chimneys. *Home.* "That's what friends are for."

"Thee is more than a friend to me. Thee is a Weighty Friend."

"Was. Once I was much more to you." He glanced at her. "You were right, Phoebe. We were much too young to marry. Too young to make that kind of decision."

"If things were different . . . if thee had remained . . ."

"Quaker."

"If thee had not abandoned thy faith, perhaps things might have been different between us."

"I didn't abandon my faith, Phoebe. I needed to sort it out on my own, without all of the thees and thous and rules and regulations."

"And has thee? Sorted it out."

"Starting to, I think." He thought of the pact he had made with God on the beach of Abacos. *Let Phoebe live and I will make my peace with thee.* God held up his end of the bargain. Against all odds, Phoebe was standing right beside him, Nantucket approaching in front of them. He would need to make good on his end, though he wasn't really sure what that could mean. He supposed he'd have to apologize to the elders.

She smiled, but her smile was sad, as if she sensed his confusion. "I'm glad, Matthew. I want only happiness for thee."

"And you, Phoebe? Are you happy?" He cupped her elbow with his hand. She looked pale and green. He nearly smiled. She was not a woman destined for a life at sea.

"I am . . . happy to be heading home."

"Heading home as the wealthy and illustrious captain's wife. Without the captain. Well, it should be nice to have a few shillings in your pocket, assuming Sarah will share some with you. Probably not after you tell her that her father has another wife." He glanced over at Phoebe and realized he'd said too much, too bluntly. The look on her face was one of shock and despair. "I'm sorry. I didn't mean to be glib."

"I was so foolish."

"You were filled with hope and dreams for a bright future. The captain is one man in the meetinghouse, another one entirely on the ship. 'Tis not so uncommon. Angelic on land, devilish with a cat-o'-nine in his hand."

"I had been warned."

"By whom?"

"My father. He was concerned the captain would harm me."

"Barnabas should have forbidden the marriage."

"He knew I was determined."

"You're going to tell people about Lindeza, aren't you?"

She gave him a grave look. "Matthew, I do not want to bring humiliation to the captain."

"He left you for dead, Phoebe!"

"Even still. I will deal with the captain quietly, when the time is right. When he returns from the voyage." She lifted a hand as he objected. "I know that could be years from now. I must seek God's guidance on this. Before I do anything, or say anything. I do not intend to cause others pain."

"Like who?"

"Sarah, for one. She would be mortified."

He scoffed. "Sarah Foulger would not concern herself about you. Not in the least."

"I realize that. But I cannot let the actions of others change me, Matthew." She gave him a direct look. "Thee must promise me not to tell anyone about Lindeza. This is my trial to deal with, not thine."

How could she be so . . . pure? Especially after being wronged? He turned toward her. "Phoebe, the captain will get what he deserves—"

"Land ho!"

The quiet moment was interrupted by sailors hustling to trim the sails as the small ship darted through the infamous Tuckernuck shoals.

When the small schooner rounded the bend to sail into Nantucket Harbor, Phoebe and Matthew had the same shock. There sat the *Fortuna*, anchored and empty.

Constable Zacchaeus Coleman stood on the docks, waiting for them as they disembarked from the lighter, a blank look on his mutton-chopped face. "Phoebe Starbuck," he said in a stunned tone. "Thee is supposed to be dead."

"But I'm not, Zacchaeus. I'm very much alive." Phoebe reached for his hand to help her climb out of the lighter onto the dock. "Tell me, why has the *Fortuna* had a broken voyage?"

"She was severely damaged in a storm. She's a splintered mess."

Matthew stared at the ship. Several sails, including the

topgallant and the studding sail, had been torn into useless tatters. Phoebe's little cuddy was gone. The whaleboats that had been hung off the port side of the ship were missing from their davits.

"The first mate declared they would have to return to Nantucket for repairs."

Phoebe spun around. "The first mate? What of the captain?"

Zaccheus avoided her question and fixed his eyes on Matthew. "Matthew, cousin, I'm sorry to be the one to bear this unfortunate news, but I have a warrant to arrest thee. I'm . . . surprised thee didn't just stay away."

"Arrest me? I just arrived! And I promise to stay clear of the taverns."

"It's not the drinkin' this time." A frown settled over the constable's round features, and he hooked his thumbs in his waistcoast pockets as he studied Matthew. "The first mate said thee was seen coming out of the captain's cabin just before the ship made sail. Thee was heard arguing with him, by several deckhands. The warrant was written up the day the *Fortuna* sailed in."

"So I argued with him." He glanced at Phoebe. "Why is that a concern?"

He quirked a bushy eyebrow. "So thee admits it?"

"Admit what, Zaccheus?"

"That thee was the last one in the captain's cabin."

Matthew felt Phoebe glance sharply at him. "What are you talking about? Why would it matter?"

"Because the captain was found mortally wounded in his cabin."

The news hit Matthew like a fist in the solar plexus. *No,*

no, it's not possible. He was gripped by a sick feeling of dread, a dread much stronger than any he'd experienced on the *Pearl*, even worse than when the ship was dismembered and his father sent him off in a whaleboat, refusing to leave until the entire crew was accounted for.

"Captain Foulger . . . he's . . . dead?" Phoebe swayed and Zacchaeus, standing closest to her, caught her.

Sharp needles of creeping heat began to crawl up Matthew's spine, but outwardly he remained stoic. He turned his gaze directly into Phoebe's shocked eyes, trying to reassure her that he did not do this deed, then pulled his eyes away from her to answer. "Zacchaeus, do you really think I would return to the island, *this* very island, if I had murdered a Nantucket sea captain?"

Zacchaeus seemed momentarily nonplussed. "It does seem a bit foolhardy, but I'm just paid to carry out orders. I'm sorry, cousin. Thee will need to come with me." His grip was firm on Matthew's upper arm.

Matthew ground the edges of his teeth together and said nothing. He watched Phoebe struggle for control, watched her momentarily lose and regain it.

He shrugged his cousin's hand off of his arm and clutched Phoebe's shoulders. "I didn't do it, Phoebe. You believe me, don't you?"

"Your hand. There was blood on it after thee returned. After thee had received thy lay from the captain—" She stopped herself, glancing at Zacchaeus, then lowered her eyes.

In that moment of hesitation, Matthew drew back. Panic tore through him. "Phoebe, you—of all people—you must believe me."

Tears filled her eyes.

"Phoebe, the crew said thee had succumbed on an island. But thy father refused to have a funeral service alongside the captain's. He said he would know in his heart if his own daughter had left this earth. I see he is right. He'll be pleased to see thee."

She seemed to come out of her stupor, tears coursing down her face. "My father. I need to see my father."

Matthew turned to the constable. "Zacchaeus, let me at least get Phoebe to her father."

A shadow passed over the constable's face. "Thee will see him first."

Phoebe's head jerked up. "Is he not at home?"

Zacchaeus squinted, as if it pained him to say the words. "Nay, Phoebe. He is in the gaol. Debtor's prison."

<hr />

Matthew seemed to be the first to recover from the shock of Zacchaeus's news, much more quickly than Phoebe. "Let's get, then," he told the constable icily. "What are you waiting for?"

Tears filled Phoebe's wide, frightened eyes, and she pressed a fist to her lips. It was all happening so fast! She knew, before Zacchaeus and Matthew disappeared off Straight Wharf and onto Main Street toward the old gaol on Vestal Street, that she had just made one of the gravest mistakes of her life—topping what she felt was quite a long list. It had lasted only a matter of seconds, but that's all it had taken to turn Matthew cold. She had seen and felt his withdrawal like a slap in the face. And it was entirely her fault.

She had to do something to fix this. She straightened her

spine and turned her terror into vigor, her despair into determination, her remorse into a promise: *I will get to the bottom
of this, Matthew Macy. I made this mess, and somehow, I
will unmake it.*

A burst of emotion flooded through her chest, and then
astonishing clarity filled her mind: she had things to do. First,
to gather missing pieces of information. And that would
begin at the Pacific Bank.

Ten minutes later, she stood in front of Horace Russell's
desk at the Pacific Bank. His small mouth dropped in an
O and his bespectacled eyes widened. "But, but . . . thee is
dead," he said.

"I am not," she answered. "I am much alive."

Captain Phineas Foulger, Phoebe learned from Horace
Russell, had not provided funds for the defaulted mortgage
on 35 Centre Street as he had promised. The morning after
the *Fortuna* set out on its voyage, Phoebe's father had been
evicted from the house, passed from one relative to another,
until his welcome ran out.

"Thee put my father into debtor's prison! Nantucket law
allows a man one year to repay a debt, but thee put him into
prison and put our Centre Street house up for sale."

"That was not my decision, Phoebe. That is to say, yes, I
did put the house up for sale to pay off his debts. But I did
not instigate sending him to debtor's prison."

"Who did?"

"The entire Starbuck clan. Led by thy aunt Dorcas after
her house was burned down by thy father's own hand."

Apparently, Horace explained, Barnabas had been experi-
menting with candle making and blew up the home of Dorcas
Starbuck. Dorcas pressed charges, no one else would shelter

Barnabas, and that meant the constable had no choice but to take him to debtor's prison.

Phoebe's spirits sank. There was one bright spot, Horace told her, nodding his head until his wattle wobbled. "The Centre Street house has not yet sold. In fact, the bank has had trouble getting any interest in it." He came around his desk and leaned toward her, so close she could smell his breath. Horrible breath! "Everyone assumes it has bad luck."

Phoebe felt the glimmer of a spark within her, small and flickering at first, then it grew to a flame. Her stomach did not twist and clench at the smell of horrible Horace Russell's breath. She had two legs firmly on the ground, the horizon was not tipping and swaying, and she was not dizzy or nauseated!

She strode out of Horace Russell's office feeling strangely emboldened. She hurried to 28 Orange Street, walked right in the front door, and ignored the startled looks on the servants' faces. "Where is she?" she said in a loud voice. "Where is Sarah Foulger?"

Dressed in black mourning clothes, Sarah appeared at the door of the front room and gasped when she saw Phoebe. Her face blanched and her hands flew to her mouth. "Thee! Thee was . . . said . . . to be dead," she stammered. From behind her, Hiram Hoyt appeared. His eyes widened in disbelief at the sight of Phoebe, and the perpetual pipe dropped from his mouth, spilling tobacco ash on the wooden floor.

An odd will-o'-the-wisp floated through Phoebe's mind, but she had no time to reflect on it. Where had she seen that before? "I nearly did die. Thy father had me gone and buried. But God had a different plan. When I recovered, I returned to Nantucket as quickly as possible. Just now, as the schooner arrived, I learned of thy father's passing."

"Murdered," the first mate mumbled. "Forgive me for interrupting, but he was killed in cold blood. By Matthew Macy."

Phoebe ignored him. "Sarah, I am truly sorry."

Sarah's eyes filled with tears, and Hiram pulled out a kerchief for her to wipe her eyes. "If thee is here to inquire of my father's last will and testament, thee should know thee is not in it."

Were the situation not so serious, Phoebe would have laughed. "I am not here for my sake, but for my father's. The captain had promised to leave one hundred pounds at the bank to provide for my father."

"One hundred pounds?" Sarah repeated sardonically, then laughed once, mirthlessly. "'Tis a pity that issue was not resolved prior to my dear father's untimely death."

"My father is in debtor's prison because the captain, my *husband*, did not provide for him."

Sarah walked up to Phoebe with her eyes narrowed to slits. "Does thee know what the crew has said about thee and Matthew Macy? The man accused of killing my father?"

"Matthew Macy is no killer."

"I heard that there was a dalliance between thee. That he built thee a special love nest on the *Fortuna*. Why else would he have remained on the island when my own father left? Oh, it all makes perfect sense."

Phoebe was shocked by the accusation. "Sarah, I have done nothing dishonorable. Nor has Matthew. What thee heard is a vicious rumor." Her eyes shifted to Hiram, whose eyes were fixed on the ground, then shifted back to Sarah.

"I heard it from a very reliable source. So thee had better say goodbye to thy lover. He is headed for Gallows Field.

And even if the Friends frown on my delight, I will be there to watch!" Sarah opened the door for Phoebe and practically shoved her over the threshold. "Cast off, Widow Foulger! Cast off without delay!" The door slammed in her face.

The awful reality hit Phoebe full force. *Widow* Foulger? Widow Foulger? *I am a widow without ever really being a wife.* Her blood ran hot, leapt into her veins, and fired her heart.

Phoebe had not expected much from the captain's only daughter, but she had gotten even less. Who was Sarah Foulger, this cold and proud woman, to judge Phoebe and find her worthless? Right then and there, she decided: *No longer!*

Mary Coffin

10 August 1661

Two terrible things happened, both in the same day.

James returned from the Cape with news that Granny Joan had died peacefully in her sleep a fortnight ago.

Father was distraught and went out for a long walk. He came back cheered, saying he had come across an oak tree and where did Stephen leave his axe?

My tree! My beloved tree.

I had to think quickly. "Oh Father! I know just the tree. 'Tis Granny Joan's favorite tree on Nantucket! She loved it so dearly. Last summer, she sat under its shade and commented how it brought her such joy." I clapped my cheeks for effect. "To think you discovered it on the very day you learned of her passing. 'Tis no coincidence. Does it not seem right to honor her by keeping it?"

With that, the tree was declared sacrosanct. Granny Joan's tree, he now calls it.

14 August 1661

The weather went from cool and rainy in June to beastly hot and humid in July and August. My hair refuses to stay pinned. I fear I look like the poor woolies, with fleece sprouting every which way.

15 August 1661

Yesterday, James returned from the Cape with news that the General Court is going to excess in several towns there. He was told there were upwards of a hundred people in jail for not attending church, or worse yet, attending Quaker services. Imagine that!

How quickly things can change.

25 August 1661

There has been a cooler spell, and although we know that summer is not over, the heat is gentle today and things are growing everywhere, not looking so scorched as they did in July. I am making jam from berries to set up for winter.

I had finished picking berries that grow near Hummock Pond and happened upon Nathaniel Starbuck and Elizabeth Macy. They were sitting under a tree with their heads together over a book. I said hello but kept on my way. I heard Elizabeth whisper something in her squeaky mouselike voice. I wonder if she was whispering to him about me.

I wept all the way home. I was in such a state that I walked past the house and straight to Granny Joan's tree and sat underneath it until I felt composed enough to go home.

19

There was only one place left Phoebe could turn, one person who would welcome her in. She knocked on the door of Libby Macy's modest house on Easy Street. When the older woman opened the door, she froze, stunned. "Phoebe Starbuck! As I live and breathe!" Matthew's mother opened her arms and Phoebe flew into them to be gathered high and hard against her. Her motherly touch brought forth one sob, then another. She had a sudden overwhelming need to be gentled and comforted, but what of the news of Matthew she had to give? Who would ease a mother's misery?

They sat at the table near the fire and Phoebe told her the whole story, start to finish, leaving no sordid detail unsaid. "There is convincing evidence. Sarah Foulger told me of the crew's accusations. If Matthew is found guilty, he will be sent to Gallows Field."

His mother suffered a moment's pause, then in a voice that was as unruffled as if she were discussing the weather, she announced, "That is not going to happen. My son is innocent of this deed."

"Of course, of course he is. But there are witnesses, and evidence. It does not look good."

"We will hire the best attorney in all New England."

"We will?" Libby Macy's staunchness suddenly put starch in Phoebe's spine. She sniffed and mopped her eyes. "Who?"

"My cousin's son, Ezra Barnard. He's a genius. And he lives just over in Cambridge." Libby rubbed her hands together. "We are going to need money. Plenty of it." With that, for the first time, a frown crossed her face. The Macys were deep in debt from the *Pearl*.

Money. Here Phoebe was again, desperately needing money. Where was she ever going to find the kind of money needed to defend Matthew? She paced nervously up and down the small keeping room. Suddenly, a light broke through her fog. "I'll be right back!"

"Where is thee going?"

"To the docks. I believe an answer lies there."

Hurrying down toward Straight Wharf, Phoebe picked her way between clusters of townspeople who gaped at each other in shock at the sight of her. She paid them no mind but hurried down to the dock. There she found Silo stretched out on top of hers and Matthew's sea chests, napping in the sun. "Silo! Oh Silo. Thee is a sight for sore eyes. And look, sweet boy—thee is protecting our chests!"

He bolted up, but seemed not at all surprised by the sight of her. She realized he must have seen them arrive on the lighter a few hours back. "Would thee bring the chests to the Macys' house on Easy Street? I will reward thee." She wondered where he was living and suspected, by the smell of his salt-caked slops, that without the captain looking after him, he was bereft of a home. She gave him a head-to-toe appraisal. Too thin! "And food. Thee needs a good meal."

⸻

Matthew lay in his cell facing a whitewashed wall, smelling the fetid odors of old urine on a stale-smelling mattress. He thought about crying but lacked the heart. He thought about fighting the charges—but for what? And with what resources? He had none. On the way to the gaol, Zacchaeus had told him the case was a solid one. Any hope was snuffed out the moment that Phoebe looked at him with doubt in her eyes.

When would he learn? When would he stop thinking that life would turn right side up for him?

The door opened and in came Barnabas Starbuck, led by Zacchaeus. "I got him up to speed," the constable said. "But I thought you two might have some catching up to do."

Despite their dismal circumstances, Barnabas looked overjoyed. "Matthew, could it be true? Is my Phoebe alive?" The old man's face, lit with hope, brought warmth and brightness to the dingy, filthy surroundings.

Matthew rolled over and stood up. "'Tis true, Barnabas. I'm sure she'll be coming to see you soon." *Not to see me, nor do I care to see her.*

The old man embraced Matthew with surprising strength, tears streaming down his face. Then he sat down in the dank and dismal cell as if it were a cozy keeping room, beaming. "Tell me everything. Start to finish. Leave nothing out. Not one thing!"

No sooner had Matthew finished the long tale than the

gaol door opened and in walked Zacchaeus, this time followed by Phoebe.

When Phoebe was a schoolgirl, she and her friends would dare each other to run up to the old gaol, touch it, and run back to the street. Not one of Phoebe's friends, herself included, could ever do the deed. They were too frightened. The boys, being braver, would stand at a distance and throw rocks at the small windows that were covered in thick iron bars.

Tucked deep on Vestal Street, the grim-looking gaol had become the stuff of school yard legends: haunted by ghosts of criminals and lunatics, filled with hardened sailors from foreign lands. It had the look of a Nantucket saltbox, two stories tall, covered in weathered gray shingles, bookended by two small chimneys. Phoebe had stopped for a moment at the end of the long path that led to the gaol and took a deep breath, shaking off those silly schoolgirl jitters that still lingered. Inside this awful place, she reminded herself, sat her dear father. And loyal Matthew. She had to get them out of here.

But as she followed the constable into the gaol, she wavered. Wobbled. The dank smells of forgotten men surrounded her, and she could feel her spirits dampen, but then her eyes grew accustomed to the dimness . . . and there was her father! Hale and hearty despite his bleak circumstances. Next to him, seated on the floor with his back against the wooden bunk, was Matthew, chin to his chest, refusing to look at her.

Barnabas rose to his feet, clasping his hands over hers. "Daughter, thee is returned to me! Like Lazarus." His voice shook precariously.

"I'm going to get thee out of here, Father. Give me a little time. I am working on a plan."

Her father waved that away. "Concern thyself not with me, daughter. I am not at all dissatisfied with my accommodations. I've been able to continue my experiments with candle making right here, with Zacchaeus's help."

Zacchaeus snorted. "There's nothing to blow up in a stone gaol."

"I have a few difficulties still to work out." Barnabas turned toward Matthew. "Mayhap thee would be willing to help me."

Matthew looked up coldly. "Why not? I find myself with a surfeit of spare time . . . at least for now." He rubbed his hand along his throat.

"See?" Barnabas chuckled. He squeezed her hands. "He told me about thy plight. Daughter, how is thy health?"

She took a deep breath. "Better, now that I am on dry land. To stay."

"I, myself, was afflicted with a similar malady when I was but a greenie. The jouncing sea never did my stomach any kindness."

Phoebe stilled. "Thee was afflicted with mal de mer? How severely? Such that it would not end?"

"Aye," Barnabas said, chagrined. "'Twas my first and last voyage. I was bedeviled by seasickness. Matthew's father talked me into joining a fisherman's fleet. I spent the entire voyage heaving over the side of the ship." He lifted his shoulders in a half shrug. "I have kept my feet on solid ground e'er since."

"Father, why did thee not tell me?"

"Truth be told, I forgot. Like a mother forgets the pain of childbirth."

"Thee could have saved me a great deal of anguish."

His voice was quiet. "Would thee have listened to me? Thee seemed determined to forge thy own path."

Soberly, she nodded. That was the truth. She would have been convinced her experience on sea would be different. That she was different from her father. But it wasn't, and she wasn't.

Listening. The very thing emphasized by the Friends. Listen for God's voice. Listen for the Spirit to inform, to guide. *Listen, listen, listen.*

Oh, she was a foolish, foolish girl.

But no longer! She was making changes. This time from the inside out, not the outside in.

Look at him. She felt a nudge, as real as a sharp elbow jabbing her ribs. *Look at him. See him.*

Phoebe studied Matthew warily. His elbows rested on his knees, his hands were clasped tightly together, his head hung low. Utterly defeated. She had never seen him so hurt, so angry, nor so desolate. Remorse spread through her and she felt as if her heart would break. "Matthew, do not lose heart."

"Don't lose heart?" Abruptly he swung to his feet with his fists balled. "Don't lose heart? I'll be hanging from Gallows Field soon, and you think I shouldn't lose heart?"

"This is not over."

"Isn't it? I saw it in your eyes, Phoebe, so don't deny it."

"Matthew, I am sorry. Please forgive me. I was in shock by what Zacchaeus told us, all that he told us—about the captain, and the *Fortuna*, and the accusations against thee. And then I remembered that thee had blood on thy hands."

"You should know by now what kind of man I am."

"I do," Phoebe whispered. "I've always known." For several

long seconds, they stared at each other. Then she swallowed and dropped her hands, stepped back, and spoke levelly. "Father, there are a few things I need to take care of. I'll return, as soon as I can, to get thee released."

Only when she left the gaol and walked down Milk Street did she relent to tears. They came fast and hard, pouring down her face. She was ashamed to admit it, but Matthew was right. He had been faithful to her despite all she'd done to him . . . and when he needed her to believe in him, she didn't. Because, for just one brief moment, she did think he might have killed the captain.

Back at the Macys' house on Easy Street, Silo had arrived with Phoebe's and Matthew's sea chests and sat at the kitchen table, carving a piece of scrimshaw. Jeremiah sat beside him, watching his every move, fascinated by him. Phoebe smiled at the sight of the two boys, different in every way yet so similar.

Libby turned from stirring a bubbling stew over the hearth. "How is Matthew?"

Phoebe's smile faded. "He's . . ." She glanced at Jeremiah.

"Don't worry. He's already heard it all. This island is too small for secrets."

Tell *that* to Captain Foulger, Phoebe thought, then grimaced as she remembered that the captain was no longer. She wished many things for him, but not to be dead.

Jeremiah nodded. "I know of a way into the gaol. I go in and out all the time, to visit Matthew. Sometimes other fellows too. The gaol is where I've learned my best insults and swear words."

"Jeremiah Macy!"

His mother sent him a black look, but he paid her no mind and leaned toward Silo. "I'll show thee how to get in, if thee wants."

"I had promised Silo a good meal as a reward for lugging the sea chests here."

"Ah! That's what he's waiting on. I'm sorry, lad. I'm all adrift, with the news of my boy back on land. And of Phoebe's return to the living." Libby cut some fresh-baked bread for Silo and lathered it with creamy butter, then heaping spoonfuls of jam. She ladled a bowl of stew and set it on the table. Silo watched her every move, licking his lips. She nodded to him, and he dug into the bread as if he'd not eaten in far too long.

Phoebe had opened her chest and dug through it, lifting up salt-caked clothes and setting them on the ground. She was thrifty by nature, but those clothes would be burned.

"Phoebe, what is thee looking for?"

"Money. I have none, but I thought of someone who could help. My great-grandmother."

"Great Mary?"

"Her journal. In it, she speaks of buried treasure." Phoebe looked up at Libby, catching the skepticism that flitted through her frank eyes. A face much like Matthew's, she just now realized. "'Tis true. Mary Coffin and Eleazer Foulger found a treasure chest that drifted ashore after a shipwreck. They decided to bury it for a time when it was needed. For someone who faced great opposition. Someone worthy. Like Matthew Macy." She glanced at Jeremiah, then at Silo. "This is one secret that must stay here, in this house. Is that a promise?"

Both boys' eyes were wide with interest, then they nodded. Phoebe unfolded the journal from the cloth she had wrapped it in, lit a candle, and sat by the window, reading through the pages for a clue as to where that live oak might be. This was one hundred years ago. What if it had been cut down for lumber? What if someone had found it?

But then . . . the captain wouldn't have been so determined to seek it out if it had been found. He would have known if someone had absconded with the treasure.

And then the answer dawned on Phoebe. She sat back on her heels. She thought she knew of this grand old oak tree! It was in the Founders' Burial Ground. Great Mary was brilliant. Who but her would think to bury treasure in plain sight?

If one woman like Mary Coffin could move a mountain, two—plus two curious boys—could turn tides. "I need thy help tonight. Something to help Matthew and my father. Libby, Silo, Jeremiah, would thee be willing?"

Silo looked at the loaf of bread left on the table. She took it and stuffed it into his sack. She added a crock of butter. Then he smiled.

That night, after the night watchman had made his first rounds, they stole out of the Macys' house and took turns pushing a cart filled with tools collected out of Matthew's cooperage. As quietly as possible, they hurried down Cliff Road to the Founders' Burial Ground.

Mary Coffin

10 September 1661

News of world events is slow to reach our little island, but James returned from Massachusetts Bay today with earth-shaking news. We are all stunned.

There has been a royal decree to free the Quakers. The English threw out Oliver Cromwell's son and created a new parliament. The new parliament invited King Charles' son to return to England from his exile and they crowned him King Charles the Second.

And there's more!

The Puritan church has lost its position and the official church is once again the Church of England.

Still more to come! King Charles II sent a letter ordering Governor Endicott of Massachusetts to stop jailing the Quakers and to send them to England for trial if there were any complaints against them. James told Father that Governor Endicott had the Quakers released from jail and did not bother shipping them off to England.

All evening, I have been wondering if Father had been more patient, would we have moved to this faraway place?

11 September 1661

A letter from Tristram Jr. came with James. He had not thought of it until late last evening, when we sat round the hearth and Father smoked his pipe. If only he had forgotten! Better still, dropped it in Nantucket Sound for the fish to nibble on.

So troubled am I that I could not sleep last night.

Tristram Jr. sent word that he wants me to join his family in Newbury and help with their newest baby. (A red-faced boy infant, James confided, who has an ear-piercing howl that never stops. James wondered if he might be possessed of a demon. I have oft wondered the same of Tristram Jr.)

You can imagine what I think about that.

Far more marriage prospects for me, Tristram Jr. reports, than a barren island. My mother's interest lifted with that thought. There is truth in that, as currently there are only two bachelors on Nantucket, and one of them is interested only in minke whales and Miss Mouse.

I wonder if it might be best for me to return to the mainland. I do not think I can remain here if Nathaniel and Elizabeth become betrothed. The island is too small to endure such heartbreak.

And then I worry that I might be more like Father than I want to believe . . . always looking for satisfaction in the next place.

I am all at sea.

20

29TH DAY OF THE ELEVENTH MONTH IN THE YEAR 1767

Clouds scudded in front of the nearly full moon, causing on-again, off-again lighting and eerie shadows on the pathway to the Founders' Burial Ground. The air smelled of coming rain, but thankfully not snow, and Phoebe prayed it would hold off. She led the small convoy straight to the live oak tree, the very one she assumed her great-grandmother had been buried under. Libby followed, with Silo and Jeremiah pushing the cart through the bumpy meadow to reach the tree. Phoebe walked around the tree once, then twice, before stepping back to peer at it. *Think, think, think.* Where would Mary Coffin have buried the treasure? *I've grown to know her well. Think the way she would think.*

North side. Mossy side. Easy-to-remember side. Phoebe laid a blanket on the ground to capture the sod and make it easy to replace. She marked off six strides—woman-sized, not man-sized. She remembered that Mary had taken those six strides, not Eleazer Foulger, to the edge of the branches. That was one hundred years ago, and the branches extended much farther now. "Here," she pointed to a spot on the ground. "We'll start here and dig."

"Here? Dig up a graveyard? *This* graveyard of all graveyards? Has thee gone barmy?" Libby's hands were on her substantial hips. "If we get caught, we could end up as gaolbirds right along with Barnabas and Matthew."

With that the two boys glanced nervously around.

"Hush, lower thy voice. We won't get caught. Not if we hurry." Phoebe looked through the cart and pulled out one shovel, then another, then a pick.

"What if we dig up a body?" Jeremiah asked and Libby shuddered.

"I don't think that will be the case." Phoebe jammed the shovel into the earth—blessedly soft due to recent rain—and turned to the three as they watched her, wide-eyed. "Thee is free to leave. But if thee trusts me, I need thy help."

Silo was the first to respond. He took the shovel out of Phoebe's hands and began to dig. Jeremiah grabbed the second shovel and dug. Libby hesitated, ever practical, and Phoebe could almost read her thoughts: weighing back and forth the likelihood of success for this crazy venture. It did sound crazy. But then she exhaled, and pulled a pick out of the cart. "So what are we looking for?"

"A box. A chest. I don't know if it would be made of wood or metal."

Libby dug the pick into the earth, as did Silo and Jeremiah, using all the tools they had brought. Phoebe kept pieces of sod separate from the dirt, so that she could cover up the hole when they were done. Here, she thought, as they dug and dumped, dug and dumped, was where sandy soil was beneficial. It was a laborious task, digging through tree roots and mud and peat, but then Silo's shovel hit something that made a *ting* sound. He looked up at Phoebe, then dropped into the hole and used his hands to scoop around the edges. Jeremiah leaned down into the hole and worked alongside him. Before long, enough was exposed to see it was made of metal. All four tugged and tugged, and the chest eased out of the ground. It was a brass chest, not much bigger than a hat box.

Silo used the backside of the shovel to break the rusted latch. They all looked to Phoebe to open it. She crouched down and took a deep breath before opening the lid. A dark cloud obscured the moonlight. She put her hand into the box and felt first a slip of paper, then below, the cold metal of round coins. Her heart pounded, she squeezed her eyes shut with a prayer: *Thank you.* Gently, she closed the lid. "This is it."

"Well, I'll be blowed," Libby said. "Phoebe Starbuck, I'm sorry I doubted thee."

"Now we need to fill the hole as best we can, cover it with sod"—Phoebe looked up at the sky—"pray for rain in the morrow, for no one to pass by until the sod grows back, and return to the house without anyone seeing us."

Rain started sprinkling on them as they hurried back to town, trying to get home before the night watchman made his rounds. She could hear his deep singsong voice in the quiet of the night: "Twelve o'clock," he cried out, "and all is well." She was glad for the rain, glad even as it peppered them, glad for the cold as well, as it would keep others away from the cemetery.

* * *

The morning brought rain again. As soon as the bank opened, Phoebe stood at the desk of Horace Russell and emptied a sack of silver on his desk. Polished silver. She and Libby had stayed up to the wee hours, polishing each coin until it shone. "This is to pay off the mortgage on Centre Street. 'Tis enough?"

He looked at the silver coins scattered on his desktop, picked one up, held it up to the light, examined it closely. "A Spanish piece of eight." He closed his palm, hefting its weight. "One ounce bit." He held it up to the light, ran his finger around the unmilled edge, bit down on the coin, then lifted his head. "Where in the world did thee find these coins?"

"Does it matter?"

He frowned at her. "Phoebe, are they stolen goods?"

"Nay!" She looked at him, astounded. "Nay! Not at all." Why, the very opposite. For she had found two notes tucked into the chest, one written by Great Mary, one by Eleazer Foulger. Each note stated how small amounts had been used— one to ransom a fugitive slave, one to provide seminary training at Harvard College for a grandson of Eleazer. Mary's note, written in her spidery handwriting, said that the money was meant to be used for the betterment of their families, and she hoped whoever found the treasure would keep that in mind. Stolen goods, indeed.

Horace peered at her. "But . . ."

"I asked thee a question, Horace Russell. I do not know the value of these coins, but I think thee does. Will the coins cover the mortgage and my father's indebtedness?"

Horace inhaled a deep breath. "Come back in a few hours. I will have them weighed and be able to give thee the full value of the coins. If they are indeed silver and not counterfeit—"

"They are not counterfeit! Thee knows that. When thee

bit down on it, thy teeth made a mark, is that not so? That is the mark of high purity."

"'Tis *a* mark, but not the only mark. I need to verify the value of these coins, Phoebe. For thy security as well as the bank's." He tipped his head. "But if they are as valuable as they appear, then aye, 'tis likely the Centre Street property's lien will be cleared. Thy father will be set free. And thee will have some coinage to spare, I suspect."

"In that case, Horace"—she gave him a determined smile—"I will be back before the noon bells toll."

Matthew lay on the too-short wooden bunk of the gaol, wasting away more of his life, wondering what would happen to him. If convicted of murder on Nantucket Island, it meant he would be sent to the gallows. There had only been nine hangings on the island, all Wampanoag Indians. Even the hangman was a Wampanoag. Matthew would be remembered as the first white man to be hung on the island. He rubbed his neck, already feeling the tightening of the noose.

The gaol door opened and a stream of late-day sunlight fell into the dark room. "Matthew?" It was the voice of Zacchaeus Coleman. "You got a visitor. Phoebe's here."

His heart started pounding and he flew from his bunk. "Just a minute!" He dragged his fingers through his hair, four swift strokes, as she crossed over the threshold.

For a full ten seconds they stared.

"Hello, Matthew." She greeted him with a sad smile in her eyes.

"Hello." Matthew's palms were sweating and his neck felt

hot as he drank in the sight of her. He turned to Zacchaeus. "Cousin, can you give us a moment of privacy?"

Hesitating, Zacchaeus looked at Phoebe for assurance and she gave him a nod. "I'll be right outside. Holler if thee needs me. I'll leave the door open."

She waited until Zacchaeus left the room. "I was able to get my father released."

Matthew scoffed. "Barnabas is hardly in here. Zacchaeus gives him day privileges. Lets him fiddle around with candle making right in his office. By night, we sit by this lovely fire"—he extended a hand in the direction of the cold chimney hearth—"and have scintillating discussions over how to refine spermaceti oil."

"Even still. His debt has been paid."

She didn't volunteer how she was able to pull that off and he didn't ask.

"Matthew, I'm going to find a way to prove thee innocent."

"Assuming that I am." Her eyes skittered aside at his sarcasm, but he couldn't help himself.

"Matthew . . ." She stopped, then started again. "Matthew, if thee would only look inside, seek the Light of God, thy circumstances would be far more bearable. Not just this present one . . . but past ones too."

"Such as?"

"Such as coming to grips with the calamity of the *Pearl*. Of thy father's death."

"I worry about you, Phoebe," he said quietly. "You are simply too naïve to survive very long in the real world. You think God sets the rules, but it's really people like the captain who pull all the strings."

"I don't believe that, Matthew. I hope, deep down, thee

doesn't either." She lifted her face. "I must away." She backed up a step, and he saw her chest begin to heave as if she were trying to stifle a sneeze.

As Zacchaeus locked the door behind her, for the first time in this old gaol, despite many, many, many nights spent in it, panic swamped Matthew.

Phoebe did not come to visit Matthew in the gaol again, but his mother did, the very next morning, with a look in her eyes he hadn't seen since he was eleven years old and had tarred the tail of the neighbor's cat. Zacchaeus didn't even need to be persuaded to leave them alone; he seemed eager to flee the ill temper of Libby Macy.

Matthew, on the other hand, was delighted to see her. "Mother! Did you bring me any victuals? You know how bad the cooking is here."

"Nay. Nor did I bring thee anything for the chip on thy shoulder." She glared at him. "What did thee say to Phoebe?"

"What?" His eyes widened in surprise. "When?"

"She came back from the gaol weeping yesterday."

Crying? Over him? "If you came here to tell me that, you can—"

"That's precisely why I came here. And don't speak to me in that tone of voice!"

She paced a few feet, pivoted, and paced back to the door. "If there was ever a time when thee needs to stand by her, this is it."

"Me stand by her?" He stiffened and splayed two hands on his chest. "Ask her about standing by me!"

"Oh, I suppose thee thinks thee has a right to sulk because

273

she arrived in Nantucket to a plethora of disturbing news and needed a moment to absorb the shock."

Absorb? Absorb! "Phoebe thought I did it! She actually thought I killed Captain Foulger!"

"Oh, she did, did she? Then why is she sailing to Boston this very minute to find a lawyer to save thy hide?"

"Sailing to Boston?" It came out as a squeak.

"She refuses anyone's financial help, even mine."

Matthew found himself with nothing to say.

"Son," she said, softer now, "thee is so like thy father. Hiding behind thy cynicism, just like thy father did. Stubborn. Proud. Refusing to ask anyone for help. So sure of thyself. But what happens when thee gets to the end of thyself? Now is a good time to look up, outside thyself. To ask God to open thy eyes and heart to trust the outcome of thy difficulties."

"To apologize to the elders and get a bellyful of scoldings and rebukes, you mean."

She walked around the awful gaol, not saying a word, which worried Matthew more than if she lashed out at him.

Finally, she turned to him and crossed her arms over her ample midsection. "Matthew, did thee ever listen to the story of the prodigal son?"

"Aye, I remember," he said flatly.

"When the prodigal came to his senses and returned home, his father did not greet him with scoldings and rebukes, but with open arms. 'The lost is now found,' he said. Give the Friends a chance to do the same."

She made her way to the door. "'Tis time to make thy peace with God." Her gaze swept the gaol. "Thee certainly has plenty of time for it." His mother sailed out the way she sailed in, loud and clear, leaving him feeling as if he'd just taken a Nantucket sleigh ride.

Zacchaeus poked his head in the door. "Your mother can sure take a man to the woodpile."

"That's the truth," Matthew replied, running a hand through his hair. "Can she ever."

He paced the dark room, cracking his knuckles. Phoebe . . . sailing to Boston? *For him!* Imagine that! After seeing firsthand how sick she was at sea—and she was willing to face it again, head-on. For his sake.

But then, Phoebe faced all of life head-on.

It struck him what his mother had set out to do—in her own unique, no-nonsense way, she'd made him realize that Phoebe must, deep down, still believe in him. Mayhap, still love him.

Later that night, he lay on the bunk facing the ceiling. He couldn't sleep.

Look up, his mother had said. Look inside, Phoebe had said.

But to accept God, he would have to accept his own abject humility. He heard a dog bark outside the door, then smelled a skunk. It occurred to him that his present circumstances could not be any more humble. No man could sink any lower than lying in a grim, stinking gaol, facing a murder charge.

God . . . I can't see how this will end. I just know that I am utterly, thoroughly helpless. I want to believe you are there, that you're here. That you see this shipwreck of my life. I want to believe. He squeezed his eyes shut. *I want to believe, but Lord, help my unbelief.*

Slowly, he opened his eyes. He experienced a curious reaction, a minute exhilaration. His torpor disappeared, replaced by a sense of . . . hope.

Mary Coffin

15 September 1661

*Just when I thought that I might, indeed, consider Tris-
tram Jr.'s invitation to come live with him, James gave me an
idea. He has complained steadily about running back and
forth to the cape for supplies . . . and then it dawned on me! I
might have found just the thing to solve my restlessness without having to live with Tristram Jr. and his screaming baby.*

Two birds, one stone.

*I had to wait for the right moment to spring this idea on
Father (remember, it always works out best if an idea seems
like it is his in the first place). So when Thomas Macy came to
the house today to see if there were any nails to be had on this
island and offered to trade for them, I seized my opportunity.*

"Father," I said, "you may be the cleverest man on Nantucket."

"How's that?" He looked at me, interest piqued.

*"Having James buy those extra nails on his last trip to
the Cape. Everybody on this island needs nails, with so many
houses to build. Nearly everyone on Cliff Road has stopped
in this week to barter for them." I paused for a long moment,
letting that sink in. "There's talk of our house as if it's Nantucket's trading post."*

Father stroked his beard. "A trading post."

*"Now there's an interesting notion!" I feigned innocence.
"And it makes sense to stock up on the very items our neighbors need, whenever you or James go to the mainland."*

"What sort of items?"

"We could stock some furniture, clothing, building supplies, tools, wood. Then there are items needed for fishing."

"But we wish to be self-sufficient on this island."

"Certainly, yet that will take time. In the meantime, we can supply our neighbors with items they need now."

"But what of cash? We have little need for it."

"Barter," I told him. "Just yesterday, two Indians wanted a basket of wool. I asked if they would consider plowing the garden for us and they were in agreement."

Father lit up at that news. The garden was long overdue for a plowing, and Mother was anxious to get the vegetables planted. He was never keen on farming, Father wasn't.

He finished the last bit of tea and went to the hearth to fill his pipe with tobacco. If he lit the pipe, I knew the matter was settled. If he did not, he was still thinking, and he would chew on the end of his pipe until he had made a decision.

He picked up a stick from the bundle of kindling Stephen had brought up from the beach, poked one end into the fire until it lit, then held it to his pipe and took in a deep draught.

And in that moment, I became keeper of a store. The first store on Nantucket Island.

21

Without Barnabas, the gaol felt darker and colder. The old man's enthusiasm for candle making was a distraction for Matthew, and they had discussed methods and trials of the refining process long into the night. Barnabas might just be on to something, Matthew thought, yet it would require help from others to see it through. He sat cross-legged in front of the fireplace, pondering candle making, and the sorry reality that he would not be here to find out if a business venture ever turned out right for Barnabas. He hoped so, for he was a good man, Barnabas. Matthew stirred the cold peat ashes with his finger. He'd get no warmth from an empty fireplace, but still its presence brought comfort. He wished for a candle to dispel the gloom in this room, as he was overflowing with pity for himself.

Zacchaeus unlocked the gaol door. "Your attorney's here."

"My what?" Matthew craned his neck around.

Standing at the gaol door threshold was a skinny man dressed in an ill-fitting brown coat and black trousers. The man gazed around the dark room in wonderment, as if he'd never seen such a primitive gaol before, or any gaol, for that matter. Then his eyes adjusted and his gaze settled on Matthew. "Ah! Now I see thee." He ambled into the room.

Who was this man? Not much more than a boy. He didn't even have side whiskers yet. Something about him seemed vaguely familiar to Matthew.

"I'm Ezra Barnard, hailing from Cambridge. Phoebe Starbuck Foulger came to see me, asked me to be thy advocate."

"Matthew Macy." Rising, accepting the handshake, Matthew thought, *She actually did it. Phoebe sailed to Boston. Hired an attorney for me!*

But what kind of lawyer? He looked nearly as youthful and fresh-faced as Jeremiah. Matthew almost expected his voice to crack as he spoke. "Do I know you?"

"In fact, we are related. Distantly. Third or fourth cousins. Thy mother Libby is my mother's second cousin. Something like that, I believe."

"And you're an attorney? Of the law? Criminal law?"

"Indeed. From Harvard College. Recently graduated."

Matthew wondered if he might be better off defending himself.

Ezra Barnard studied Matthew for a full minute before he leaned close to him to ask, "Matthew Macy, did thee kill Captain Phineas Foulger in cold blood?"

Matthew fixed his eyes on this boy-lawyer and replied with a firm "Nay."

Ezra leaned back. "Has thee any idea who might have done the dastardly deed?"

"Nay, I do not."

Again, a lengthy silence. "Thee must have some suspicions."

"Nay. None. Truly."

"Was the captain admired by his crew?"

"Admired? I would not say admired. He was feared."

"Then is it not possible that the crew mutinied?"

Matthew mulled the thought over, then dismissed it. "The crew was made up of boys, mostly." *Hardly younger than yourself*, he thought but did not say aloud. "A few foreigners, but they had no quarrel with the captain, nor the first mate."

"What about the first mate? How did he get along with the captain?"

"Hiram Hoyt is his name. He revered him. Carried out his orders without question."

"And the second mate? The cook?"

"Old men, both. You see, this crew all wanted something from the captain—wages for retirement or whaling experience. They would not have reason to do the captain in—he was each man's bounty, and he knew it."

"Thee did not admire him, I take it?"

Matthew stiffened his back. "I had no respect for the man. For many reasons."

Another lengthy silence that gave Matthew the impression that Ezra was puzzled. Matthew half expected him to decline the case, but Ezra surprised him again. He slapped his hands on his knobby knees and said, "Well, I don't want thee to get thy hopes up, but I do believe in thy innocence."

"Have you had many criminal cases?"

"Nay, actually thee is my first." His lawyer beamed, as if that was a grand thing.

Matthew squeezed his eyes shut. Oh, boy. Again he felt the

280

rawness of the noose around his neck . . . but then he stopped that line of thinking. Skepticism had done him no good.

In spite of Ezra Barnard's youthful appearance and complete inexperience in trials of accused murderers, he had confidence in his defendant. His first defendant.

Plus, Matthew had no other options.

It took a few days for Horace Russell to reverse the defaulted loan for the Centre Street house. When Phoebe was allowed to move back in, she took Silo with her, and only Silo. Jeremiah and Libby had work of their own to do, her father said he was on the verge of a breakthrough and did she mind terribly if he continued his work at Zacchaeus's office? She minded not a bit.

The house was in terrible condition, worse even than she had expected for it being boarded-up. It had only been closed for months, yet there were dead mice in the corners, dead flies and bees on the windowsills, mold growing on the ceiling and windows. The two worked side by side, sweeping and scrubbing each room. At one point, she went outside for fresh air, and when she returned, she found Silo in the back room, scrubbing the rust off those iron pots her father had bought to sell. After Silo's scrubbing, they looked good as new. She pulled out a wooden box and opened it. Rusty iron horseshoes. She opened a sack. Rusty iron nails. With rumblings of skirmishes brewing between England and the colonies, anything made of iron would be highly valued.

She looked at all the . . . flotsam and jetsam . . . her father had collected. Everything in it could be cleaned up and sold, if marketed right.

A thought tapped Phoebe. Tapped and grabbed. Mary Coffin had started a store.

Hands on her hips, she gazed around the small room, mentally measuring its width and length. There was space enough for a table. She envisioned shelves against the walls. She envisioned the shelves stocked with neat piles of wares—pins, needles, buttons, coffee, tea, herbs, and spices. Mayhap fabrics and threads. Assorted dry goods. She could see it, could imagine it! The Centre Street Shoppe.

Why not? There were other women who kept shops. Catherine Hussey sold baked goods from her home. Leah Mitchell had a haberdashery. There were all kinds of ship chandleries, but no shops for a woman's everyday necessities. Like iron pots! How had it never occurred to her before?

"Silo! I have an idea." She gave him a broad smile. "I am going to support myself—and my father—by becoming a shopkeeper. The first store on Centre Street, run by a woman!"

He crinkled his face in puzzlement.

"Thee doesn't approve the idea?"

He pointed to the chest they'd brought over from Libby Macy's, hidden under blankets and buckets and brooms.

"Ah, I see what thee is thinking. Why don't I just use the Spanish silver? Is that what is running through that fine mind?"

He grinned and dipped his head in a single nod.

She wondered if anyone had ever told him he had a fine mind. For he truly did. "The silver was buried to help others in need. Oh, I know what thee is thinking. We are in dire need!" She looked around the dusty, dirty house. A window had been broken, and the loose shutter had finally fallen to the ground. One could argue that repairing the home could be considered for the betterment of the family, but it didn't feel right. "I did use the silver to lift the debt off the house and free my father from debtor's gaol. Using it to defend Matthew is a valid use for it. But if Mary Coffin and Eleazer Foulger didn't use it to provide needs of daily life, and they were the ones who found the chest on the beach, then I am going to follow their example." She sighed, contentedly, hands on her hips. "And Silo, I do not want to be a seamstress! I've always hated to sew. It's too lonely. But . . . I think I *do* want to be a shopkeeper. Nantucket needs it. And I think I need it too."

One week later, with help from Libby Macy, Jeremiah, and Silo, and much advice from Barnabas, Phoebe opened up the Centre Street Shoppe. Customers would need to come to the front door and through the keeping room, so she set the table with mugs of cold lemonade (and she paid a dear sum for lemons from a ship on the docks that had just sailed in from the Caribbean—worth the price, she felt). Libby made her famous shortbread cookies, shaped like stars.

Her father helped himself to lemonade and cookies. "Daughter, thee has always had a head for business. I sense a great endeavor has begun today. Thee might be naturally cut out as an entrepreneur."

Oh, she hoped not. But to Barnabas she smiled, kissed the top of his head, and flittered nervously around the back room, dusting and adjusting the stock. She started to feel greatly satisfied. It was a new feeling for Phoebe.

By midafternoon, after not a single customer had crossed the threshold, she started to feel greatly distressed. (Not a new feeling, not at all.) When Libby arrived to check on how things were going, Phoebe nearly cried. "What if no one comes?"

"Oh, Phoebe, thee is just frightened!" Libby's motherly arms surrounded her, dragging her close.

Jeremiah and Silo interrupted, appearing behind her with shortbread cookies in their hands. "I heard Sarah Foulger has warned others not to frequent the store."

"She's a vile woman," her father said. Everyone had crowded into the lean-to. Everyone but customers.

"I expected there might be some of that," Phoebe said, fully aware of the icy reception she'd been given by Sarah's relatives and friends. "But Nantucketers are practical people. They appreciate a good deal."

"But do they know of it?"

Phoebe looked at Libby blankly. Then she grabbed her bonnet and cloak and told everyone to stay put and watch the shop, that she would return within the hour, and she hurried down the street to find the drummer and pay him to drum through the streets: "Fine quality kitchen wares for bargain prices at the Starbuck house on 35 Centre Street!" The drummer cried out the chant, over and over, between rolls on his drum, quite literally drumming up trade.

Lo and behold. It worked!

At three o'clock, in came Leah Mitchell and her sister Lydia. They bought a cast-iron pot—the first sale. Phoebe gave the coins to Silo, for it was his fine polishing that made the rusted pot salable. Not ten minutes later, Obed, an old fisherman who spent most days sitting on a bench on Main Street, came in and had a cookie and lemonade with Barnabas. Then he shocked Phoebe by asking to buy all her extra lemons.

"Name thy price," he said. "I need them for m' grumbling gut."

She named a ridiculous amount to Obed and he didn't even blanch. He reached into his pocket, pulled out the coinage, and dropped them on the table, then scooped up the lemons.

Phoebe had learned her first lesson in shopkeeping: advertise, advertise, advertise.

Mary Coffin

6 October 1661

My store is under way. In fact, I am overwhelmed. I have created a greedy monster.

Keeping a few things in stock for neighbors who needed them has now created a growing expectation on their part that I can be relied on to provide them with anything and everything they might need. I am quite perplexed by the variety of things, many of which I do not have but must arrange to procure.

I expected these items to be in demand: goose grease, corn seed, cloth, needles, thread, buttons, herbs and spices, nails, axes, hammers, chisels, flints, powder, shot, fishhooks, and sinkers.

I did not expect these whispered requests: rum, grog, ladies' unmentionables. Some men's unmentionables, too. I blushed after asking what those particular items were and the men laughed and laughed. I did not know such items existed.

Through trial and error (mostly errors), I have found the balance of bartering. Thomas Macy wanted gunpowder and had too many goose feathers. I traded gun powder for feathers (an odd pairing!) and then traded the goose feathers to old Rachel Swain for her lumbago, and in return, she gave me four red hens. The hens were wanted by an Indian, who was willing to trade them in exchange for labour: three plowed acres.

It all worked out quite nicely, but that is not always the case. Last week, I ended up with too much fresh fish and fowl (the Indians fish and bird hunt), milk and butter, on a too-warm day in which no one seemed to require anything perishable, and the produce soured. The house smelled to high heaven and Mother was furious.

12 October 1661

The store has been removed from the house. Mother has tired of having men and Indians in the kitchen, as they tarry too long. The store is now in a small shed formerly used for the horse and cow.

6 November 1661

I have been too busy to write of late.

There is so much activity in the store that I am losing track of who wants what and who owes me what. I traded away the last package of tobacco and Father was quite miffed. He does enjoy his pipe at the end of a long day. For the last two nights, he has sat by the fire with a frown on his face, feeling quite pitiful.

I wonder if an account book might help me keep track of the things I provide for different settlers and Indians, and of their time and manner of repayment.

15 November 1661

Each time I resolve to turn my thoughts aside from Nathaniel Starbuck, to face the truth that he feels nothing for me, he does something to turn my resolution upside down.

He had been on the mainland last week, and took with him a load of tanned sheepskins to trade. He went to a printer's shop and purchased excess paper. Then he created a book *for me. It is eight-and-one-half inches by twelve-and-one-half inches, with a sheepskin cover and leather clasps. An accounting book. For me to use. For keeping the store.*

Nathaniel made this for me. Nathaniel? I did not think he gave me any thought. I am confounded.

22

13TH DAY OF THE TWELFTH MONTH IN THE YEAR 1767

Early one morning, Jeremiah and Silo came to the gaol with a pot of rabbit stew made by Matthew's mother. Jeremiah walked around the room, showing it off to Silo as if he were lord and master. "Can I bring my school friends over?"

"Nay, not a good idea," Matthew said. "I think you are taller, Jeremiah."

Jeremiah squared his shoulders at that compliment, and rubbed his chin hopefully.

"Still whiskerless, little brother," Matthew said, smiling. He appraised Silo, who seemed more of a boy around Jeremiah, less of a sad little man. 'Twas his brother's happy nature, he thought. *He has the same influence on me.* "So you two have become friends?"

"He's teaching me to carve scrimshaw." Jeremiah showed him the little piece he'd been carving.

"What is it?"

"Can't thee tell? It's a whale." He frowned. "Mama thought it was a dog." He stuffed it back in his pocket. "Thee should

289

see some of his." He gave Silo a nudge with his elbow. "Go on. Show him."

"I remember seeing some of your work on a piece on the *Fortuna*." Matthew noticed a large scrimshaw tooth sticking out of Silo's trouser pocket. "Can I see what you've made?"

Silo took the scrimshaw tooth out of his pocket and handed it to him. Matthew looked at it closely, marveling at the artistry and intricacy of his carvings. Then his eyes caught something small, and he went to the window to look at it more closely. "Silo, is this what you saw? On the *Fortuna*'s last voyage, is this the sight you saw?"

The silent boy nodded.

"Have you more of these?"

He nodded.

"Zacchaeus!" Matthew bellowed. "Zacchaeus, get in here!" He clattered his tin cup against the bars of the window.

"Hold your horses," came a voice from the distance.

"Hurry up, Zacchaeus!"

"I'm comin', I'm comin'." The constable opened the door. "What is it?"

"Go get Ezra Barnard. Tell him I need to see him. Now!"

"Who? Oh, that lawyer-laddie. I don't know where he is."

"Phoebe will know. If she doesn't, then my mother will know." When Zacchaeus hesitated, Matthew turned to Jeremiah and Silo, both wide-eyed, watching the exchange. "Boys, remember this moment. Nantucket's constable is unwilling to help justice prevail."

Zacchaeus cursed. "I'll get word to Ezra Barnard." Then the door slammed.

290

At the end of the day, just as Phoebe was turning the closed sign on the door, Ezra Barnard arrived with a request she had not expected. "Matthew seems to think thee might know something more about the captain that could help his case. Something to prove that the captain had enemies?"

"Enemies? But I don't know of enemies."

"Secrets, then?"

She bit her nail.

"Matthew would not reveal more. He said it was up to thee."

She came *this close* to telling Ezra she had discovered the captain had another wife—*this close*—and he must have sensed she was withholding something vital. He waited a long while, watching her, but the words would not come. They were clogged with shame. If others found out, especially if it were just based on her word, without any proof, she would be the laughingstock of Nantucket. Her store—barely begun—would be finished, she would have to move far, far away to start a new life.

"Phoebe, remember that Matthew's life is at stake." Ezra went to the door. "I must prove that others had a motive to do the captain in. Right now, evidence is pointing right at Matthew Macy. I need something. Anything. To prove the captain had other enemies than Matthew."

After he left, Phoebe paced the keeping room, biting her nails. There *was* proof. Lindeza's letter. She had to get onto the ship and into the captain's cabin. She knew Hiram Hoyt remained on the ship while it was being repaired as acting guardian of the ship for investors. He was hoping, she believed, to be offered the chance to captain it. He would never allow her access to the ship, much less the captain's cabin. But she had to retrieve that letter from Lindeza that was hidden in the shipbox. How, how, how? If she couldn't get onto the ship, who could?

Of course. *Of course.*

"Silo. Would thee help me with another errand?" She handed him the small brass key to the shipbox, retrieved from the bottom of her drawstring purse. "This one, I hope and pray, will be the one that will hold the key to set Matthew Macy free."

The jury for Matthew's trial had been selected, all men of Nantucket, varied ages and occupations. All men whose hearts belonged to the sea. The lawyer for the island of Nantucket was Josiah Swain, a humorless man whose sister had married Captain Phineas Foulger's second cousin. The entire town crowded into the courtroom, as a criminal trial on Nantucket was exceedingly rare and provided a unique entertainment.

Early this morning, Zacchaeus had brought in a bathing tub and filled it with hot water for Matthew to bathe. He even brought a small mirror and razor to give Matthew a shave. Matthew dressed carefully, taking great care to tighten the knot in his tie, adjust his cuffs, unbutton and rebutton his jacket. He paced, cracked his knuckles, checked his reflection in the mirror once more. Again he ran his knuckles over his jaw, worried that Zacchaeus's shaky hand didn't give him enough of a clean shave—not for a jury, but for Phoebe. And then the door opened and Zacchaeus appeared again.

"'Tis time, my friend." The constable's eyes seemed unusually watery and his deep voice was preciously shaky.

Matthew stuck out his hand to offer his cousin a handshake. "Whatever happens today," he said, his heart in his throat, "know that I will always be grateful for how kind you've been to me."

He lifted his eyes as he entered the courtroom and his collar felt suddenly tight. Phoebe sat in the first row, sandwiched between his mother and Barnabas. Gratitude swamped him but again. When Phoebe's eyes met his, he felt his heart leap.

"Have a chair," Ezra Barnard told him, holding out the chair next to him.

Matthew hardly recognized his youthful attorney for his ill-fitting, powdered white wig. Powder was sprinkled on his shoulders. He leaned close to Ezra and whispered, "So how does the case look?"

"Depends on the witnesses. Criminal cases always do."

"So it's entirely dependent on the prosecution's witnesses?"

"The defense has witnesses too. We go last."

"How did you find witnesses? Who would talk?"

"Henry Coffin, Silo Foulger."

Matthew's heart dropped into his shoes. An old man with an axe to grind, a mute cabin boy. "That's it? That's your entire list of witnesses?"

"There's more. One more, anyway. Phoebe Starbuck."

Nay. "I don't want Phoebe to have to testify."

"She seems competent. I did not detect any muddled thinking."

Matthew shifted in his chair slightly so that he could see Phoebe. "She's more than competent."

"Then, is she an atheist? The court won't permit testimony from an atheist."

"She's devout. I just . . . don't want her put under that kind of scrutiny. She's been through enough."

Ezra's thin eyebrows lifted. "Ah, I see. So the rumors are true."

"What do you see?"

"Thee is in love with her."

Matthew sighed. This wasn't going at all well. "Ezra, I want you to put me on the stand."

"Nay. Absolutely not. Thee will end up convicting thyself."

Matthew was appalled. "May I remind you that you are my attorney?"

"True. And may I remind thee that I was hired by Phoebe Starbuck and thy own mother, not by thee? To save thy sorry hide, I believe Aunt Libby said."

"All rise," the bailiff called dryly.

The judge entered, garbed in black robes, white wig neatly tucked in place. His eyes scanned the courtroom, paused on Matthew and moved on. Matthew had one thought: by whatever miracle, thank God, the judge was not a Foulger.

"All be seated," the judge ordered.

And the trial of Matthew Macy began.

Mary Coffin

22 November 1661

The weather has turned bitter cold. Winter has come early.

James returned from the Cape with tobacco for Father and men's unmentionables for those unmentionable men.

All is well.

25 November 1661

Eleazer arrived at the house today with a pair of peacocks. He was given them by an Indian, traded for a pair of shoes. The peacocks screech like howling babies, but he said it's worth the racket for the quill feathers. He thought a feather might fetch a shilling or two in the store. "After all," he said, "how many fine establishments on Nantucket Island boast that they keep peacock feather quills in stock?"

None, I said, nor do I want those screechy-sounding birds anywhere near Capaum Harbour, for they would scare away my customers.

"Hardly," he said. "I believe they would flock to the store, curious about which cruel person was pinching a baby to cry in such a horrible manner."

I said he was crazy. He laughed and said he was. Crazy in love.

I stilled. No one has ever told me he loved me before.

I am more confused than ever.

27 November 1661

A mere look from Nathaniel touches something deep inside me. When he is close, my heart pounds and I can scarcely draw breath. Eleazer is kind and sweet and treats me like I'm a precious pearl . . . and yet I feel nothing at all in return.

30 November 1661

Eleazer Foulger asked me to marry him. I am thinking on it.

23

Judge Samuel Coffin, despite his discomfiting name, was round and roly-poly, with a face half framed by several chins. Matthew had stood before him many times, and the man's eyebrows rose in recognition, but he said naught. As the judge settled himself into his chair on the dais, he nodded to the two attorneys. Opening statements were given by both men, Josiah Swain went first for the island of Nantucket, then Ezra Barnard presented the defense. Listening to the two men, Matthew sat tensely. He couldn't help but think his chance for acquittal was hopeless. In his sixties, Josiah Swain had an abundance of courtroom experience, flourished by a deeply authoritative voice and an intense gaze that swept back and forth over each jury member. Novice Ezra Barnard stammered, lost his train of thought, and apologized to the jury, before stumbling over a chair leg as he returned to the defense table.

"The prosecution calls Constable Zacchaeus Coleman."

From the very ill-at-ease constable, the jury heard of

297

Matthew's excessive time in gaol since he returned from the disastrous *Pearl* voyage, his drinking and brawling, and the confession to Zacchaeus Coleman on the dock as he arrived with Phoebe Starbuck Foulger last month, that he had, indeed, interacted with Captain Phineas Foulger in his cabin before the *Fortuna* set sail from Abacos.

When Ezra Barnard rose to his feet for a cross-examination of the constable, his coat sleeve swept papers on the floor. Snickers and chuckles broke out in the courtroom and the judge banged his gavel to restore order. Ezra spent so much time pondering each question before he delivered it that the jury exchanged curious glances with each other. Matthew shifted nervously in his seat. Ezra's cross-examination of the constable revealed that Matthew had served his sentence compliantly, been a cooperative prisoner and released by recommendation of Captain Phineas Foulger, who trusted him implicitly and implored him to sign on the *Fortuna*, offering him a substantial lay. Before Zacchaeus stepped down, he looked at Matthew, eyes brimming with tears. "He didn't do it. I know he's innocent."

"Objection!" shouted Josiah Swain. "The constable is a distant relation to the defendant."

"Overruled." Judge Coffin rapped his gavel once, then twice. "So is everyone on this island."

From the ever bad-tempered cook, Matthew learned that the captain's body was discovered sometime between six and seven o'clock, when Cook brought in his evening meal because he couldn't find Silo to deliver it. "That boy is unreliable," Cook volunteered. "I don't know why the captain kept him on." He would have continued on his rant, but the judge reminded him that Silo was not on trial.

First mate Hiram Hoyt was called next. With stooped shoulders and a crackly voice, he described the cause of death of the captain—a mortal blow to the head—and from the back of the courtroom, Sarah Foulger started to weep. Loudly. Matthew saw the look on each juror's face, heartstrings tugged by Sarah's sorrow. This wasn't going well.

From Hiram came critical evidence. He had seen Matthew arrive sometime before six that evening, had seen him go into the captain's cabin and shut the door. And then came condemning facts, ones Matthew could not deny, for they were true. "I heard them arguing, the captain and the cooper," Hiram Hoyt said. "Everyone on the upper deck heard, thee can ask them all."

Josiah stood, facing the jury with his hands clasped behind his back. "Did thee hear what the argument was about?"

"Something about how the captain had treated his wife, Phoebe." Hiram Hoyt leaned forward and said, apologetically but right to the jury's ears, "The cooper and the captain's wife, they spent quite a bit of time together on the ship. *Quite* a bit."

It was all testimony that Matthew had expected, yet he felt shaken at how incriminating it sounded when stated by witnesses under affirmation—a solemn declaration to tell the truth. Legally binding, accommodated for the Quakers' refusal to swear oaths.

He could feel the noose tighten.

Then the tide changed. Ezra Barnard cross-examined Hiram Hoyt and detoured from the present case. "The *Fortuna*'s voyage, just prior to this broken voyage, the ship came in with an astounding amount of whale oil. A full belly of barrels."

"Aye. A greasy voyage."

"Indeed. What I don't quite understand is how the *Fortuna* was able to strike such good fortune in scarcely—what was it—two years' time?"

The first mate lifted his shoulders in a shrug. "I suppose that's why she's called *Fortuna*. Good fortune." His shoulders lifted again in a sigh. "Until now."

"And how many barrels of sperm oil?"

Hiram hesitated. "I don't recall."

"How many sperm whales did the *Fortuna* capture?"

Again Hiram hesitated. He scratched his skin and dropped his gaze to his hands on his lap.

"First mates usually know that kind of information, do they not?"

"Aye, but the last few months . . . there's been such tumult . . . the captain's murder, then the storm . . . " He sighed a grievous sigh. "I could get the information from the counting-house."

"That will be all for now, Mr. Hoyt." He turned to the bailiff. "The defense calls Silence Foulger, cabin boy for Captain Foulger. Goes by the name of Silo."

Josiah Swain jumped to his feet. "Objection! He's a half-breed."

Ezra looked calmly at the judge. "The captain gave him his name. In the British colonies, to have a surname means an individual is a full citizen of the Crown."

"Objection overruled."

"But he's deaf and dumb!" The prosecutor was indignant.

Ezra kept his attention on the judge. "Silo might be unable to speak, but he is not deaf, nor is his intelligence diminished in any way. He speaks in a different way than thee and me, but he does have a voice."

Judge Coffin looked a little uncertain but allowed Ezra Barnard to carry on.

The bailiff repeated the affirmation for Silo, who nodded when asked a question. "Silo," Ezra said, "how were you treated on the ship?"

The boy's eyes swerved nervously around the courtroom, then his dark eyes landed on Phoebe, and she gave him an encouraging smile. Slowly, he unbuttoned his thin shirt, peeled it off his shoulders, and turned around. His skinny back was ribboned with red scars.

"The whippings this boy received were from a tool like this one. It's called a cat-o'-nine-tails. There are nine knotted lines in it." Ezra Barnard set the whip in front of the jurors and turned to Silo. "Did this happen often, Silo?"

Silo nodded.

"Silo, why did the captain order those punishments for you?"

Cook interrupted from the back of the courtroom. "I told y'! He's lazy and unreliable. Stole food from m' galley!"

The judge rapped on his gavel and told Cook to be quiet. "Is this at all relevant, Mr. Barnard?"

Ezra seemed to grow in stature before Matthew's eyes. "Aye, 'tis very relevant, sir. I do not believe Silo was punished regularly for small infractions such as stealing a loaf of bread. I believe he had information. These punishments were reminders to keep silent." He turned to Silo with a smile. "There are other ways to tell one's story beside talking, are there not? Would thee show us thy voice, Silo?"

Silo reached into his leather bag and brought out a large scrimshaw whale tooth, carved with etchings.

Ezra Barnard held it up for all to see before handing it to

the judge. "Silo Foulger is a skilled artist of scrimshaw. This is a scene of two Nantucket whaling ships. One ship is in the background, its bow tilted as if it hit a sandbar. Sailors are unloading barrels from the ship into a whaleboat. The ship in the forefront is sitting low in the water. Sailors are hoisting barrels up to the deck." He turned to the judge. "Would thee read the name of the ship's quarterboard in the foreground?"

The judge squinted his eyes, took out a magnifying glass, and peered at the scrimshaw. "*Fortuna.*"

"And now would thee read the name of the damaged ship?" The courtroom hushed. "The quarterboard says . . . ," the judge paused, and the entire jury leaned forward in their chairs, ". . . the *Pearl.*"

There was a gasp in the courtroom, then a murmuring. The judge sounded his gavel.

"Silo, did thee see this occur on the *Fortuna*?"

Silo nodded.

"And did the captain return to Nantucket with the *Pearl*'s contents in the belly of the *Fortuna*?"

Again, he gave a firm nod.

Matthew leaped to his feet. "Foulger absconded with two years' worth of whaling! The ambergris—that belonged to the *Pearl*! Captain Foulger went after right whales. He'd never even seen a sperm whale! He stole it all . . . and let the *Pearl* go under. He could have saved my father's life and he did not!"

Ezra hurried to his side and pressed him back into the chair. "Sit down and be quiet!" he said. "Thee is making a case against thyself!"

"I won't be quiet! There was something amiss with the *For-*

tuna's return. The ship was unloaded during the night. The warehouse was kept locked." He spun around and pointed to Henry Coffin. "Henry was fired from his job as Foulger's warehouse guard, for no reason."

"'Tis true," Henry shouted, waving his cane. "No reason at all."

"Barnabas Starbuck overheard the accountant at the countinghouse say what the weight of the ambergris was. It was the same weight! That was too much of a coincidence. I tried to see the ambergris. I would know it belonged to the *Pearl* if I could only lay eyes on it. But each time I went to the warehouse, I was turned away. It was kept locked. Guarded twenty-four hours a day."

The judge rapped for order with his gavel. "May I remind everyone that this is not the case on the docket!"

Matthew ignored the judge, ignored the tugging of Ezra on his sleeve. He pointed to the first mate, seated in the back next to Sarah Foulger. "The *Pearl* foundered after hitting a coral reef near the tip of the Bahamas. My father sent the crew off in the whaling boats to the nearby island to seek out help. He refused to abandon the ship. When we returned, the ship had gone under. All that was left was the top of the masts." He choked up. "We were too late. Too late returning." He pointed at Hiram Hoyt. "The crew of the *Fortuna* stole everything from the *Pearl*, and did not have the decency to even save my father's life! May God smite you for what you did!"

The courtroom exploded with murmurs and gasps. Hiram Hoyt's face turned a dark shade of red.

"Get a warrant!" Matthew said, his voice cracking. "Get a warrant and send Zacchaeus to the countinghouse. Find out the weight of the ambergris! Twenty-nine pounds, three ounces. High quality, white in color." He pleaded with the judge. "Your honor, please! See if I'm wrong!"

The judge rapped and rapped on his gavel. It took nearly a minute for the din to die down. "Mr. Macy! Sit down! Sit down now or I will add contempt of court!"

Ezra pressed Matthew back into his chair and whispered to him to be quiet, that he was only incriminating himself to have sufficient cause to kill the captain.

The judge did motion to Zacchaeus, Ezra, and Obadiah to approach the bench, spoke to them all, and then the constable hurried out the side door.

"What did he say?" Matthew whispered.

"He sent the constable to the countinghouse to look at the *Fortuna*'s books." He gave Matthew a look. "Let's just hope that ambergris matches the weight that thee said it did."

"What if it does? Then what?"

"The question thee should be concerned with is: what if it doesn't?" Ezra waited for the judge to give a slow nod to begin again, then he took a deep breath and stood. "Silo, 'tis no small thing to keep a secret on an island like Nantucket. How did Captain Foulger keep the crew from talking about the *Pearl*?"

Josiah objected. "There is no proof to this story other than a piece of scrimshaw! Carved by a mute boy!"

The judge gave him a look, but acquiesced. "Mr. Barnard, keep the prosecution's remarks in mind. The looting of the *Pearl* is a theory. Nothing has been proven."

"A man's life is at stake here, thy honor. If thee will allow me to finish questioning Silo." When the judge nodded, Ezra repeated the question to Silo. "How did the captain persuade his crew to not tell others about the *Pearl*?"

Silo held up two fingers and rubbed them together.

Matthew threw up his hands. "Of course! He silenced them with money."

Ezra whirled around and pointed at Matthew to be quiet. Then he turned back to Silo. "And thee, Silo? Did he provide thee with any money? Anything at all?"

Silo shook his head.

Ezra thanked Silo and dismissed him. After he returned to sit next to Libby, the bailiff called, "The defense calls Phoebe Starbuck Foulger."

Phoebe tried to keep her voice from quivering as she repeated the affirmation. Ezra helped her onto the witness stand. He circled for a while, asking her a few standard questions—when was she born, where, her wedding date to the captain. She wasn't sure how necessary were the questions, as everyone in the room knew the answers, but she suspected he was trying to help her nerves settle. Unfortunately, Ezra took so much time that the jurors grew restless. Finally, Ezra got to the point. "Why was Silo, in particular, not given any money to keep information about the *Pearl* to himself?"

Phoebe opened her drawstring purse and pulled out a letter. She handed it to Ezra, who handed it first to the judge. The judge read it, handed it back to Ezra, and in a solemn voice, said, "Inform the jury of its contents."

Ezra read the letter from Lindeza aloud. He leaned into the jury box, making eye contact with every single juror. "Captain Phineas Foulger had another wife. A legal, binding marriage that preceded the one on Nantucket Island to Phoebe Starbuck."

In the rear of the courtroom a gasp was heard from Sarah Foulger, then a chorus of shocked *ohhs* from the jury. Phoebe saw the color drain from Sarah's face. She saw the perpetual pipestem slip out of Hiram Hoyt's mouth and drop onto the floor as his mouth opened to a surprised O.

The courtroom erupted again. The judge did not bang his gavel this time.

That nagging will-o'-the-wisp feeling returned. Pipe? Poke-weed tobacco?

Suddenly she remembered where she had seen ash on the floor, where she had smelled it! Her house, after it had been ransacked.

The judge let the murmurs settle down of their own accord.

Phoebe was dismissed from the witness stand, and again, Ezra called Silo up.

Ezra stood in front of the witness stand, hands clasped. "Silo, the letter mentions that Lindeza wants the captain to bring Quiet with him."

Silo nodded.

"Is Lindeza thy mother?"

He nodded again.

"And Silo, is thee the 'Quiet' she meant?"

Another nod.

"Silo, is thee the true son of the captain?"

Another nod. From the back of the courtroom, Sarah Foulger let out a whimper.

"Silo, did thee witness the captain, thy father, being mortally wounded?"

Silo reached into his bag and brought out another scrimshaw piece. It was of two men, locked in battle. The captain was one of the men.

"Is the other man in this picture the one who killed the captain?"

Silo nodded.

"Is he in this room?"

Silo's gaze shifted over the entire courtroom, from the judge to the jury, over all those who sat in the courtroom. He shook his head. Phoebe's heart fell.

Mary Coffin

14 December 1661

I have not said no to Eleazer, which makes him feel greatly encouraged. Nathaniel has not stopped by the store in weeks, which makes me feel greatly discouraged.

15 December 1661

I saw Nathaniel and Elizabeth together today, walking toward the Macy house.

I have decided to accept Eleazer's proposal. 'Tis a wonderful thing to be loved and admired by a man.

20 December 1661

Today Eleazer happened to mention that we will have to wait thirteen months before we can marry. I asked him why, and he said that his father wants him to wait until his sixteenth birthday.

Mercy!

I had no idea he was younger than me. By **three** years! He is so tall and smart and amusing and full of plans and ideas, and besides, he is growing side-whiskers. I knew he was young but I did not think he was **that** young.

A boy has much growing up to do before he pledges his life to another. Eleazer says he would never regret it, but I do not feel peace about saying yes. How can I pledge my life to a boy-husband? He wants me to think on it and pray on it. And then to say yes.

Here I sit in the quiet of my store, trying to think of a way out of this mess I am in.

23 December 1661

Nathaniel Starbuck found out that Eleazer wants to marry me. I don't know how he found out, but I suspect Mother was the source. She fears Eleazer will turn me into a Baptist.

This afternoon Nathaniel marched into the store and said to me, "Are you going to marry that boy?"

I told him that it was none of his business. He has made that perfectly clear to me.

He puffed out his chest and said that it certainly was his business. He said that there was no way I could consider marrying a man I did not love, not when I loved another man.

I told him that it wasn't so much about whom I loved, but that I wanted to BE loved. I wanted a man to love me the way Sachem Autopscot loved Wonoma. He looked very confused. I sighed and explained that I wanted a man to love me with his whole heart.

"But, Mary Coffin," he said, in a loud voice, the loudest I have ever heard him, "I do! I do love you with my whole heart."

"You have an odd way of showing it," I said, in just as loud a voice. "I would not think you cared a lick for me, the way you treat me sometimes. Ignoring me. Seeing Elizabeth Macy . . . and don't think I don't know."

His eyes got glassy and his cheeks went red. "Mary," he said. "I am not like you. I don't have the words you have."

"You have plenty of words when you have something to say."

He shook his head. "Not those words. Book words. I never learned how to read. I struggled as a boy and I struggle now. I fear it's too late. I've been trying to learn. Elizabeth Macy has been trying to teach me. But I can't seem to learn."

Hold on. My mind started racing. "That's why you've been spending time with Elizabeth?"

He nodded. He looked miserable. "I know you deserve a husband who can read and cipher. I can't do either."

"But you tried?"

"I've been trying for over a year. Ever since that day on the beach. The day when a ship went down, and the sailor had me rescue his reading pigeon." He took a step closer to me. "Do you remember it?"

"I remember."

He reached out for my hands and squeezed them. "Don't marry Eleazer. I'll keep working at reading, Mary. I'll keep trying."

In that moment, I realized that Nathaniel Starbuck did love me the way Sachem Autopscot loved Wonoma. I don't think there's anything more dear to a man than his pride, his dreadful affliction. Nathaniel may not have risked his life for me, but he has risked his pride. And that is enough for me.

I think, nay, I know, 'twill be a wonderful new year ahead.

24

The door to the courtroom opened and in walked the burly constable with a firm grip on Hiram Hoyt's arm. Zacchaeus marched Hiram Hoyt up to Judge Coffin and whispered something to him.

"I was getting the information of the barrel count from the countinghouse for the little lawyer, 'tis all!" Hiram said, loud enough for all to hear.

Ezra's clear voice filled the room. "Silo, I ask thee once again, is the man who killed the captain in this courtroom?"

Silo stood up, lifted his thin arm, and pointed right at Hiram Hoyt. A hush fell over the entire courtroom.

Phoebe's heart began to thunder with excitement. Matthew turned to catch her eye. His entire face lightened with hope.

Hiram Hoyt charged the witness stand. "God'll strike thee dead!" Reflexively, Silo cringed and covered his head with his arms. The constable leapt forward and grabbed Hiram before he reached out to choke Silo.

"'Twas an accident!" Hiram spun around to look at Sarah, whose face was ghostly white. He blinked three times, opening and closing his mouth. "Sarah, m' love, 'twas an accident! I was trying to get his blessing on us!" He whirled to face the judge, panic in his voice. "We want to be married, Sarah and me, and I figured the time was right to tell the captain after he abandoned *that one*"—he pointed to Phoebe—"but the captain, he refused me! Said he'd never allow it. I wasn't good enough for his daughter, said he. Said my skin color was all wrong. But I knew what he'd done with *that one*"—again, pointing to Phoebe—"I knew about Silo, I knew about the other wife, about the *Pearl*. This Lindeza—she lives like a queen down there in the Bahamas. Lives in a mansion, has servants. She wove some kind o' spell on the captain. He went barmy over her, wasn't thinking clearly. He gives her everything she wants, but she keeps after him for more. She'd threatened to tell Sarah about the two of them, about Silo. That's why the captain took Silo on as cabin boy. To keep an eye on him, y' see."

Then his face grew purple and he choked out disconnected words. "And then"—he looked at Phoebe—"he takes another wife! It might've worked if *this* one would've stayed in Nantucket, but no, she sweet-talks him into sailing along on the *Fortuna*! He thought he could manage it all, could get away with it. He's the captain, after all. I warned him, time and time again, the sea always wins. The sea *always* wins. She's a jealous mistress.

"And then *that* one"—pointing right at Phoebe—"he said she'd be easy to manage, being so young. But she weren't. If she wasn't hurling into Cook's pots, she was trying to reform the crew. 'Twasn't long before the captain realized he'd made a terrible mistake, letting her tote along. That's why he left her on the island.

"I just held my tongue. I'd been nothing but loyal to the captain, all through the years. I did all his bidding. All his dirty work. Never questioned his orders. But then, when he refused me his blessing to marry Sarah—I told him I would tell it all, back in Nantucket. I was trying to . . . to . . ."

"Blackmail him," Ezra volunteered.

"Nay! Nay. I was trying to make the captain hear me. But he wouldn't! Wouldn't even look at me. Told me to get off his ship and stay off. I grabbed him . . . just to scare him . . . and we wrestled, and then he tottered and toppled and . . . and fell . . . hit his head on the corner of his desk. And then he . . . he lay still, blood oozing from his ear. I didn't mean to kill him! 'Twas an accident!" Hiram looked to the judge, pleading. "Judge, y' have to believe me." His voice drizzled to a whisper. "'Twas just an accident."

Ezra didn't let up. "And yet thee accused Matthew Macy of the crime. Right here, under affirmation, thee said he was the murderer, that he fled the ship. That thee would see him hang at Gallows Field."

Matthew stood up, anger pouring out of him. "After stealing from the *Pearl*! The ambergris! Every last barrel! Over two years of the crew's hard work . . . and you helped yourself to it all and sailed away."

Ezra pushed Matthew back down in his chair.

"It weren't like that!" Hiram looked at Matthew in utter shame. "We'd had dreadful poor luck on the voyage, hardly more than a few whales caught and captured, and then we came across the *Pearl*, foundering. Listing on her side. She was going under at high tide, that was clear. The captain didn't plan on stealing from the *Pearl*. In a way, your own father gave us the idea. Your father, he refused to leave the ship. He told us he would rather die on the ship than abandon it and leave this earth as a coward, for his boys to think their father a lowly coward. Here was the *Pearl*, a belly full of barrels"—he lifted one palm, then another—"and then there was the ambergris. The ship was deserted, there was no sign of the crew, and your father wouldn't come with us. It was too good to be true."

Phoebe's hands clutched Libby's.

"Pride, pride, pride," Libby whispered, tears running down her cheeks. "That stupid, prideful, wonderful man."

Ezra wasn't finished. "Hiram Hoyt, I ask thee . . . did Matthew Macy kill Captain Phineas Foulger?"

Shame-faced, Hiram Hoyt looked up at the judge. "Nay. Matthew Macy did not kill the captain." He hung his head. "I did."

Phoebe stopped breathing. The entire courtroom fell in a hush, all eyes fixed on the judge.

The judge banged once on his gavel. "Constable, take Mr. Hoyt out of the courtroom and lock him up."

Before Zacchaeus reached the door with Hiram in his grasp, Hiram stopped and turned to look at Sarah, who was sobbing steadily. "I always thought the captain was a little barmy over women. Risking everything for them." He let out a deep sigh. "But then, I've gone and done the same thing." Sadly he added, "The sea, she always, always wins."

The judge turned to Matthew. "Because of the confession of Hiram Hoyt under affirmation, thee is declared innocent in the court of England of the death of Captain Phineas Foulger."

And with that, the bailiff presented a pair of white gloves to the judge. A Nantucket tradition, signifying the purity of a court having no criminal cases on the docket.

Pandemonium broke loose. Matthew spun. Phoebe clapped her hands over her mouth and started crying. She had a single thought . . . to reach him.

***

Phoebe woke before dawn to head up Cliff Road to the great live oak tree, Granny Joan's sacrosanct tree, in the Founders' Burial Ground. Although it was First Day, a day meant to be set apart from physical labor, she took a shovel with her, along with the treasure chest of Spanish silver. She did not think God would mind so very much if she bent the rules, just for today, for a very good reason.

She dug and dug in the soft sandy soil, dug to bury the treasure deep, as deep as Mary Coffin and Eleazer Foulger had once buried it, in the very same spot. There it would remain, save a few coins that had arrived in a timely manner, until the next descendant of Great Mary was in need. She had tucked a note in an envelope, to lie along with Mary and Eleazer's notes:

A bit of silver was used in the year 1767 to protect the innocent.

~Phoebe Starbuck

It had puzzled her for a long while why the captain was so eager to find this treasure. It wasn't until Hiram Hoyt filled in the missing gaps about Lindeza and her lust for finer things, coupled with Sarah's appetite for opulence, that she realized the captain's extravagant lifestyle was all smoke and mirrors.

Last night, she had wrapped the journal up snug and tight in a linen sack and set it in a barrel in the cellar. It had served its purpose for her, and she felt satiated. The rest of Great Mary's story could wait for some other wisdom seeker. But before she set it deep in the barrel of sand—to keep it from deteriorating—she had held it close against her and whispered thanks to her great-grandmother. "Mary Coffin, thee has become a Weighty Friend to me."

As dawn lit the sky, she tamped down the sod and prayed for rain to cover it up. Even better, snow. She would need to rush home to dress for Meeting. She did not want to risk tardiness today of all days. For today, Matthew Macy was going to officially apologize for his irreverence and be reinstated back into the Friends' membership. He was ready to swallow his pride. "Apart from dyspepsia," he told her wryly, "it brings me great peace."

Phoebe hurried back down Cliff Road as the sun started to rise over Nantucket Island. It was a new day, a new year, a fresh start, and her heart felt full to bursting.

Epilogue

Silo Foulger set sail for the Bahamas, to join his mother Lindeza and his new sibling, after the court of Nantucket Island awarded him half of the estate of Captain Phineas Foulger. It did not end up to be much more than his fare to Nassau, as the court reimbursed the crew of the *Pearl* for the stolen ambergris and oil, and sold off 28 Orange Street to pay off creditors. However, true to his nature, Silo had expected nothing, thus was very content with his inheritance.

His departure was a sad day for all, particularly Jeremiah, for they thought they would not see Silo again. It turns out they were wrong, as Silo's talent for scrimshaw became world renowned, thanks to help from Ezra Barnard. Seven years later, he returned to Nantucket Island as a famous Island scrimshander. He purchased 28 Orange Street. He brought with him his little sister, Angelica Foulger. Their mother, Lindeza, chose to remain in the Bahamas.

Greatly helped along in the legal process by Ezra Barnard, and in the science of refining by Matthew Macy, Barnabas Starbuck was able to take out a patent for his process of refining spermaceti oil into making candles ('tis all in the pressing, they discovered). Barnabas and Ezra partnered to build the first chandlery on Nantucket Island. It was, at long last, a success for Barnabas.

For the remainder of her days, Sarah Foulger made her residence with one relative to another to another—a large circle, as she quickly wore out her welcome. She would not leave the house except for First Day Meeting. Hiram Hoyt, after confessing to the murder of Captain Phineas Foulger, was hanged at Gallows Field. Sarah chose to never acknowledge her half-siblings, Silo and Angelica.

One year after the hanging of Hiram Hoyt, on a sunny First Day in June, Phoebe Starbuck and Matthew Macy were married at the meetinghouse. They lived in the Centre Street saltbox where Phoebe had grown up, and raised a large family—three boys and four girls. Matthew continued to work in his cooperage, teaching the art of barrel making to his sons. His brother, Jeremiah, joined him in the business, until he turned sixteen and set off on a whaling voyage of his own. A bittersweet day for Matthew. A bitter day for Jeremiah's mother. She knew she would not see her boy again. Unlike Silo's return to Nantucket, she was correct in her prediction.

Phoebe never set foot off the island again. Not even in a dory. She ran a dry goods store out of her home. Other women took hold of Phoebe's example and ran shops and businesses on Centre Street while their husbands were off chasing whales around the world. It wasn't long before Centre Street became known as Petticoat Row.

As for "what happens next" in the life of Mary Coffin, well, that is another story.

KEEP READING
FOR A SNEAK PEEK AT

Minding
the Light

As Daphne Coffin made her way onto the wooden planks of Straight Wharf, she heard someone call her name and whirled to see her sister Jane hurrying to catch up with her. Holding each of Jane's hands was a towheaded child, a boy on one side and a girl on the other.

"Has thee heard the bells?" Jane said, her face bright with happiness. "Ren's ship is in!"

"The *Endeavour*?" Daphne's eyes widened in disbelief while her mind took hold of this stunning surprise. Ren was home? At long last! "I heard the bells but didn't realize they rang for Ren's ship."

"Imagine, Daphne. Ren has not even met his own children yet."

Her sister looked exceptionally pretty, though her face was flushed with heat from the warmth of this sun-stippled day. Jane Coffin Macy was one of the loveliest girls on Nantucket Island. She had high, wide cheekbones and a dainty, pointed chin that gave her face a charming sweetheart shape. Brown eyes, blonde hair, a peaches-and-cream complexion, with lips that were always red, as if she'd been eating berries. "I'm so glad thee is here this morning, Daphne." She straightened the organza fichu that draped across her shoulders and smoothed her skirt. "Thy presence will help me stay calm."

Daphne looked a little closer at her older sister. There was a trembling air about her, a vulnerability that was nearly palpable. "Thee must be beside thyself with excitement. Here, let me take Hitty." As she reached out to take her niece's hand, Jane suddenly swayed, as if she were on the verge of fainting.

"M-Mama!" Jane's son, Henry, shrieked in alarm.

Daphne grabbed her sister's shoulders to steady her. "Jane, is thee not well?"

Jane dipped her chin so that her black bonnet shielded her face from the sun. "I'm fashed, 'tis all. A bit dizzy. I'm sure 'tis from anticipation."

Daphne spun around as she heard the rhythmic slap of oars on water. The lighters were coming in now, slipping through the calm waters of Nantucket Bay, bringing the crew off the ship *Endeavour*. As captain, Ren would be the last one off, that much she knew. It would be a long wait this morning, but they would not budge from their waiting post on the wharf. The wharves were no place for maids, so unless a ship was arriving into port, she did not go near them. But how she loved being down by the harbor! So many strange accents, unusual skin colors, piercings, tattoos.

The *Endeavour* stood black-limned behind the bar that lined Nantucket Harbor. Lighter after lighter sailed up to release crew to pour onto the wharf and hustle down to greet their loved ones or make their way to the taverns to celebrate their return.

Jane's eyes were fixed on each lighter as it docked, gazing over the sailors, nodding to each one as they hurried past them, sea chests hoisted on their shoulders. Overhead, seabirds circled with shrieks and cries. "Over six *years*, Daphne," Jane said in a low voice. "He's been gone six *years*. Nearly seven."

Daphne grinned. "I wonder if Ren might be covered in tattoos. Or wearing a thick tangle of whiskers that hides his chin." She wrinkled her nose as some rank seamen went past. "Hopefully he will not smell like a beached whale." When she caught the solemn look on her sister's face, she quickly added, "Jane, 'tis a jest. Hand over heart, I was only jesting. Ren will return as the same man."

"How do I know what he's like after six years at sea? We were married less than a month when he set sail."

Daphne's smile faded. "I suppose that is the plight of a captain's wife. More goodbyes than hellos."

"Still, I did not expect an absence of six long years."

"He's missed quite a bit."

"He's missed everything. The birth of his children, the death of Father, and everything in between."

Daphne glanced at Jane and noticed a drip of perspiration trickling down the side of her cheek. "He is home now, sister. Safe and sound."

"But for how long?"

"Today is not the day to concern thyself with the next voyage."

Jane paused a moment, as if she'd become lost in thoughts, or memories. "Thee is right." She pushed the words out on a sharp expulsion of breath, then flashed a rueful smile. "Not today."

She was a fine captain's wife, Jane was. Reynolds Macy chose well, Daphne thought. She'd never heard her sister complain of loneliness, not once, not even after Hitty and Henry were born. Not until this moment.

Jane's eyes were fixed on the ship. "I have changed much in these six years."

"Not so much."

"But I have. Starting the Cent School, for one. Who knows what Ren will think of that venture?"

"It provides a great deal of help for island women, Jane, whose husbands are at sea. I'm certain he will understand."

"I'm not at all certain. And while thee might jest, no doubt Ren has changed too. What if we don't feel the same way about each other?"

Daphne put an arm around her sister's small shoulders, a vivid reminder of how opposite they were. Jane was delicate and fine-boned where Daphne was sturdy and curvy. Jane was reserved, graceful, as even-keeled as a ship, instinctively knowing how to react in any situation, while Daphne could be clumsy, blunt, at times socially awkward. In Daphne's eyes, her older sister was as close to perfection as a Quaker woman could be, one whose Inward Light reflected such a strong and steady beam. Despite being reprimanded by the Friends for marrying out of unity, Jane's faith never wavered.

They heard a shout and pounding feet coming up hard on them. "Any sign of him yet?" Tristram Macy, cousin and business partner to Ren, flew past them, turning his head for an answer.

"Nay, not yet," Jane called back, smiling. It was hard not to smile when Tristram was around.

Daphne lifted her hand in a wave to Tristram, whom she had seen only yesterday. He gave her no greeting, she noted. Jane noticed as well. "He's distracted, that's all."

"Of course." Of course he was. And yet, and yet . . . there was always something off between them.

"Mayhap, with Ren safely returned, Tristram's thoughts will turn to the future. Thee knows how worried he's been about the business. Soon, I think, he will propose marriage." Jane squeezed Daphne's hand. "Everyone hopes so."

All the world, or at least all of Nantucket, considered Tristram Macy to be Daphne's intended. The man she would marry, although he hadn't gotten round to ask her yet. How many times had Daphne thought Trist was going to propose marriage? Just the other day, they were walking along the beach at sunset—a perfect Nantucket evening. He had taken her hand and covered it with his own, and she thought, *Tonight. Surely, tonight he will ask.* But he didn't.

So how did Daphne feel about him? She and Tristram had known each other all their lives. She knew him when his stutter made him the target of school yard mocking. He knew her when she was round as a barrel, much like Hitty was now, before she started to grow and grow and grow, and her body rearranged itself.

She had watched as Trist evolved into a very handsome man, dashing and decadent, whose charming personality had a dazzling effect on women—including her own mother. Daphne did not feel dazzled by Tristram Macy, which might be why he favored her. Her feelings for him were akin to sitting by the hearth on a rainy day with a well-loved book to read and reread, warm and cozy.

Daphne saw Trist make his way toward the far end of the wharf, darting between clusters of townspeople, clapping hands with the crew as they emerged from lighters. By the pleased looks on their sun-weathered faces, and the fact that the *Endeavour* sat low in the brine, it seemed the rumors were true—it had been a greasy voyage. Mayhap Jane was right—now Tristram would believe the business he and Ren had started was on solid footing and he would make plans for the future.

The two cousins had a business arrangement that suited them well. Reynolds captained the ship, Tristram found and managed investors. Or, as Trist liked to describe it in his cheeky way, "Ren makes the money. I spend it."

Before long, Straight Wharf nearly emptied of sailors but for stevedores who unloaded the heavy wooden casks of whale oil off the lighters, rolling them down a wooden gangplank with a loud rumble—precious cargo ready to head to the warehouse. The same four remained in a tight clump: Jane and Daphne, Henry and Hitty. And Tristram, of course, though he was engaged in a deep conversation with the *Endeavour*'s first mate at the wharf's edge.

Jane's eyes snapped to a lighter approaching the dock. "There he is," she said. "I'm sure of it." Her fingers tightened on both of her children's hands. "Come. It's time to meet your father." She started down the wharf to meet the lighter as it docked.

Ren stood at the bow with legs straddled, hands on his hips, elegant and graceful on the swiftly moving lighter. When he spotted his wife, he lifted both arms in greeting and she raised her hands locked with her childrens', laughing.

Daphne was so pleased to see her brother-in-law return hale and hearty, she nearly lifted her skirts and ran down the deck, shouting his name. Five years ago she might have—nay, *would* have—done such a thing, but it would hardly be proper now. Then, she was still a girl, only fifteen. Today, she was a woman, trying to be proper, but it made her feel so stiff, like the whale-boned spikes that squeezed her middle so tight she could hardly breathe. How she missed the freedoms of girlhood! She squelched the desire to tumble straight into the family's sweet reunion and watched demurely from a distance.

She'd forgotten how alike in looks Tristram and Ren were. Both with those broad Macy faces and deep-set eyes, dark hair. Ren's hair was sun streaked but cropped close, Tristram's was held back in a queue. Both with striking figures: tall, trim, upright, confident. Standing behind Ren was a dark-skinned sailor she did not recognize. And then a familiar and weathered face, Jeremiah Macy, Ren's father, who coopered on the *Endeavour*. She hardly knew Jeremiah but by reputation—his older brother, Matthew, had married Phoebe Starbuck, great-grandmother to Daphne and Jane. Like most Nantucketers, they were all distantly related.

When the lighter drew within a rod's length, Ren leapt onto the deck, not even waiting until the mooring lines had been tied to the cleats. As soon as his boots—cracked white with salt—touched the solid planks of the wharf, he strode toward his wife and lifted her up in an embrace, swinging around in a circle. He gently set Jane down and bracketed her face with his two hands, holding it as if it were a precious treasure, gazing down into her eyes as if memorizing every feature. Jane was the one who broke the intimate moment as she remembered the boy and girl who peered up uncertainly at the stranger. "Ren. Oh Ren. There will be time for us later. But now . . . come meet thy children."

Daphne watched a sudden transformation come over Ren. He blanched, losing that ever-imposing captain's countenance, and drew in a deep breath, as if recovering from having the wind knocked out of him. As he turned his attention to his children, he seemed . . . ill at ease, uncomfortable, unsure of what to do next, so he did nothing. Nothing but peer back at them. Prompted by Jane's elbow, Henry extended his hand for a shake. Ren bent over to shake his son's small hand. "Um, lad, hello."

Henry kept a quizzical expression on him. The boy was so like Jane, reserved and formal. He poked his glasses up on the bridge of his nose, staring at his father, until he received another elbow jab from his mother. "Hello, Captain, sir. I am Henry James Macy."

Jane gently pushed Hitty forward. "And here is Mehitabel."

Ren turned to the girl. He crouched down to her eye level. "Mehitabel. Hello, lass. I am pleased to make thy acquaintance."

"Everyone calls me Hitty," she replied and curtsied very low, as if she were a lady.

"Then, Hitty it will be."

"Did thee bring us presents?"

Again, Ren seemed baffled. "I'm certain," he said at last, "that I have a few treasures in my chest." With that, Hitty threw her arms around his neck. Daphne saw Ren's eyelids slide closed for a moment as his daughter's small arms clung to him.

Jane glanced up to see Daphne and raised an arm to her to bring her into the circle. "Ren, thee remembers my sister Daphne."

Ren lifted his chin over the top of Hitty's head. His dark eyes moved back and forth over her face, wide with surprise. "Daphne? Why, thee was just an awkward foal of a girl when I saw thee last."

328

Daphne took a few steps forward to join them. "When I last saw thee, Reynolds Macy, thy hair was in a queue—"

He brushed a hand over his short-cropped hair. "Cut off. The entire ship. A lice outbreak."

"—and thee was wooing my favorite sister and stealing her away from our childhood home."

Ren laughed, as did Daphne. She turned, expecting to see Jane smiling too, and was startled to see the color drain from her sister's face as if a stopper was pulled from a sink. Her eyes rolled back in a most unholy manner, and she wilted onto the deck.

Discussion Questions

1. Pre-Revolutionary Puritan America is not something most people know much about, other than the Pilgrims on the *Mayflower* at Plymouth Rock. Did you discover anything new about this time period? Did anything surprise or shock you?

2. This novel has two stories in it—Mary Coffin's and her great-granddaughter Phoebe Starbuck's. Did you resonate more with Mary Coffin or with Phoebe Starbuck? Compare the two women. How are they similar? Different?

3. What twists in the book did you figure out early on? Anything you guessed wrong? What plot twist took you most by surprise?

4. Mary Coffin grew up during a time when higher learning was closed to women. But her quick mind and quicker tongue never stopped her from being learned. Was it difficult for you to understand why she loved an illiterate

man? Would you have preferred Eleazer to be her choice of a husband? Why or why not?

5. As Mary grappled with learning of the General Court's severe persecution of Quakers in New England, she summed it up with a thought-provoking comment. "People oppress people. It is in their nature." Do you agree or disagree?

6. Which character in the book did you empathize with the most? Do you recognize yourself in any of the characters?

7. One of the novel's themes was the pride of man (or woman). Mary Coffin called it a "dreadful affliction." The greatest gift Nathaniel gave to her was admitting to her that he had been trying, unsuccessfully, to learn to read. "That was enough for her," she said. What did she mean by that?

8. Did you ever think you were meant to marry one person, only to discover in hindsight they weren't the person God intended for you after all? What would you tell a young person pining for someone who doesn't return his or her affections?

9. Captain Phineas Foulger was a complicated character. At times, he was kind and protective. Other times, he was cold and unfeeling. Did you feel any sympathy for Captain Phineas Foulger? Like him at all? Wish the author had given him a different ending—or do you think he got the ending he deserved?

10. Phoebe is determined to marry well, within the conformity of her Quaker faith. She thought the love of the esteemed captain would prove her worthy. At one point,

Phoebe realized that she just kept exchanging one set of problems for another. Have you ever struggled with similar feelings of insecurity? What changed for Phoebe ... and when?

11. The use of laudanum might've surprised you, but it was not an uncommon drug in that time period. It was available without prescription, thought to be harmless, and used for all kinds of ailments, from depression to dysentery. Can you think of a modern equivalent of a cure-all? First, you control it. Soon, it controls you.

12. Let's consider Silo for a moment. He was a half-breed boy, considered deaf and dumb, unacknowledged by his own father, not particularly valued by his mother. Phoebe felt a tenderness for Silo because he had to live on the fringe of Nantucket society (she understood *that*, she said). Later, during Matthew's trial, when Silo was called to testify, Ezra Barnard explained to the judge that there were many ways to have a voice. How would you describe Silo's voice?

13. Contrast Phoebe with Matthew. Here's an example: Phoebe had an unwavering faith. Matthew doubted everything he'd been taught. What self-perceived inadequacies did they operate under? How did this thinking affect their decisions and choices?

14. Discuss God's faithfulness to Phoebe and to Matthew, despite their obstinacy.

15. How did God use others to draw Mary Coffin away from a strong aversion to hypocritical religion and toward a genuine relationship with him?

16. "The sea always wins," Hiram Hoyt declared during

Matthew's trial. What do you think he meant by that? Did the sea win in this story?

17. Finding true faith is another theme in this book. Discuss the moments when faith became real to Mary Coffin, to Phoebe Starbuck, and to Matthew Macy. Could it be possible that faith is the metaphor for the sea? As in, "the sea always wins." So does our God.

A Note to the Reader

I've always loved Nantucket. And yet it's not the modern Nantucket I've always loved. What is compelling to me is the history of the island, its development over the centuries, and the critical structure that the Quaker faith brought to it during the whaling years. For me, this is quintessential Nantucket: rich with stories of brave, determined pioneers who forged lives that would inspire future generations.

A few years ago, I spent a rainy day in the Nantucket Historical Society, eager to see the famous accounting book of Mary Coffin Starbuck. I had to sign my life away to the Society's highly attentive keeper, leave my purse and camera in a locker, fill out paperwork, and wear a pair of white gloves. When the book was brought to me out of the vault, chills ran up and down my spine. Here it was, a sheepskin book over three hundred and fifty years old, penned by a woman I had grown to greatly admire.

I learned a few things about Great Mary as I paged oh-so-carefully through her book: she had exquisite penmanship with few spelling errors, her trading was carefully accounted for in pounds and shillings and pence, and she had dealings with everyone on the island. Indians and farmers, men and women. Clearly, she was a learned, open-minded woman. And yet her husband, Nathaniel, could not read or write. How curious! This woman, I knew, had a story to tell.

Unfortunately, other than one letter to a granddaughter, the accounting book is all that is left behind from Mary Coffin Starbuck. As I imagined her personality and penned a journal for her, I kept in mind what I had gleaned about her and sought to create a woman ahead of her times, intelligent, wise, admired by all, yet a believable character too. It's a heavy responsibility to try to re-create the complex personality of a woman who lived three centuries ago. I hope I have done her justice.

There's more to discover about Great Mary and her impact on young Nantucket, but that will have to wait for the next book in the series.

Historical Notes

What's True and What's Not?

True or False: Did whaling captains take their wives along on voyages?

True. The addition of tryworks on a whaling ship, along with seeking out new breeding grounds for whaling, meant that voyages could last as long as four or five years. In the nineteenth century, more captain's wives did come along, as well as their children.

True or False: Could anyone really have a bout of seasickness like Phoebe Starbuck?

True. Mystic Seaport contains the *Charles Morgan*, the only wooden whaling ship left in the United States. On it is a "cuddy," a small wooden room built for the captain's wife who could find no relief from seasickness. That's where I got the idea for Phoebe's mal de mer. Most people are affected by seasickness; most recover as their bodies adjust, but not all.

True or False: Could Phoebe Starbuck have gotten addicted to opium (laudanum) after just a few uses?

True. Opium has a highly addictive nature. One can become addicted to it after just one use. Frenchman Hector St. John de Crèvecoeur visited Nantucket in the eighteenth century and wrote of his observations. He claimed that this "Asiatic custom . . . prevails here among the women."

True or False: Mary Coffin was a historical figure. Was Phoebe Starbuck?

False. Phoebe Starbuck was entirely fictitious.

True or False: Is there really a man named Peter Folger (or Foulger) who Christianized the Wampanoag Indians?

True. Peter Foulger was a fascinating man . . . and just so happened to be the grandfather of Benjamin Franklin. You can see the resemblance in their keen intelligence and curiosity about all things. The Whaling Museum in Nantucket is named for Peter Foulger and is well worth a visit.

True or False: Quakers were severely persecuted in the colonies in the 1600s, yet in the 1700s, Nantucket was predominantly Quaker.

True. It is amazing how quickly public opinion can change. As for Nantucket Island, you can find out more about its rapid transition to Quakerism in the next two books of the Nantucket Legacy series.

The Quakers
of the 17th and 18th Centuries

Quakers are members of the Religious Society of Friends, a faith that emerged as a new Christian denomination in England during a period of religious turmoil in the mid-1600s. The movement was founded in England by George Fox (1624–1691), a nonconformist religious reformer.

At the age of nineteen, George Fox left home as a seeker, filled with unanswered spiritual questions. A few years later, he heard a voice: "There is one, even Christ Jesus, who can speak to thy condition." He felt a direct call from God to become an itinerant preacher and promote the concept of the Inward Light, or Inner Voice. He believed God's Spirit to lie within every person's soul. Everyone had the capacity to comprehend the Word of God and express opinions on spiritual matters. His belief came from Scripture: "The true Light, which lighteth every man that cometh into the world" (John 1:9 KJV).

The tenets of the movement's foundation soon developed:

Every man and woman had direct access to God; no hired clergy or "steeple houses" (churches) were needed.

Every person, male or female, slave or free, was of equal worth.

There was no need in one's religious life for elaborate ceremonies, rituals, creeds, dogma, or other "empty forms."

Following the Inward Light led to spiritual development and toward individual perfection.

Fox taught his followers to worship in silence. At meetings, people would speak only when they felt moved by the Holy Spirit. Fox promoted simple living and prohibition of alcohol; followers were against holidays, frivolous entertainment, and opulence of any kind. They distanced themselves through simple clothing and plain language—such as the use of "thee" and "thou" in place of the more formal "you." Fox's early followers thought of themselves as friends of Jesus and referred to themselves as "Friends of Truth" (John 15:15), eventually shortened to "Friends."

The movement came into sharp conflict with England's Puritan government: Friends refused to pay tithes to the state church, to take oaths in court, to practice "hat honor" (doff their hats to the king or other persons in positions of power), or to engage in a combat role during wartime. They showed an intense concern for the disadvantaged, including slaves, prisoners, and inmates of asylums. They advocated for an end to slavery, and for improvements in living conditions in penitentiaries and treatments in mental institutions.

Fox was imprisoned many times. Once, when hauled into

court, he suggested that the judge "tremble at the word of the Lord." The judge sarcastically referred to Fox as a Quaker and it stuck. It became the popular name for the Religious Society of Friends. During the second half of the seventeenth century, over 3,000 Quakers spent time in English jails for their religious beliefs; many hundreds died there.

The Quakers sent missionaries to the New World despite the fact that most of the colonies viewed them as dangerous heretics. They were deported as witches, imprisoned, tortured, or hanged. In 1688, a group of Friends in Germantown, Pennsylvania, took a public stand against slavery. It was considered the first stirrings of abolitionism in the New World.

Initial opposition toward Quakers eventually lessened and they became accepted as a denomination. As a group, they became identified and respected for their industriousness and high moral character. Today, worldwide, there are over 300,000 Quakers.

Acknowledgments

Special thanks to . . .

. . . Karen MacNab, a docent at the Peter Foulger Whaling Museum, who met with me through a request by Matt Parker, the owner of the Seven Sea Street Inn. She answered countless questions about early Nantucket, Quakerism, and whaling. She also provided me with resources, including a printout of her thoughtful "Quaker Lecture."

. . . Andrea Doering, Michele Misiak, Barb Barnes, Hannah Brinks, Karen Steele, Cheryl Van Andel, and the entire staff of Revell Books, for their dedication to make each author's book the best one possible. It is a privilege to work with all of you.

. . . Wendrea How, Tad Fisher, and Lindsey Ciraulo, for your honest critiques. Your feedback is invaluable, always listened to, and hugely influential!

. . . And you, my readers. Thank you for your enthusiasm about my books and for sharing them with your friends and book clubs. I'm thankful for each and every one of you!

. . . Above all, thanks and praise to the almighty God for this wonderful opportunity to share the wonder of story. Great is thy faithfulness.

Resources

These books provided invaluable background information that was helpful to try to imagine and re-create what life was like for Mary Coffin in the seventeenth century as well as Phoebe Starbuck in the eighteenth century. Any blunders belong to me.

Cook, Peter. *You Wouldn't Want to Sail on a 19th Century Whaling Ship!* Danbury, CT: Franklin Watts, a Division of Scholastic, Inc., 2004.

Forman, Henry Chandlee. *Early Nantucket and Its Whale Houses*. Nantucket: Mill Hill Press, 1966.

Furtado, Peter. *Quakers*. Great Britain: Shire Publications, 2013.

Karttunen, Frances Ruley. *Law and Disorder in Old Nantucket*. North Charleston, SC: Booksurge Press, 2000.

Karttunen, Frances Ruley. *Nantucket Places & People 1: Main Street to the North Shore*. North Charleston, SC: Booksurge Press, 2009.

Karttunen, Frances Ruley. *Nantucket Places & People 2: South of Main Street*. North Charleston, SC: Booksurge Press, 2009.

Karttunen, Frances Ruley. *Nantucket Places & People 4: Underground*. North Charleston, SC: CreateSpace Publishing, 2010.

Philbrick, Nathaniel. *Away Off Shore: Nantucket Island and Its People, 1602–1890*. New York: Penguin Books, 1994.

Philbrick, Nathaniel. *In the Heart of the Sea: The Tragedy of the Whaleship Essex*. New York: Penguin Books, 2000).

Philbrick, Thomas, ed. *Remarkable Observations: The Whaling Journal of Peleg Folger, 1751–54*. Nantucket: Mill Hill Press, 2006.

Whipple, A.B.C. *Vintage Nantucket*. New York: Dodd, Mead, 1978.

Suzanne Woods Fisher is the bestselling author of numerous series—Amish Beginnings, The Bishop's Family, Lancaster County Secrets, The Inn at Eagle Hill, and Stoney Ridge Seasons—as well as nonfiction books about the Amish, including *Amish Peace*. Suzanne is a Carol Award winner for *The Search*, a Carol Award finalist for *The Choice*, and a Christy Award finalist for *The Waiting*. She lives in California. Learn more at www.suzannewoodsfisher.com and connect with Suzanne on Twitter @suzannewfisher.

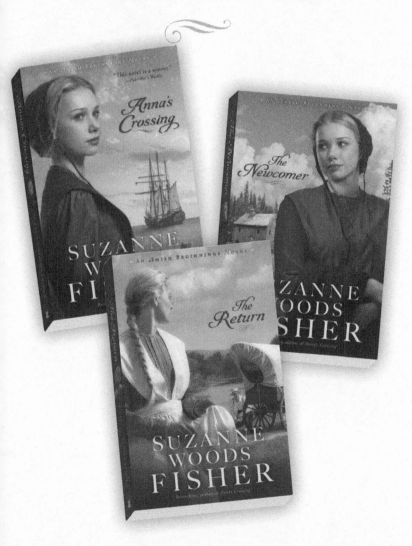

Don't Miss Any of The Bishop's Family

"Suzanne is an authority on the Plain folks. . . .
She always delivers a fantastic story with
interesting characters, all in a tightly woven plot."

—Beth Wiseman, bestselling author
of the Daughters of the Promise and the Land of Canaan series

WELCOME TO A PLACE
OF UNCONDITIONAL LOVE AND
UNEXPECTED BLESSINGS

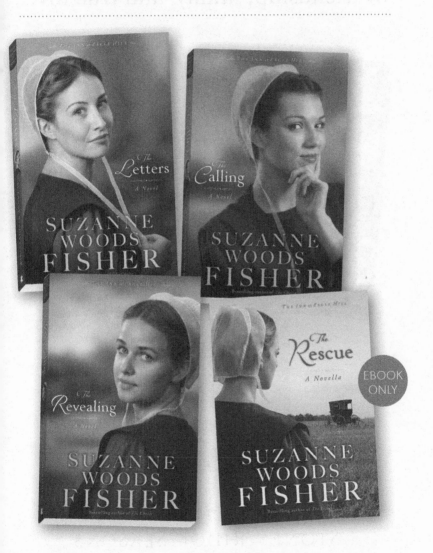

⟋ THE INN at EAGLE HILL ⟍

Fisher intrigues and delights with stories that explore the bonds of friendship, family, and true love.

STONEY RIDGE SEASONS